On the Sidelines

ON THE SIDELINES

Copyright © 2024 by Ashley Bear.

All rights reserved. Printed in the United States of America. No part of this book may be used or reproduced in any manner whatsoever without written permission except in the case of brief quotations em- bodied in critical articles or reviews.

This book is a work of fiction. Names, characters, businesses, organizations, places, events and incidents either are the product of the author's imagination or are used fictitiously. Any resemblance to actual persons, living or dead, events, or locales is entirely coincidental.

ISBN: 123456789

First Edition: Month 2024

10 9 8 7 6 5 4 3 2 1

On the Sidelines

Ashley Bear

To anyone who wants a golden retriever guy with possessive tendencies

Warning

This book
contains scenes
of sexual
assault, death,
and trauma.

1

Evie

Breathing was a mistake. The lungful of air I was greedily trying to suck in, sends me into a fit of coughing. It draws the attention of the few passing students, but none stop to ensure I'm okay. But that's all right by me, I'd rather they left me alone.

After the atrocious first impression I left on my new roommate, I'd like to crawl into the nearest ditch and rot away until I'm nothing but bones and dust. Unfortunately, I won't be allotted that luxury. The numbers blaring at me from my phone warn me of the limited time I have left to make it to my counselor's office before her hours are over.

My lungs burn from exertion, but I'm forced to ignore their screaming. My time slot is quickly shrinking, not only to meet Ms. Carlton but to fix this scheduling mistake. I am NOT supposed to be in this class, I can't be. I'm an English major, I should never have been put into a theater class. But not just any theater class, a musical theater class!

I've always had a way with the written word, but my talent has never extended to the spoken word. My friends can atone for my lack of communication skills. Talking to people freaks me out on a normal day. Performing in front of them while singing is an absolute no-go.

I push my way through the crowds that have congregated in the main courtyard area, I think it's called a quad. It's more of a small park but that's not important right now.

I get glares from the people I shoulder past, but I'll worry about it later. I have five minutes before she locks her doors and I need to be in them before she does that. Someone to my right squeals like a pig, damn near fainting in front of me. I give her a quizzical look but ultimately shrug it off, I don't have time for this. I can see the other side of the crowd, I'm almost there, just a few more people and- I'm free! Voices to my right try to call my attention. Well, not mine specifically, but I can't say I'm not curious about what's causing all the commotion.

I cheer quietly to myself, allowing myself the small victory. I race across the rest of the quad and barely make it before I'm locked out and stuck with a class that would likely cause me nightmares. As much as I wanted to look, I just don't have time right now.

Ms. Carlton looks happy to see me, the sweaty panting mess I am. "Oh-" I suck in a large breath. "Thank-" the breath leaves me just as quickly. "God." She's laughing at me, chuckling softly.

"Good evening, Miss Campbell, what can I do you for?" She appears professional but the laughter in her eyes gives her away. I've only met her a few times, but I already know we'll get along.

"Can I close this?" I motion the large oak door behind me, wide open. She nods. I take a seat across from her in the large black armchair. "There's an issue with my schedule. Oh, thank you!" My hands grasp the cold water bottle she hands me, greedily taking gulps as the cool water soothes my burning lungs.

"What's wrong with your schedule." Her attention is glued to her monitor as she types in my information. She mumbles as she lists off my classes for the first semester. "English 101, I'm surprised you didn't test out of it."

"I did but it's a prerequisite for a class I want to take next semester."

"Ah, that makes sense. Now let's see. Math 111, BIOL 160, CIT 101, and Musical Theater. I don't see anything off about this." Her eyes filter back to mine.

"I shouldn't be in Musical Theater! Why am I?" Her mouth forms an O as understanding sets in. She's quick to start typing again, letting the silence drag on. My nerves can't take this.

"You can drop the class with no repercussions and considering you have four classes already; you don't have to fill the slot. You could if you'd like too though." I down the rest of my water but it doesn't stop the lump in my throat from growing. God, when did I become such a crybaby?

"What are my options to fill it?" I fail to keep my voice flat which draws her attention back to me. I can only imagine what I look like. Red-faced, lip trembling, watery eyes.

"Oh sweety, why are you crying? It's not a big deal, we can fix this." I nod while wiping my eyes, hoping to stop the tears before they fall.

"Sorry, I cry a lot. I know it can be changed but I was worried I wouldn't make it in time." Her smile portrays patience as she pats my hand in a reassuring beat.

"It's all right, cry all you want, I won't judge." I nod again, feeling a little like a bobblehead. "Well, there's an opening in the Intro to Psychology class. It won't affect any of your other classes, would you like me to add you?" Again, I choose to nod, not trusting my voice. "Okey-dokey, you're all set. Was there anything else?"

"No, that's all. Thank you." She hands me a paper version of my new schedule and sends me on my way.

Walking out of the office building, my shoulders feel a lot lighter, and I don't feel like crying anymore so I guess today was a success. At least this chore was.

To my surprise, when I entered my shared dorm room thirty minutes later, Ella was nowhere to be seen. Maybe I scared her off already. I wouldn't blame her for wanting a new roommate. I mean, what type of adult screams bloody murder when their new roommate tries to introduce themselves? Me, I'm that type of adult.

I blame it on being the only child in the house when I was younger. My older half-sister chose to live with her mom. I never had to worry about someone sneaking up on me when I was minding my own business.

I'm only half-unpacked so I take this chance to finish. I'm putting the last of my clothes away when Ella returns. I give her a sheepish smile that she returns with a frown.

"You're not going to scream again, are you?" My cheeks heat while I fidget.

"No, sorry. I'm not used to people walking up behind me. My mom drilled stranger danger into me since I was old enough to understand the words." Her eyes bore into me, the bright blue orbs rooting me to my spot. Ella is the quintessential idea of beauty.

Blond hair, blue eyes, tiny waist, legs that go on for days. She has big boobs, a big butt, and pouty lips.

A huff passes those lips of hers, arms crossing under her boobs, pushing them up. "Whatever, as long as it doesn't happen again. By the way, my boyfriends coming over tonight, so I'll need the room to myself until two."

I'm shell-shocked. My first night at a new school and I can't even spend it in my room! Judging by her bored expression, this will be a regular occurrence, so I better get used to it. At least I have one more week before classes start up.

"Uh, two a.m.?" At her nod, I sigh. "Okay." My voice comes out meek but she doesn't notice. Ella's already leaving the room.

"Be out of here by six. I don't need my boyfriend knowing I have a loser for a roommate." She's out the door before I can respond, leaving an overwhelming scent of Jasmin in her wake.

I grab my phone off the charger and balk. It's five-fifty! I look at the door hoping she was kidding, but she was not when she didn't come back.

I don't want to be the annoying roommate so I spur into action, grabbing anything I might need in the next eight hours. I stuff my phone charger and laptop charger into my messenger bag, along with my laptop and my wallet.

5

I make it out of my dorm with a minute to spare. The elevator dings open as I meander toward it. Ella and some jock step out, completely ignoring my existence. As I pass them, I can hear her tell him that her roommate 'offered' them the room for the night and that she'll be back around two a.m.

I bristle at the blatant lie but my hate for confrontation has me biting my lip. I'm starting to think I shouldn't feel bad about screaming earlier.

I watch them enter the dorm, my dorm, as the elevator doors close. I open my phone and send off a quick text to my best friend, asking her if she wants to meet me for dinner at the twenty-four-hour diner on campus.

I'm sitting at a booth when she finally responds.

> **Bestie: Sorry, can't**
> **Bestie: New roomie wants a get to know you night together**
> **Bestie: Another time?**
> **Me: Sure, have fun**

The waitress brings me my water and inquires whether I want to wait for the rest of my party to order. "Nah, she can't make it. Seems like I'm on my own."

"Oh, okay. Well, are you ready to order or would you like a few minutes?" Honestly, I haven't even touched the menu but I'm not really hungry.

"A few more minutes please." Despite that, I still flip through the menu. It's mostly breakfast with a few burgers. When the waitress returns, I order a waffle meal with a scrambled egg and a coffee. I'll be here for a while, so I need to stay awake.

I've watched far too many tables come and go but it's only ten. Even my original waitress has left, handing me over to someone new. I gave her the same run-down, informing her that I'll be here until two.

She seems okay with it so at least I'm not upsetting anyone.

I've managed to tackle a good chunk of the short story I'm working on. It's coming along well enough. I'm about halfway through with it and another character is about to be killed by the demon when a group of rowdy guys walk in.

I lose my focus, fingers stuttering to a stop. They're talking too loud for the time of night but no one else seems to care. Actually, everyone is staring at them like they hung the moon. I don't understand why, yeah, they're attractive but they're just boys. They're nothing special, but I guess I am because my waitress seats them in the booth behind me.

They roughhouse, shaking the backrest, making it impossible to get any work done.

They've been here all of ten minutes and I already want to strangle them. New record for me. While I come from a family with anger issues, I was saved from the same fate, though I am still quick to anger sometimes. Now seems to be one of those times.

I try my best to keep my focus on my story and succeed for a little bit. Unfortunately, one of the guys from that table takes an interest in what I'm doing, and I can feel him watching me.

I turn my head to meet his stare head-on but he's not looking at me, he's looking at my laptop. Embarrassment heats my skin as I snap it shut.

"Hey! I was reading that!" I ignore him. I text my bestie again, but this one goes unanswered. She must be asleep. Makes sense, it's almost ten thirty and we've both always been quick to go to bed.

A hand reaches over my shoulder, straining for my laptop. I yelp when his arm brushes me, my fight or flight kicks in and my hand instinctively reaches back and slaps him.

The air stills as silence descends over the diner. My hands fly to my mouth, I'm horrified, and it seems the rest of the room is as well.

Suddenly, loud boisterous laughter breaks out from three of the boys behind me. The ones whose arm still hangs over me has started chuckling. "Damn, it's been a while since a chick has slapped me."

"You deserved it, Tanner." The others agree in quick procession. Tanner, who I slapped, wears a fake shocked expression.

"How dare you, Sean! I was unfairly hit. Anyone can see that." Sean rolls his eyes, his head shaking.

"What did you expect? You were eavesdropping on whatever she was doing and then you infiltrated her personal space. From my angle, you totally deserved it!" Tanner's arm retracts into his own space.

The table starts arguing as to who was in the wrong, to my surprise, they all gang up on Tanner. At some point, he's had enough. He stands and takes the seat next to me.

I stare at him awestruck at his brazen move.

The waitress decides that's the perfect time to check on me. "Is there anything I can get you, ma'am? More coffee?"

I stare at her wide-eyed with flushed cheeks while silently begging for her help. But she either doesn't care or doesn't notice. With a defeated sigh I ask for more coffee and a side of fries. She nods then looks to Tanner like he's my date and asks for his order.

He orders a double cheeseburger with a double side of fries. I gawk at him, where does all that food go? He catches me looking and winks. He fucking winks!

I huff and turn away from him, deciding it doesn't matter if he reads over my shoulder. I need a distraction and writing is my best bet. This is going to be a long night.

His friends whine behind us about him abandoning them for a woman, but he doesn't budge, though he also doesn't read my screen. He's chosen to watch me instead and it's making me extremely uncomfortable.

Finally, I've had enough and address him. "Please leave."

"Why should I?" I glance at him briefly before returning to the task at hand.

"Because you're making me uncomfortable, and people are looking. Leave, please." The fucker just laughs. He laughs at me. My annoyance spikes.

"Maybe I want to stay."

"I don't want you to." He fake pouts like that will change my mind.

"But I'm great company, just ask my friends."

"No thanks," I glance over my shoulder while scrunching my nose, "they make me uncomfortable too." He laughs beside me, the sound as smooth as Tennessee whiskey. I cringe to myself at the thought, Mom must be rubbing off on me. The sayings might be the worst part of growing up in a small town.

The food arriving saves me from whatever he has to say. His attention is solely focused on his burger, and I couldn't be happier. That is until I see him inhale the thing. Like he literally inhaled it. I've never seen someone devour something so fast.

His fries don't last much longer and then he orders more! He's still hungry!

While his head is turned, I take the opportunity to check him out. He's insanely attractive with dirty blond hair, a chiseled jawline, green eyes, and a dotting hair that serves as a beard. Then there's his body, his absolutely humungous body. He dwarfs the booth, I've never been claustrophobic before, but I feel it now. I shift closer to the wall.

He's a behemoth of what feels like pure muscle if his arm is anything to go by. I'd wager he's an athlete which explains why every woman in the building is glaring daggers at me. I want to scream at them that they can have him, that I don't want him. But I refuse to draw more attention to myself, what I have is already enough.

I've lost the inspiration to write so I turn everything off and take to staring blankly out the dark window. I slowly snack on my fires, not missing how Tanner snags a few here and there. If he won't leave because I asked him to, maybe he will if I ignore him.

"What's your name?"

"How old are you?"

"What's your major?"

He continues to badger me with as many questions as possible. I must not be the only one who's annoyed. The friend he was sitting beside earlier turns to me and offers his hand. I stare blankly at it but that doesn't seem to bother him, he instead tucks it under his chin.

"Names Oliver. A piece of advice? He won't stop. The man's got more energy than a newborn golden retriever. You might as well give in, or at least throw him a bone, something for him to chew on for a bit." He turns back around to continue his conversation.

"English." I throw him the word, or the proverbial bone, hoping it will be enough. It's not.

"English? Really? Why?"

I sigh and whisper to his friend. "Oliver," I wait until he looks at me, "it didn't work." He takes a page out of Tanners' book and laughs, leaving me to deal with the puppy on my own.

Not even his third side of fries shuts him up. I keep ignoring him and he keeps asking questions for the next hour. God, does he ever shut up? I check the time, happy to see its finally Midnight.

"So why are you here alone? Were you stood up?" I've finally had enough and slap a hand over his mouth.

"No, I wasn't stood up." I manage to bite it out with as much venom as I'm capable of.

"So why are you here?" His words come out muffled but even my hand can't shut him up.

"My roommate kicked me out for sexy time with her boyfriend." He stares at me before flicking his eyes down to my hand and back up again. Sighing, I release his mouth.

"When did you move in?"

"Today." His eyebrows rise up his forehead.

"When did she?"

"Today." They rise impossibly farther.

"That's a bitchy move." I shrug.

"Not really. The bitchy move was to tell her boyfriend I

offered while ignoring my existence because she doesn't want her boyfriend to know she has a 'loser' for a roommate." I add air quotes around loser, so he knows they're not my words.

"Yeah, that too."

I shrug again, if I act like it doesn't bother me then it won't. "It's not a big deal, I can head back in two hours."

"How long have you been here?"

"Six hours." I don't know what to expect will happen but it's not him calling the waitress over and paying for both of our food. Nor is it him dragging me to my feet with all my stuff in tow while his friends follow suit.

"What are you doing?" I manage to squeak out as he drags me out of the restaurant.

He doesn't respond.

His friends flank us, talking amongst themselves and acting like this is a normal night.

In the ten minutes it takes to drag me to wherever we're going I learn the other guy's name is Dillian. He seems nice enough. He looks like the male version of Ella with blond hair and blue eyes. He has dimples that he loves to show off, the same with his blinding white teeth. He's tall, I think he said he was six-three. He's smaller than Tanner, height-wise and build-wise but he's still muscular, all of them are actually.

Oliver is the same height but otherwise, he's completely different. Black unruly hair, deep brown eyes, crooked smile. He's a wet fantasy. If I was in the market to date, he'd be just my type.

Seans' the same. A little taller but with brown hair, hazel eyes, and a smile that seems to promise wicked things. I think I can also see a few tattoos creeping up his chest and onto his neck.

I'm surrounded by massive men whom I met not too long

ago yet, I feel completely safe. My mama would have a heart attack if she heard me say that but it's true. I feel safe.

2

Tanner

Why am I dragging a woman who won't tell me her name across the campus? I have no idea. I've asked myself the same question countless times.

I just need to see her smile. Know that she can be happy.

My boys follow behind us as I drag her behind me through the quad. They're talking amongst themselves, occasionally bringing her into their conversation. She's surprisingly quiet, not complaining about being forced away from her *invigorating* evening.

"Are we almost there?" Her voice comes out nervous but when I glance at her, she seems confident and calm. A lot calmer than a random girl being dragged across campus by a group of strangers should be.

"Yes." No, I don't know. I don't even know where I'm taking her. Her roommate is a bitch for throwing her out of their room on the first night and I guess it pissed me off enough that I needed to do something.

"Dude, where are we even going?" Dillan comes to my side; he's whining but I saw the stiffness in his shoulders when he heard what she said. I'm pretty sure she's a freshman, which makes it even worse. I would have seen her around if she had gone here last year. She's far too pretty for me to have never noticed her. "You don't have a clue, do you?" Thank God he whispered that.

At the shake of my head, he starts spouting off different locations nearby that we can go to. He's a lifesaver and he knows it. "The library is still open, the bar off campus that we like, we can't go to the rink. Coach would have an aneurysm if he saw one of us swipe in at this time. Ooo, we can go to the club." I take back the life-saver comment.

Oliver pops his head up and adds his ideas into the mix. "The coffee shop by the rink is open at this hour, you could tell her that if she's drinking coffee, she might as well drink good coffee." Now *he's* a lifesaver.

So that's where we go. She complains that she had coffee at the diner, but I throw Oliver's excuse out and it shuts her up. Of course, that earns me a wink from Oli and him my middle finger.

"Will you ever tell me your name?" I'm hoping she'll say yes but I'm not betting on it.

"How do I know I can trust you?"

"What does trust have to do with a name?" She giggles and the sound goes straight to my ego. She may not want to talk to me but at least I can make her laugh.

"A lot actually. What would stop you from calling my name out in a crowd? If you don't know it, you can't call it." A crowd? Why would it matter? Oh. OH!

"You don't like attention being drawn to you, huh?" She shakes her head, the strands of her black hair swishing behind her. I don't know if her hair is long or she's just short, maybe both? I'm six-five and her head grazes my chin so she's probably five-four, five-five. So, the scene we made in the diner made her uncomfortable. Fuck.

"I come from a small town where if you did anything, everyone knew. I hated it. My mom was upset when I chose to go to an out-of-state school but, I chose Hayes University for its size. I chose West Virginia for its distance from home. It also helps that my bestie Alysa was accepted as well."

"Where are you from?"

"A small town in Montana." Damn, she's a long way from home.

"Holy shit!" Yeah, Sean, I agree.

"What town?" Dillan just has to pipe in, doesn't he?

"Libby, Montana. A population of 2,800 or so." Her words boast but her tone is dead, like she never wants to go back. I wonder why. I'm from a small town an hour from here and I loved growing up there.

I pull her to stand next to me, motioning for her to order. Her pointer finger rests on her plump lips as she asses the menu. The cashier looks like he'd rather be anywhere but here as he waits somewhat patiently for her to order. "Are you able to do a half French vanilla, half mocha iced latte?" A long sigh passes his lips.

"Yes, what size?"

"Oh, wonderful. A medium please." I stop her hand that reaches for her wallet and motion for the boys to order something. Oliver orders his regular Chia tea, Sean orders a French vanilla, and Dillan orders as he says, 'the most chocolatey drink you can make'. I step forward last and scan the menu quickly and settle on the same thing as the woman next to me. We all ordered mediums and I paid. The fuckers didn't even try, they figured if I didn't let her pay, I wouldn't let them. They're not wrong but an effort would have been nice. My family isn't rich but we're pretty well off, plus my summer jobs give me a lot of financial freedom.

We take a seat in the corner booth while we wait. "If I tell you a secret, will you tell me your name?" She considers it for a moment then nods.

"It has to be blackmail worthy but yes."

Sean bursts into laughter. "Why blackmail worthy?"

"Well, wouldn't that be the only kind of secret you would want?"

"Tushe." Damn, now I have to think of a secret. I mull over multiple options. It takes until we get our drinks for me to think of one and I'm tempted to try to think of another.

"Your time frame is shrinking." Time frame? What the hell?

"I didn't realize I had a time frame."
"You do now. You have less than a minute to spill or I leave." My boys chuckle but none of them offer any help. Maybe I need better friends. Though I'm glad to know she knows her time is valuable.

"Fine. Let's see, my favorite color is pink."

My so-called friends laugh harder, and Sean even calls me out on the lie, it's blue. "Fuck you, man." She giggles next to me while sipping on her coffee. It's almost twelve-thirty, none of us should be having coffee yet here we are. What a great way to start a new year.

"Ok, fine. Does is count if my brother helped."

"Maybe, is it embarrassing for you?"

"Very." She smirks and damn if it isn't the sexist thing I've seen all year. "Ok, so, my brother and I wanted to prove to our high school girlfriends that we were hot shots, so we lit various types of balls on fire. First it was a golf ball, then it was a baseball, and so on and so forth. We were out in an open field; it was near the park that we grew up next to. I wanted to show off, so I grabbed my dad's football and set it on fire. We didn't see them at the time, but two police officers were walking toward us and my dumbass threw the football to my brother. Well, he didn't catch it and it barely missed the cops by a few feet." Chuckles surround us, they know this story, it's their favorite. They love hearing about me getting in trouble with the law.

"We tried to explain to the cops that it was harmless, but they disagreed. Told us if we wanted to be 'hot-shots' then we'd get the hot-shot punishment. Our dad wasn't too happy when he had to pick us up from the police station. Nor were the girls' parents who forbade them from seeing us again. They were forced to move to a new school a week later and I had a record for six months as a part of my punishment. It almost cost me my scholarship to this school." I don't know if that was her idea of embarrassing but it sure is mine.

"Is he serious? That's what he considers embarrassing?" She's addressing everyone else which causes an uproar of laughter from them.

"Dude," Oli pants, "Dude, tell her about the first week of freshman year. That was embarrassing." My cheeks heat from the reminder of THAT night.

"Freshman year? What happened?"

"I'll tell you if you promise to let me off the hook after."

She grabs my hand in hers and gives it a surprisingly strong handshake. "Deal."

"It was what, the third night of the new year?" I directed the question to Sean who was my roommate that year. He considers it for a moment but shakes his head.

"I think it was the first Thursday. I know it wasn't quite Friday cuz she was complaining about a morning class the next morning."

"Okay, so it was the fourth day then. I invited a girl over to my dorm; Sean here was my roommate that year and he graciously offered me the room for the night. Well, she agreed, and we went back to my room. Sean hadn't left yet, he had forgotten something, so he got to witness everything.

"She didn't mind that he was there, actually I think it kind of turned her on. At least for the first few minutes. But she started taking my clothes off during a steamy make-out sesh. Well, she refused to take hers off because we weren't alone, so Sean took the hint and left. As he said, she mentioned a morning class so it would have to be quick. Unfortunately for us, the fire alarm went off. I don't know if she did it on purpose, but she grabbed me and pulled me out of the room stark naked. She was far too strong for a girl her size. Well, half my hall saw my ass and the other half saw my dick.

"Sean was thankfully still there and, in his rush, to help, took his fucking pants off and gave them to me. There are still some videos circulating of me jumping into his pants while rushing out of the building."

"Oh, and the kicker was," Sean buts in, "the alarm went off because someone tried to put instant noodles in their microwave without water." He's busting a gut, laughing so hard I'm surprised she can understand him.

"Evelyn." My boys are laughing so hard that I almost miss it.

"Evelyn," I repeat, tasting the word on my tongue. "It suits you." She smiles at me, so broad and wide it takes my breath away.

"God, it's almost one! How late do you have to stay out?" Dillan pipes up from where he's squished in the middle of the round booth.

"Until two. Who knows if she'll be done by then though, her boyfriend looked like an athlete." Really, maybe I know him then. I'm sure he'd like to know what his girlfriend did.

"Did you catch his name." Evelyn shakes her head.

"Nah, she didn't mention a name. He might just be a hookup that she calls a boyfriend. I knew a girl in high school who did that." She sighs wistfully into her coffee. I finally take a sip of mine and ho God is it sweet. I must make a face at it. "If you don't like it why'd you order it?"

"Because you ordered it and I didn't know what else to get. Here, it's all yours." Pushing the coffee over to her earns me another giggle but she takes it gratefully. I didn't notice until now but hers is almost gone.

Everyone dissolves into different conversations. Evelyn sits quietly, taking it all in while I take her in. Long black hair brushes the dip in her waist, she's pale, like snow white pale. Big brown doe eyes with long lashes to frame them. Rosy cheeks but I think that's from her smiling, a natural reaction since the blush wasn't there in the diner. She has a heart shape face, a slender neck, and tiny shoulders. Actually, now that I take a good look at her, she has the same body type as a few of the cheerleaders I've been with. I think they called themselves flyers? Eh, who knows?

Oli catches my attention with practice talk. "Does it start tomorrow or the day after?"

"Like later today tomorrow, or tomorrow as in tomorrow?" We all fall silent, just blinking at Dillan.

"What the fuck?" The words are out of my mouth before I can stop them. Like seriously, what kind of crazy talk is that? Why would today be tomorrow?

"Okay, are you talking about the twenty-fourth, twenty-fifth, or twenty-sixth?" Jesus Dillan, you couldn't have asked that first? We're athletes for a reason, well not really. Oli is like super smart, so is Sean. I'm decent at school but I want to go pro after college, so it doesn't really matter as long as I pass my classes. But Dillan is sort of a genius.

I slip my phone from my back pocket and check the schedule. "First practice is tomorrow the twenty-fifth. So not later today." Oli nods his thanks but not after sending a glare at Dillan.

"What sport do you play?" Evelyn is looking at me so the question is obviously meant for me but the others don't seem to care.

"Hockey." They all reply in unison.

"Oh, my grandpa's a big fan of the NHL. My dad doesn't understand, says football is superior." A collective scoff arises from everyone around the table. "I agree with my mom who says baseball is best."

"Baseball!" She looks at me with a curious gleam in her eyes.

"Yeah, what could possibly be better than watching of bunch of fit men run around in white leggings? Those uniforms make their butts look amazing." She sighs dreamily, leaning on me like she needs support as she clasps her hands in front of her and looks to the roof.

"Hockey's better." I say it as a statement, because what the hell? You can't tell a table of hockey players another sport trump theirs because the uniforms are sexier!

"Why, because that's what you play?"

"Of fucking course! I bet when I put my hockey uniform on, you won't be able to keep your eyes off of me."

"Is he always this cocky?" She doesn't ask anyone in specific so everyone replies. Oli says yes, Sean laughs and says yea, and Dillan, the fucker, say 'what else would he be?'

"Come to our first game Sweetheart and I'll prove myself right."

"Who says I want to go to a hockey game? I don't even like the sport." She meets my gaze head on, challenge in her eyes.

"You wouldn't want to make me sad, would you?" She huffs before turning to Oli and start talking to him about something else. Well, it seems that's the end of the conversation.

She's drinking my coffee, so I take the initiative to throw her empty cup away. The clock on the wall reads one thirty so there's only a half an hour left before she can head back to her room.

By the time I return to the table, she's talking about walking back to the dorm buildings. "It's about a twenty-minute walk to my dorm from here so I should get going. Hopefully my roommate and her boyfriend are asleep when I get back." She starts to stand so I offer my hand for her to latch onto. "Thanks." She climbs out of the booth, everyone else following suit.

"I'll walk you back. I don't have anything to do until late today so I can afford to lose an hour of sleep." Sean is quick to pipe in, saying he will as well. Normally I'd be upset but he had a good point, with it being so late. Another shot of annoyance shoots through me at the audacity of her roommate to force Evelyn to stay out this late.

"Oh, thank you."

Oli and Dillan bid us a goodnight, heading back to their shared apartment. We all head our separate ways, answering any questions Evelyn throws our way. "Do you still like on campus?"

"Nah, we rent a three-bed house with a buddy of ours, I'm sure you'll meet him soon enough." She looks at me quizzically.

"You seem so sure I'll see you again. It's a big campus, and you're a Junior. We have different classes. There's a good chance I won't see you for a long time." It kind of hurts that she doesn't seem the least bit sad about that. Her tone blank as she stares at me.

We're nearing her dorm building when something, or someone, catches her attention. "Oh, that's the guy my roommate brought into our room!" I look up and sure enough, I know him. Joshua Silvosh. He's a good guy, a basketball player I've had a few classes with. "Well, thanks for walking me back. Goodnight." Evelyn disappears inside the building, leaving Sean and I outside.

"You thinking what I'm thinking?" I look at him.

"Sure am. Hey Josh!" He stops in his tracks. His bright blue eyes can be seen even from this distance. The distance he eats up in a matter of seconds. He pulls us into a bro hug, smiling from ear to ear. His smile alone can light up the night from how white his teeth are. His blond hair, blue eyes, and devilish smile draw in the ladies quicker than you can call his name.

"What's up, man? Haven't seen yous in a while. Whatcha doing out so late?" He's looking between us and the dorm building suspiciously.

"Don't look at us that way, you're the one who just left the freshman dorms." Damn Sean, way to call the man out.

"True, true."

"Hey, were you just hooking up with someone named Ella?" I had to badger Evelyn for her name, took me about an hour to get it.

"Uh, yeah?"

"Are you two together?" He seems thoroughly confused now.

"Nah, why? Is she saying we are?" He definitely seems upset now. I don't blame him. No one wants someone you're just sleeping with to tell people you are together; it causes unnecessary drama.

"I don't know about others but that's what she told her roommate while kicking her out for the night." His blue eyes blink, once, twice, three times.

"Ella kicked her out? She told me her roommate offered her the room. Told me that she had plans for the night." I knew it!

"Nope, met her a few hours ago in the dinner on the other end of the campus. Took me a little while to figure out why she was out alone so late but eventually she told me it was because her roommate decided to spend her first night on campus with some guy and kicked her out of her room. Actually, it's both of their first nights. I figured, given you reputation, you'd like to know."

Well, I don't think Ella will be seeing Joshypoo any time soon, he's fucking **pissed**. "Good to know. Though how'd you know it was me that was with her?"

"Evelyn made a comment when we were walking up. Pointed you out as the guy she saw Ella bring to their room."

"How did this Evelyn know who I was? I don't think I met her?"

"Nah, but you did pass her when she was heading to the elevator. You and Ella were getting off while she was getting on. That's how she knew that Ella told you that she offered their room up. It annoyed her but she didn't say anything. Well, I just wanted to let you know. See ya in class, I'm sure we have at least one together." It would make sense; we do have the same major.

"Thanks, dude, see ya." Josh heads back in the direction of the Junior dorms while we head back across campus to where I parked my truck earlier.

"You plan on seeing her again, don't you?" I smile to myself.

"Yeah, I think I'm done with the random hookups. It was nice for a while, but I'm bored."

"So, you want to date a freshman?" There's no judgment in his voice, though I didn't expect there to be. Sean's always been open-minded when it comes to the age differences in relationships. He has to be considering his parents are eleven years apart.

"Maybe, she's pretty and gets along with you guys. I can see myself with her but I don't know if she'll be open to it. She did say she doesn't like hockey so we might not be the best match." Sean chuckles at my obvious joke. We both know that if I wanted to, I could convince her that hockey is far superior to baseball. Especially if her only argument is how good the players look in their uniforms. However, something tells me hockey won't be why she doesn't want to go out with me. Her reactions and lack of reactions have me worried.

"We'll see. She may be just what you need. I mean, how often do you meet someone who gives you a run for your money? She slapped you first thing." He sucks in a breath, a playful glimmer in his eyes. "Maybe I should chase her. That slap *was* sexy." I shove him off the sidewalk. My trucks in view and if he wasn't my best friend, I would consider leaving him here. Oh, who am I kidding, I'm definitely considering leaving him here.

"Don't even think about it. Just watch, I'll make her mine." Hopefully.

3

Evie

Ella ignores me when I enter. She doesn't say anything while I get ready for bed and put all of my things away. I set my alarm for eight a.m. and crawl into bed. The tension in the air is so thick it could be cut with a butter knife but neither of us tries to break it. It's nearing two-thirty and if I'm tired, she's exhausted.

After a few minutes, the room is filled with snoring, which when I met her, she swore she didn't do. My annoyance wracks up with every passing minute. Under normal circumstances, I wouldn't care but she snores so loud I'm worried we might get a noise complaint.

I could go to the office tomorrow and ask for a new roommate, but I'm worried I might be paired with someone else like her. But I can't risk a bad roommate bring my grades down. I send off a text to my Aunt Jenessa, if anyone would know what to do, it would be her.

> **Me: Hey, I need advice**
> **Me: My roommate is awful**
> **Me: Should I ask to be moved to a different dorm?**
> **Me: What if they put me with someone worse?**
> **Me: Auntie, I need help**

I set my phone down before I send more and accidentally wake her up. She lives in Seattle and works two jobs just so she can afford the live there. It's two a.m. here which means it's eleven p.m. there but I think she works at four a.m. so she's probably asleep.

I shut my eyes, hoping to wake up to a text from her with my much-needed answers.

I turn my alarm off while climbing out of bed. Ella is still snoring softly and relief rushes through me. I really don't want to deal with her this early.

I throw on a pair of leggings, a sports bra, and a loose T-shirt before grabbing my headphones and phone. I close the door with a soft click, locking behind me. I would prefer to be awake earlier, but I was up way too late for that.

I gear up for my morning walk, I've already planned out my route, three miles around the campus. I'm hoping there won't be too many people awake.

As I enter the elevator, I get caught up on my notifications. I'm elated to see Aunt Jenessa replied.

> **Auntie J: It wouldn't hurt to try**
> **Auntie J: What kind of awful is she?**
> **Auntie J: Bratty or bitchy?**
> **Me: Bitchy**
> **Me: She kicked me out last night from six to two so she could 'have fun' with her boyfriend**
> **Me: Didn't give me a say in the matter**

Before I know what, I'm doing, I'm walking into the dorm office. The woman behind the desk looks up as I walk in.

"Good morning. How can I help you, young lady?" She's a sweet old lady that I met a few weeks ago when I found out what dorm I'd be in.

"Oh uh, I was wondering if I could move dorms. Like, get a new roommate? I don't think I'll do too well with my current one." She's typing away before I can finish my sentence.

"What's the matter with her? Or is it you? Before I can re-assign I need a reason."

"Well, I had just finished unpacking yesterday when she walked in and told me to leave. She was having her boyfriend over and she needed the room from six p.m. to two a.m. Once the semester starts, I'm afraid she'll continue, and it will affect my sleep and therefore my grades." She stops typing to study me.

"Well, she seems to be here for the right reasons." I crack a smile at her slight animosity. I was informed when I was accepted that while it is looked down upon, it is completely okay to have the opposite gender in your room. I know a few schools I applied for that was grounds for expulsion.

"It doesn't bother me, but I don't want it to impact me in the wrong way. I worked so hard to get here, I don't want a bad roomie to be my downfall."

"I get you, sweetheart, let me see here." She continues to type away for a few minutes. "Well, I don't see anyone wanting a room change right now but there are a few empty rooms up for grabs. I can put you in one of those. This is actually unusual, we have a much smaller class size this year which has left quite a lot of rooms open. Though, it might have something to do with the apartment building that was built a town over. I've heard its reasonably priced. Anyway, with how this year is looking, there is a chance you won't have a roommate, but it's not guaranteed. You won't know until the second week of the semester." She looks over her monitor at me and I'm ecstatic.

"That's more than okay! When can I move my things?" She chuckles at me but gets back to work, clicking around and typing.

"After three today. We still have students moving in but roommate changes aren't as common as people think, at least not here. There's not much I can do to ensure that you have your own room. Although I can flag your room since you were an early acceptance, the school does tend to favor those."

"Early acceptance? I thought I got my letter at the same time everyone else did." Actually, I'm pretty sure I did. I opened my letter with Alyssa.

"That's odd. You should have received it well before others. I wish I could tell you why you were among the small amount to be accepted early, but I'm not privy to that knowledge. We're a fairly small school so we tend to fill up quickly. Chances are it was something you put in your letter, it must have pulled some heartstrings. Well, here's your new room key, and when you are done moving just drop off your old key in the drop box outside the door."

I grab the key from her hand and bid her farewell. It didn't say anything on my acceptance letter that I was hand-chosen but I guess they might not want to inflate someone's ego. But if I was early acceptance, why didn't I get my letter early?

I go about my walk, listening to a podcast about life. I pass a lot of people, but none pay me any mind. Well, most don't. The guys from last night spot me and start walking my way and I'm surprised to see Ella's hookup with them.

I don't feel like talking right now so I ignore them and walk faster. I can't hear if they call out my name but I'm hoping they don't. I think I made it clear last night I'd rather not get more attention than necessary.

I see one of the many college restaurants. Well, restaurant may be a bit of a stretch but whatever. I veer into a juice and smoothie shop and get in line. Once I get to the front, I order a strawberry banana smoothie and pay. While I wait for them to make it I see the group of guys walk past the window.

I breathe a sigh of relief, grab my smoothie, and walk the opposite way of them. It's almost nine and I'm hopeful Ella will be somewhere that is not our dorm. But just in case, I text Alyssa, wanting to get this move over with quickly.

Me: Hey, morning!

Me: I got a new room assignment, can you help me move my stuff?

Me: I get access to my new room at three

I slip my phone into the pocket of my leggings, knowing she's probably still asleep. My dad used to make comments about how different we are and how he couldn't understand how we were friends. The last time he said that she was spending the night. He got really drunk that night and did some unspeakable things.

That was the last time I talked to my dad. I'm still pissed he wasn't held responsible. What a great message to send the boys in my high school. A message they got loud and clear.

A large hand lands on my shoulder, yanking me to a stop. My heart skitters to a stop, panic blinding me.

I turn to look at the owner and of course, it's Tanner. And he's talking. A lot. I bet he doesn't even realize I have headphones in. But his friends do. Sean was it? Is laughing his ass off behind Tanner. Which catches said man's attention. My heart starts back to a normal beat as I watch them.

They start arguing and I try to dip but Oliver stops me and takes one of my headphones out. He pops it in his ear despite my displeasure at the idea. "Great, now I'm going to have to wash that." The asshole just laughs. I mean, come on! That's so gross!

"What is this, a talk show?"

I gawk at him; he can't be serious! Yet, he is. "No. It's a podcast. Now gimme that back!" I make a scene trying to grab it out of his hand but he easily dodges my advances. I almost spill my smoothie and Tanner is the only reason I don't. He grabs the cup from my hands before it falls to the ground and spills everywhere.

"Dude, give her the headphone." If it weren't for the amusement in his voice, I might actually think he cares. I give up trying to reach my headphone. He's too damn tall.

"Nah, this is actually interesting." He smirks but I know how to wipe it from his face.

I grab my phone out and search for the podcast I heard yesterday. It's by the same women but this one is all about menstruation and how young girls should handle it.

I click on it without hesitation.

"All right! The topic today is one many of you wanted us to talk about." Oliver's brows scrunch as he listens intently. I still have one of the headphones in so I hear it a the same time he does, but even if I didn't, the look on his face would tell me he heard the topic.

"How young girls should handle their periods. Let's start with pads," he's tossing the headphone at me like it's caught fire. Tanner catches it while I die of laughter. I'm holding my stomach but it's not enough. My knees feel weak as I crouch down, hoping to get a breath in.

I notice Tanner put the headphone in his ear right before he starts laughing with me. "That's a good one."

Ella's guy friend walks up looking extremely confused. "What's so funny?"

"Oli didn't want to give Evelyn back her headphone, so she turned on a podcast about periods."

"It's not funny, Josh!" Except Josh is now also dying of laughter and either can't hear him or ignores him. I will never understand why men find periods disgusting. It's funny though.

Tanner hands me the air pod and my smoothie once I've recovered. "Thanks." My phone buzzes in my hand and I see Alyssa answered.

> **Bestie: Of course! Brunch?**
> **Bestie: Wait! Is it too close to lunch for you to have brunch?**

I laugh at her antics because no, no it is not too close to lunch but that wouldn't have stopped me anyway. Food is life.

> **Me: Where do you want to go?**

Tanner peaks over my shoulder, reading my texts like he has a right to. "Is that the friend you were talking about last night?"

"Yes." I move my phone out of his vision, but he follows it. "Please don't read my texts."

He just shrugs but does back away.

> **Bestie: I have no idea**
> **Bestie: Meet me at my room?**
> **Bestie: We can decide together**
> **Me: Deal**
> **Me: See you soon!**

I manage to leave the group without them noticing my disappearance and head back to the dorms. Alyssa is on the second floor while I was one the third. I look at my key and the little note that tells me my room number is 410. Now I'll be on the top floor which means lugging all of my things up another floor but it's worth it if I won't have a roommate.

4

Tanner

I turn to say something to Evelyn but she's not there. I look around but there's no sign of her. Sean comes up beside me to pat my shoulder. "There, there buddy. She seemed to be in a rush to get somewhere, or maybe she just doesn't like you." He shrugs like it's no big deal but at least I know it's the former thanks to my eavesdropping.

"She's having breakfast with a friend."

"And how do you know that?"

"I read her texts over her shoulder." He rolls his eyes at me but they both should have expected that considering I met her by reading over her shoulder last night. Which reminds me, I want to know what she was writing. I read a few paragraphs before she noticed me, and I'm hooked!

I reach for my phone but stop. I didn't get her number. Damn.

I blink at my empty hand like it burned me. Josh notices and makes fun of me for it, but I flip him off. I don't have much to do today, classes don't start for a few more days and practice doesn't start until tomorrow.

I don't work during the school year so I can focus on my classes and practice so I can't lean back on that. I could go to the gym; except I don't want to be sore for practice tomorrow. I've already walked my class schedule. It's too early for a party, but that doesn't sound fun anyway.

While I'm deep in thought I don't notice the woman sidling up to me, plastering herself to my side. I only notice when her arms snake around mine. She's batting her eyes at me, giving a sashay smile. That smile falls faster than I can blink when I shake her off and take a very obvious step away from her.

I know who she is, Brianna Jones is a Junior like I am and probably the school's biggest puck bunny. We've never slept together, to her obvious disappointment.

She and her friends have slept with, at the very least, half the hockey team. I'm not one to slut shame and call women whores just because they're sexually active. Considering I've been considered a man-whore my entire freshman year, I know it doesn't feel too good.

I'm not saying they were wrong to call me that, I did sleep with a lot of women, most of whom I don't remember their names, let alone their faces. I'm not proud of who I was, drunk and fucking my way through the year just because I could. If my ex could see me now, she would, God I don't know what she would do. But she definitely wouldn't be happy. I miss her, with every day that goes by.

"Hey, what's up? Whatcha thinking?" Collins nudges me bringing my thoughts back to the land of the living. Rufus Collins is one of my best friends, he lives off-campus with Sean and I. He's a big dude but he kind of has to be, he's one of the team's goalies and a damn good one at that. His shaggy blond hair is now long enough for a man bun, I think his mountain man beard is too. His nose is crooked from the many hits he's taken on the ice. But the thing that draws your attention to him is his smoky gray eyes.

"I was thinking about Mia." His eyes soften. It took my buddies getting me drunk last year for me to finally talk about her but I don't regret it. They deserved to know why I was so against relationships when we first met.

"It wasn't your fault, dude. There was nothing you could do to save her." His voice is grim but firm.

"I know, that's not what I was thinking about." At his confusion, I continue, "I miss her, her smile, her voice, her kindness, just her." Sadness snakes it's way into my heart.

My high school girlfriend Mia was the best thing that ever happened to me. I met her freshman year and chased after her until she finally gave me a chance sophomore year. Her dad hated me at first and I can't blame him. From his view, I was taking his baby girl from him, she always was a daddy's girl. Her mom wasn't in the picture, she left when Mia was three. It took a year and a half for the old man to soften to me but when he did, we became extremely close. Mia loved that, she always said she loved that her two men got along.

It was our junior prom, she and one of her friends were on their way to the school. We had agreed to meet at the school because she wanted to drive separately, wanted to bring a sophomore with her who didn't have a ride.

I remember so clearly the music stopping. Our principal taking the stage, crying. "There's been an accident." His voice ringing through the silent auditorium. "At 8:32 this afternoon we lost two of our own to a hit and run." It felt like the air was being sucked from the room. I looked around the room for Mia, to comfort her, she was always emotional even when she never met the person, but she wasn't there. That's when I knew. "May Mia Reynolds and Stacey Shaw rest in peace. God bless their souls." I felt their eyes on me, everyone looking to see my reaction. I remember being told as a child that crying made you weak, but I couldn't stop the salty rivets from cascading down my face.

I don't know when he came but her dad showed up to bring me to the hospital, to see her one last time.

It didn't take long after that night for the police to find the culprit. Stacey moved to our city that year but never told anyone why. We found out why. She had a crazy ex-boyfriend. A boy who couldn't accept that she might be happy without him.

He swore up and down he didn't come this way to do any harm, he just wanted to talk to her. But when he saw her in Mia's car, smiling, laughing, he lost it. He claims he blacked out, doesn't remember anything that happened. The camera of the local bakery caught everything, him seeing her, his car speeding forward, his car hitting Stacey's door at seventy miles an hour, her dying on impact. Somehow, he was able to walk away from it, hardly a scratch on him. He didn't even remember she wasn't alone in that car.

He left Mia to die a slow and painful death, her lungs being crushed by the airbag that hadn't deployed fast enough. She was propelled into the steering wheel where the car seat forced her to stay as the airbag tried to deploy, where it stole her last breath.

I've long since blamed myself. It took a few years to accept it wasn't my fault but eventually, I realized there was no way for me to save her. Mia wanted to bring Stacey and some crazed guy took their light. It wasn't my fault; I couldn't have saved her even if I wanted to.

"I get it, dude, she was a great person, from what you told us." He offers a comforting smile. None of them have ever pushed me on the topic and I'm more than grateful for that.

"Who's Mia?" Brinna's voice irks me. She shouldn't be speaking her name or asking about her. Mia is none of her concern but for some reason, she believes all of us hockey players are her property. I've seen her get territorial multiple times.

"No one." I keep my back turned to her but that doesn't stop her from snaking her arms around my waist like she has the right to touch me. Like she has a right to me.

"It's alright, she doesn't matter anyway. I'm here now." I watch as Collins eyes grow wide, his face taking on a ghostly shade. I'm stiff under Brianna's touch, she's still speaking but I can't hear her over the blood rushing in my ears.

Seans' face comes into view, he's also speaking but he's smart and realizes I can't hear him or I'm not paying attention. I've never heard someone who knows nothing about someone else tell them that a person from their past doesn't matter. She doesn't know Mia is dead, or that she was the best thing to ever happen to me but that makes it worse. She knows nothing of this woman, just assumes she can replace her, take her spot in my life. It pisses me off to no end.

Sean is quietly conversing with Collins; I can't see his face but his body language tells me a lot. He's fucking pissed. Welcome to the party.

Brianna's hands tighten around me, and I snap. "Let go of me." My voice comes out in a growl. Her hands loosen slightly but she doesn't release me.

"Oh, come on baby. I just want to love on you." I pry her hands from my torso stepping away from her reach.

"Don't ever fucking touch me without my permission." I can see her flinch in my peripheral vision, but I don't care if I hurt her. She should learn to keep her fucking mouth shut.

My boys flank me, none of them giving her attention as we walk away. "That fucking bitch." Sean sounds as pissed as I feel. "Who the fuck does she think she is." He continues to rant, calling her almost every name under the sun, not caring if anyone hears him. Josh and Dillan break off from the group at some point, both of them needing to speak with a counselor about something.

We enter one of the various dining halls. While I grab a seat, the others grab food. I'm not hungry after the interaction earlier so I take in my surroundings.

The hall is packed, students and teachers alike grabbing breakfast and chatting away with their friends. A few groups glance my way, some people brazen enough to meet my stare head-on. Oli takes the seat to my left, Sean the one to my right, and Collins across from me.

A few people come over to talk to us, some flirt, and others outwardly try to fuck us right here. I glower at everyone who gets close to me, effectively giving me some peace.

"If you keep that expression, no one will want to talk to you." Evelyn breathes into my ear, her melodic voice bringing me temporary peace.

"That's the point." I turn to look at her, I didn't notice her sitting in the seat behind me earlier. She leans back in her seat so she can be heard over the crowd.

"What happened? You were happy when I left earlier." I see the genuine curiosity in her eyes, and I feel compelled to answer her.

"Some puck bunny didn't know personal boundaries." She makes an O with her mouth like she could possibly understand the true meaning behind my statement.

"Oh, what a shame. I thought you were all about the bunnies." A tall dark-skinned beauty sits down next to Evelyn, but her pale blue eyes are focused on me.

"Alyssa!" Evelyn chastises. "That was rude. Apologize!" Alyssa rolls her eyes, ignoring her friend's demands. "She's sorry." I look back to Evelyn, a smile pulling at my lips.

"Don't apologize on my behalf. If I was sorry, I'd say sorry!" Alyssa takes a big bite of food, avoiding eye contact.

"Why don't you like him? He's done nothing wrong." My eyes flicker between the two like they're playing tennis, batting the ball back and forth.

"You know why Evie. He's a jock, that should be enough." Evie stiffens but her eyes remain soft with a shadow passing over them.

"Sorry, I get it, trust me I do. It's just that he hasn't done anything to deserve my hatred yet. It's a new year and we left all that behind. I know I'm being optimistic, but I'd like to believe not everyone has ill intentions." She sounds sad, like she is battling tears. Alyssa rests a hand on Evie's.

"I would like to also but we're moving you out of your room today into a new one because you got a bitch for a roommate the first time around. It's not too promising." Evie nods as she wipes at her eyes.

"Yeah." She turns her back to me but I'm not the only one who knows she's there now.

"Evelyn! I was wondering where you went earlier. You just disappeared." She looks at Sean and offers a small smile that he sees right through. "What's wrong?"

"I think you should be asking your buddy that; he's scaring everyone away with his glowering. I thought Oliver told me he was like a golden retriever." I can tell she's trying to lighten the mood and it's working. Though she can't hide her watery laugh.

"Oh, yeah, I know why. Some girl stepped out of line and spoke about a situation she knew nothing of. It pissed us all off. Who's your friend?" She visibly brightens at the question and Alyssa groans.

"Evie, don't you da-"

"This is Alyssa, my best friend. I mentioned her last night. We've been friends since we were babies." Evie is beaming at us while Alyssa glowers at her supposed best friend.

"I'm Sean." He offers her his hand, which she ignores in favor of her food. The others have noticed who we're talking to and have started to attempt to get their attention. They both ignore my friends, Evie whispers something to her friend. Whatever response she gets has her nodding.

"Alright, let's go then." They both stand, Alyssa moving toward the counters to put her dirty dish where it belongs. "I'll see you later." They just got here and they're leaving already?

My hand involuntarily reaches out, stopping her. "Wait, can I get your number?"

"Oh, I don't know. I don't give that out to hardly anyone." She bites her plush lip, drawing my attention down.

"But, Evie baby, it's me." My smile falters when her reaction is not what I expected. She rips her hand from mine, a darkness floats in her eyes. I know I fucked up before she says anything.

"Don't call me that." Her voice is laced with venom as she takes a step away from me while nursing the wrist I was holding like she was burnt. Alyssa approaches and they leave without another word.

I stare dumbfounded at her back until she's out of sight. One of my boy's whistles low followed by a few chuckles. "Damn, spicy."

"Shut up Collins." He chuckles again.

"Never, Tanner, never."

I don't know what I did wrong, but I plan on figuring it out. Sean follows closely behind me as I stalk out of the dining hall toward the freshman dorms. Toward the girl I can't get out of my head.

5

Evie

Alyssa doesn't ask as I practically drag her across campus. I'm sure she heard what he said. She knows what meaning those words mean to me. Where they send me. They send her to the same place.

Freshman year of high school, when she went to grab a glass of water from the kitchen and didn't return. I went to check on her, but I heard her first. Her cries and pleas for him to stop. Her sobs filled the silent kitchen as I rounded the corner.

The terror in her pale blue eyes will be forever etched into my mind. Same with my father forcing his way between her bloody thighs as she screams in pain. His large palm covered her mouth to muffle the sound. Mom was sleeping upstairs when I heard the blood-curdling scream come from me. At least I think it came from me.

That caught his attention, his face whipping around to mine. "Evie baby, if you don't quiet down, you'll be next. Now shut up and let your old man enjoy something for the first time in his life." I didn't stop, I woke up half the neighborhood. My mother beat him with a bat when she found out what was happening. The police showed up and refused to take our statement, they asked Alyssa if she really wanted to 'ruin' his life with the allegation.

They didn't care there were two eyewitnesses; all they cared about was keeping us quiet.

While my father never touched me that night, his actions and lack of punishment did. Marcus Flocken was the first to drug me and take advantage. Jake Schelve was next, all through high school this went on. No one would do anything because for some reason their future mattered more than mine, more than my best friends. Of the five guys that raped me, three were athletes, two were from the town over.

I'm not ashamed of what happened to me. I own it. It wasn't my fault the justice system in our little town is corrupt, and it most definitely wasn't my fault when the boys took advantage of my turned head in class and spiked my drink. Where they got those drugs, I pray I never learn.

"Evie." Alyssa tugs my arm until I stop. "Evie, he's following us." She played the part of a bitch earlier, but I know better than to believe it. She's scared.

I follow her eyes and see Tanner flanked by Sean coming

closer.

We're not far from the dorms, we could easily reach it before they reach us but in an unspoken conversation, we decide to stay. "What did I do? Tell me and I'll fix it." My heart aches to believe him but Alyssa is right, he's a jock, enough said.

"It doesn't matter. You can't fix an issue that's already resolved."

"But it's not resolved. You're still upset, and I want to know why. I want to help." He's sincere but that doesn't change that my hurt is still too raw for him to fix, to help.

"Go away Tanner, whatever you think might happen between us never will." He seems hurt but that's for the best, I can never let him that close anyway. He's one of them at the end of the day, no matter how nice he seems.

"But."

I raise my hand to hush him. "No, just leave. I'm not here to make friends, I'm here to graduate and make a better life for me and my mom, you do not, nor ever will, fit into that so leave. Save your breath for someone who cares." My words hit their mark. We silently watch as the boys walk away, hopefully, I won't have to deal with them.

The first week of classes went by uneventfully. To no one's surprise, I have no classes with Tanner and his friends, though I do have one with Ella. It's basic English and when she noticed me sitting near the front, she quickly disappeared up the stairs, toward the back.

She wasn't in the room when I moved my things and I haven't seen her since the morning after she kicked me out of the room.

There's still a week to go, so still no guarantees, but so far I have no roommate. Alyssa states how jealous she is every chance she gets but I know she likes he roommate. I haven't had a chance to meet her but Alyssa gushed about her the entire time we packed my stuff up.

I'm currently walking across the Quad toward my Monday class. A headphone in my ear is playing a podcast but I'm only half paying attention.

I watch as students mull about, some speedwalking across campus to make it to their destination on time. Others congregate on blankets spread out on the grass.

A couple sits under a tree completely enamored by each other, or by their mouth more likely. She looks like she's trying to suck his face off, it looks painful.

I spot a few more couples dotted about, holding hands, kissing, hugging, I even see a girl nearly tackle a guy as she jumps in his arms. There's a pang in my heart as I watch them interact with each other. I wish I could do that.

Then again, maybe I could.

I've agreed to go to therapy after my mom badgered me about it. She made a compelling argument, I live in a new state, away from my past trauma. I need to talk to someone about this, about what was done to me. Mom hopes that one day I'll be able to move past it and maybe even fall in love someday.

After having the same conversation for the umpteenth time, I finally agreed. I'm supposed to start next week.

I was surprised when I brought it up to Alyssa, she said she'd try it with me and found her own therapist to go to. Her appointment is on Friday.

I faintly register the sound of someone coming up behind me but I don't think anything of it with as many people out here as there are.

I've made it halfway across the quad by the time the footsteps reach me. I still pay no mind, believing it to be a student in a rush. That is until a hand clasps my shoulder, the sudden shock has me jerking away, my scream echoing between the buildings.

Tanner jumps back, looking around as people start watching. He smiles at someone off to my right before turning his attention back to me. "Hey," he scratched the back of his neck nervously, "sorry, I didn't mean to frighten you. I thought you would have heard me coming. I've been told I'm a loud guy." He flashes me a sheepish smile, one I'm sure has many girls falling over themselves to see again.

My heart feels like it might jump out of my chest. It's beating so loud that I almost can't hear him. My mouth pops open in shock as his words register.

"You didn't mean to scare me?" I take a deep breath, calming my frayed nerves. The words leave my mouth in a deadly whisper, far more malice clouding them than I usually use.

"Uh, no?" There he goes again, scratching the back of his neck. He's nervous.

"Why in the world would I believe the footsteps behind me are someone coming to talk to me? Can you not see how many others are walking right now?"

His mouth pops open only to close right away. He stands there, blubbering for words as he desperately searches for words

I don't want to hear.

"It doesn't matter. I told you to leave me alone. I don't want to talk to you." I brush past him, leaving him in the middle of a grassy field. A few people snicker as I pass but no one else approaches me as I walk to class.

During the first month of school, Tanner tried to talk to me fifteen times. Each time ended the same as the first, with me telling him to leave me alone and walking away.

I overheard someone in one of my classes say that hockey season is starting so I'm hoping that means less Tanner.

The person next to me yawns as the professor drones on about similes. The time on my laptop is a harsh reminder that class has now gone over half an hour. I don't know how the professor hasn't realized, or maybe he has and he doesn't care, but I do.

Just like most of my classmates, I pack up my belongings and leave.

The professor glances at me when I open the door. I motion to my wrist like I'm tapping a watch as the door closes behind me. I hear his words stop just as the door closes. Hopefully, that means he's checking the time.

I slowly walk through the hall, passing by a few teachers and waving at them.

Most people are in class right now so the building is quiet as I descend the stairs. Turning the corner I notice a group of girls loitering at the end of the hall near the doors I'm leaving out of.

As I near them, blond hair catches my eye.

Ella looks over her shoulder at me and scowls. Her gaze wanders the length of my body. She scoffs at me before giving me her back.

For the most part, she's left me alone, save for the few passive-aggressive comments she makes about me. I've seen a few of her posts on Twitter that are obviously about me but nothing too bad. From what I've gathered, the guy she invited over that night won't talk to her and she blames me for it.

I guess I can't blame her for assuming I'm behind his lack of communication. She did see me talking to him while Tanner was around before school started.

"I hope you're happy." Her back is still to me but there's no doubt in my mind that she's talking to me.

"About what?" I stop walking, now standing behind her.

"Josh won't talk to me. Seems your little boyfriend is whispering in his ear." My heart falls to my feet. Tanner, she's talking about Tanner.

"I don't have a boyfriend. If someone is talking in his ear, it has nothing to do with me." I continue my way to the door, ignoring her as she tells me that she doesn't believe that I have nothing to do with Josh's silence.

The doors close behind me, shutting her and her friends up.

I've been going to therapy for two months now and I think it's going okay. I didn't like the first therapist I went to so I switched and Dr. Wilson and seemed to click.

My phone buzzes in my hands. A text from Alyssa reading, *Hope you have a good appointment :)*

I reply quickly with a thanks and tuck my phone into my little backpack. She got lucky with the first therapist she went to and has stayed with her since her first appointment. The phone on the receptionist's table rings until it eventually goes to voicemail. Miss Laura had gone to the back to discuss something with a doctor a few minutes ago.

The analog clock on the wall ticks over the hour mark reading three pm. My appointment is scheduled for now, an hour with Dr Wilson, diving into my trauma. She claims we made headway last time, which I guess she's not entirely wrong. I told her about the janitor's closet back at my high school.

We left off with her asking me to try to remember the first time I had an unusual reaction to the closet. Despite not wanting to, I did.

"Evelyn Campbell?" I look away from the clock to the door that Dr Wilson now stands in. I smile at her while standing to follow her to her office. "How are you doing today Sweety?" Dr Wilson is in her early sixties and specializes in sexual assault survivors.

"Better than last week. Thank you." I nod my appreciation for her holding her office door open for me. The door closes with a soft click. Dr Wilson walks to her desk and pulls something out, probably my file.

"Would you like to start where we left off last week?" She looks up at me as I tentatively nod.

I sit in the chair that I feel most comfortable in and relax. "It was freshman year, a few months into school." I think back to the day in question, a cold fall day, unusually cold for October. " Some of the guys on the football team approached me to ask the same thing they always asked, how it felt to watch my dad that night. I told them to screw themselves before shoving past them. The day passed by normally until lunch. I had leftovers from dinner the night before but something tasted off about them. I didn't think anything of it and continued to eat. By the next class period, I felt sick so I went to the nurse. I don't remember much after that. I remember walking past the boy's bathroom, passing the janitor's closet, and someone touching my shoulder. The next thing I remember is waking up in the nurse's office in extreme pain. I almost couldn't feel it through the pain but my thighs were sore. I had no proof but I had a really bad feeling. When I voiced my concerns to nurse Debie, she called the local police and I talked to one of the officers.

"Nothing came of it, no report, no rape kit, nothing. My mom came and picked me up. Later that night I saw blood in my underwear but I wasn't on my period. After that, I stayed away from that closet. I don't know why but I didn't feel safe walking past it. I always thought my subconscious was trying to tell me something."

An hour later I'm back in my car on my way to campus. I know it will take time to feel better, to fully heal, but after today, it finally seems possible. My shoulders feel lighter and my mind clearer. Maybe I'm not as broken as I think I am. Maybe I'm not beyond repair.

He's watching me, casting glances my way every chance he gets.

His friends are making fun of him for it but he doesn't seem to care.

I don't know how he spotted me in this crowd, but he did. He's standing in line for the buffet in dining hall three while I'm sitting tucked away in the corner.

He's in a large group of what I assume is mostly hockey players. I recognize a few of the younger ones from some of my classes but I don't know their names. I swear I try to ignore him, but Tanner is impossible to ignore. He flashes me a grin when he sees me staring.

I look away quickly and pick at my food. I'm not too hungry after the appointment yesterday but I know I need to eat. I try to ignore the fact that I didn't cook this food, so I have no idea if it's been tampered with. No one other than the cooks and I have touched this food and that needs to be enough for me.

A chair scrapes next to me as someone takes the previously empty seat. I look up to see Oliver smiling at me.

"Hey, are you okay? You seemed sad." I haven't talked to Oliver a lot but he's always seemed genuine. He's never pushed me to talk to him or do anything I don't want to do. He seems like a great guy.

"Yeah." I look away, back to the line where Tanner is watching us. He has a sad smile on his face. Oliver follows my gaze and sighs.

"Ya know, I've never seen him like this. I've known him since freshman year of College and he's always been this outgoing, funny, selfless guy that's never wanted to settle down. He wanted to have the 'full college experience'. But ever since he met you, he's stopped doing a lot of things, like going to parties. People have noticed, started asking questions." He takes a bite of his pizza while watching my face, probably looking for a reaction.

"And that should mean something to me because..?"

Oliver chuckles, shaking his head. "I guess it doesn't. Just thought you might want to know since he's doing that for you."

Finally, I focus all my attention on Oliver. "No thanks," I stand, "I didn't ask him to do that, and I don't want him to. If he feels the need to change, that's on him, not me. Goodbye, Oliver."

"I told you to call me Oli," he half whines behind me.

I glance behind me at him, "Have a nice day, Oliver."

I return my food tray on my way out, avoiding Tanner's gaze the entire time.

Another week. Another therapy session. Another conversation with Tanner.

It's getting easier to talk to him but I still don't want him to. It's starting to piss me off. I tell him to leave me alone but it's like he can't. I can see how his behavior could be attractive to some women, unfortunately for him, I'm not one of them.

He's laid off after my conversation with Oliver last week but that didn't stop him fully.

Currently, the hockey team is out of town for some away games. No matter how much I try to distance myself from him, the more he seems to sneak his way back in. The more I seem to let him sneak his way in.

I don't think I'm ready to be with someone, not by a long shot. But maybe when I am, I'll try with him. He obviously is trying, if he didn't actually want to get to know me, he would have left me be. Or maybe I'm just really out of touch with dating and attraction.

It's not like my luck with past boyfriends is good. Considering my ex left me for my sister I would say that warrants me to consider my dating life bad luck.

I live two thousand miles away from everyone who hurt me, there's no way I'll ever come across them here.

I won't have to worry about running into them at the grocery store anymore. I moved here to start a new life. A better one for both me and my mom.

For the time being, a boyfriend is not in the cards for me. In a year or two, possibly, but not in the near future. School is my priority, as it always has been. My grades got me here, and my dedication will take me further.

~Winter Break~

"I still can't believe you got so lucky last semester and got your own room!" Alyssa's roommate Sasha whines from her desk chair. "While I love Alyssa here, I would die to have a room to myself."

"Thanks, Sash, love you too." My best friend's monotone voice draws laughs out of all of us.

"Yeah, it can be amazing but lonely." I've already been informed that I will not be receiving a roommate for the upcoming semester either, though I haven't told Sahsa that yet.

"Who cares! You don't have to share your private space! You can have a guy over without asking for your roommate to leave. That sounds like heaven." Her wistful sigh pulls another laugh from me. When either wants a guy over, mostly Sasha, the other ends up in my room for the night. I won't complain, it's nice to have the company.

"Have either of you got your next schedule yet? Mine came in yesterday." That's right, new schedules are coming out this week. Classes start on Monday.

"Not yet, I'm dying to know." Sometimes I think all Sash knows how to do is whine.

"Same here, nothing." Alyssa nods to herself. She started seeing this guy a few weeks ago but I don't think it will last long. He's very demanding when it comes to her spare time. She claims she's okay with it but I can see the toll it's taking on her. She's constantly tired. She's also having trouble staying concentrated.

"So, you're still getting grief from Ella?"

"Yeah, she's the same bitch as she's always been." Once she found out I was the reason Josh stopped seeing her and blocked her on everything, she made it her life's mission to make my life as difficult as possible.

"Seriously?" Alyssa finally refocuses on the conversation.

"Yup, I think she's coming back this week, so I better soak in the peace while it lasts." We all fall into comfortable conversations for the next few hours.

Sasha is the only friend I've made this last semester. I've stayed true to my word and focused on school. I've topped all of my classes and plan on it again this semester.

I didn't think that we would become so close, but it makes sense when I spend so much time here. It was only a matter of time. Her family also offered for both Alyssa and I to join them on Christmas, which we did. It was strange not spending it with mom, but she can't afford to fly out right now and there was no way I was going 'home' for the holidays.

I facetimed her for a few hours before heading over to Sasha's place. While her parents don't know why we stayed on campus, she does. We both opened up to her about it halfway through last semester.

I bid them goodbye around nine o'clock and headed back to my room. I wasn't kidding when I said it was nice but lonely.

My room is pitch black when I unlock my door, so I flip on the light. Everything is illuminated within a second. I've claimed the bed along the left of the room when you walk in. I am thankful that I can have my bed as low as possible because the other bed in the room is raised so I can have a desk underneath.

I drop my bag next to the wall and climb into bed, my sky-blue comforter bringing me comfort. I should write another story for the website I upload onto, but I don't have the energy.

A month into school I signed up for a pay to read website and started uploading my short stories there to make some extra money. I was blown away when I got my first paycheck. It was five hundred in the first month! I put each short story at two dollars for unlimited access to that story and currently have twenty stories up. I write mystery and thrillers that are no more than fifty pages each. A lot of people seem to like my work which is a huge boost to my ego.

I'm halfway through one about a couple who wandered into a haunted house. The man wanted to scare his girlfriend and it backfired horribly.

I check the time on my phone and decide I might at least try to finish it. I'm booting up my laptop when a notification pops up on my phone.

Psychology guy: He says I should give him your number. Still against it?

I sigh at the reminder. I had to have a partner for an assignment near the end of the semester and I partnered up with a guy named Jimmy. I only gave him my number because I had too, I really didn't want to but we needed to be able to communicate. What I didn't realize was his brother is friends with someone Tanner hangs out with.

Word got back to him so now Jimmy is being used to badger me. Poor guy doesn't know why I won't give Tanner a chance but I'm not about to explain it to him, we're not friends.

Me: Yes

My computer loads up with my story open and I get to work, completely ignoring my phone. I actually threw my phone onto my bed so there were no distractions. I become so immersed in my work I lose track of time and don't end up going to bed until three a.m.

The next morning on my walk I asses my missed texts from Jimmy.

> **Psychology guy: I wish you'd tell me why. Dude really wants to talk to you.**
> **Psychology guy: He's trying to take my phone from me so if you get any strange messages, they're from him.**
> **Psychology guy: Please talk to me**
> **Psychology guy: I get you want to focus on school**

> **Psychology guy:** But that doesn't mean we can't be friends
> **Psychology guy:** Just give me one chance

I've had a few run-ins with Tanner but thankfully not a lot. With him being a Junior and me a freshman, our schedules don't mix. But every time he saw me, he dropped what he was doing to talk to me. At first, I ignored him but the longer he was next to me, talking, the harder it became.

Eventually, I would tell him to go away and he would, although he always seemed sad to do so. I don't understand why he cares so much. I've seen hundreds of girls hanging all over him, yet he doesn't pursue anything with them. Why choose the one person who wants nothing to do with you?

> **Me:** Why doesn't matter. I just don't want to talk to him.
> **Psychology guy:** You know I won't push you on it but he's desperate. He got drunk last night and cried because you hate him and doesn't know why. Dude was a MESS.
> **Me:** I don't hate him. I'm just not in a position to deal with him.
> **Psychology guy:** Deal with him?
> **Me:** He's pushy. I'm sure you noticed that.
> **Me:** I don't have the time to unpack my psyche with him. I have enough on my plate as it is. I can't add him to it.
> **Psychology guy:** I'll let him know. Maybe he'll stop asking me to text you.

**Psychology guy: I just have one question because from your perspective, you hardly know the guy. Why is he so adamant about getting to know you?
Me: I wish I knew.**

I slide my phone away as I enter my favorite smoothie store. The line is short since it's only seven, so it only takes a minute for me to reach the front of the line to place my order. I rub a hand down my face needing to wake up. Four hours of sleep is not enough.

While I wait, a group of girls walk in. I don't mean to eavesdrop but it's hard when they're talking louder than everyone else.

"I know! It's such a bummer." Blondie complains.

"Like, since when does he have a sick up his ass? We're hot, why won't he fuck us?" The red head whines. "He even stopped going to parties! What's up with that?"

I keep my head down as they continue to repeat the same questions just phrased differently. Their conversation isn't very entertaining. My name gets called so I grab my drink, but blondie stops me before I can leave.

"Are you the one he's drooling after?" I just stare blankly into her brown eyes.

"Girl, maybe she doesn't know who you're talking about?" Her friend joins us after she pays.

"Tanner Shaw." I continue to blankly look at her. "He plays hockey."

"I know who you're talking about. I just have no interest in this conversation." I try to walk away again but they block my path.

"So you are the girl." Ginger pipes up. This is ridiculous! How did they even get my name? And how do they know it's me? There must be a hundred girls with the same name that go here.

"I never said that. Now if you'll excuse me, I have things to do." Which I do. I'm supposed to get my schedule today and I want to compare with the girls.

This time when I try to leave, they let me. The sun is starting to rise, illuminating the cloudy sky. I think it's supposed to snow today. I hope so.

I pass a few people as I continue my morning walk. I'm by the library when Oli walks up and joins me. No matter how many times I tell them to leave me alone, none of them do. I hate that it doesn't piss me off as much as it should.

"Good morning, Evelyn." At least they listened when I told them not to call me Evie. Only my friends are allowed to call me that. They are not my friends.

"Good morning, Oliver." He bumps me with his arm, like he does every time I call him by his full name. I've learned he prefers Oli, so I refuse to call him that, at least to his face.

"Oh, why do you refuse to call me Oli? You know I hate Oliver." He flashes me one of his signature smiles, the one that has women begging for a night with him. What? I hear things.

"There's your reason. I'm hoping one day you'll get so annoyed you'll leave. It hasn't worked yet." He laughs next to me but of course, stays.

"We leave later today for a stint of away games." Cool, I'll be left alone for a while. "I know you don't want to talk to him and while I don't understand why, I'll accept the fact. Though, if you ever want to talk to him, here's his number." I stop in my tracks and stare at his outstretched hand holding a small sliver of paper.

"Is this why you came to talk to me today? To hand me his number!" Oli at least looks sheepish about it. If I wanted his number, I would have asked!

"I didn't want to but I lost the bet."

"What bet?"

"We played a game last night where you bet or dare someone to do something. If they fail to do so, there's a punishment, this is mine. The fucker knew I couldn't fulfill the bet, so I was doomed from the start." I don't know how to react, why does he want to be my friend, I've done nothing but push him away.

"Why?" Oli finally looks me in the eye.

"Uh, because my bet had to do with a girl, and it was a sausage party?" I roll my eyes.

"No, not the bet. Why does he keep trying? I've given him no reason to yet he doesn't stop. Why?"

"Oh, honestly I'm not sure." He scratches the back of his head with his free hand. "I told you the night we met he was like a golden retriever; he'll keep begging until you give him a bone. For some reason, that night he saw something in you. He may have a reputation of a fuck boy on campus but he's not like that, not anymore. Yeah, he's slept around but I don't think he ever really enjoyed it. He decided at the beginning of this year he was done doing that, and of course he met you the next day. He's a romantic at heart, believes in true love and love at first sight. All of that bull shit."

"You don't believe in it?" I'm genuinely curious now. Oli seems like the type who would, but he speaks about it with such venom that it piques my interest.

"Nah, I haven't met anyone who makes me believe in it. Well, that night I think he saw you and decided he wanted to at least try. Then you pushed him away and now he wants, fuck, I don't know, you interest him. He's obsessed with getting to know you. I can't say I blame him though. I wanted to get to know you from the moment you slapped him." He chuckles to himself like it's an inside joke I'm not a part of. "Look, you can toss it, rip it to shreds but if you don't take it from me, I'll be forced to bug you until you do. That's my punishment."

I sigh but take the paper from his hands. "Okay." As he's walking away, I read the none attached. "Hey Oli," he turns around, "good luck with your away games."

"Thanks Evie, see you around." I don't bother correcting him. One text won't hurt, right?

6

Tanner

Evie: **Good luck!**

Dillan has already made fun of me for staring at my phone like an idiot, but I can't believe it. When Oli texted me saying he was successful, I never imagined she would actually text me.

She's been ignoring my existence for the last few months. Why did she choose now to stop? Or maybe this is all I get.

"Dude, did you hear anything I just said?"

"Oh, sorry Dillan. I was thinking."

"Normally I'd make a joke about it but you've been staring at that text for hours." He's right. We're three hours into the road trip and I've been staring at her text for all of it. It's just hard to believe she finally gave me attention five months after meeting her.

"I know, I'm just surprised." Oli pops his head over the back of our seat.

"Maybe it was something I said. I mean, when I left she let me call her Evie." My nerves rack up when I think about what Oli might have told her. "Don't worry dude, she asked why you were so persistent so I told her that she interests you and that's probably why."

I guess she would be wondering why I'm still pursuing her after she's blatantly told me to fuck off, maybe not those exact words but close enough. It's not like she's the only one confused with my interest in her, my teammates don't understand it either.

"There's just something about her. I knew from the moment I met her that she's special. Maybe it's because she slapped me and ignored me that first night, I don't know." Johnson turns around to face me.

"She slapped you! And you still want her? Dude, why didn't you tell me you were a masochist?" Laughter erupts all around us, including from me.

Me: Thanks
Me: Gotta say I'm surprised
Me: I didn't expect you to use my number

I wait with bated breath for her response. The conversation

continues around me but I tune them out.

Evie: Don't get used to it. Oli just mentioned your team has a few games coming up. I was being polite.

I don't care if that's why she sent it, all I care is that she took the time to send it. I spend the rest of the trip smiling like a lunatic while sending her messages that go unanswered.

We won the game and set up camp in a nearby motel. We have another game tomorrow and two the day after, then we get to go home.

Me: We won!
Evie: Congrats

I can imagine the dry tone she used which made me laugh. Sean and I are bunking tonight so he's peering over my shoulder, reading my texts.

"I can't believe she actually texted you."

"Neither can I." I back out of the app and open my emails. I see one about schedules so I open my school account and see my schedule has been updated. It's pretty basic classes, math, science, history, and an elective. I choose creative writing as mine since I'm awful at writing, maybe it will help me get better. "What's your schedule? I got mine."

I have to help him log into his student portal, his login rarely works which is stupid. We have history together but that's it. "You should ask Evie if you have a shared class." His teasing tone lets me know he thinks he's funny. I flip him the bird on my way to the bathroom.

ON THE SIDELINES

We played four games over the three days. We won three of them and lost the fourth by one point. But we're still on track to play in the frozen four.

We're swarmed by classmates when we dismount the bus. All of them congratulating us. I scan the crowd knowing she's not here but wishing she was. Evie has wished me luck before every game but that's all her text consists of. If we win, she congratulates, if we lose she says better luck next time. All of my texts about anything that's not hockey related goes ignored.

Classes start tomorrow and I gotta say, I'm excited. I've been bored, there's nothing to do when I don't work and hockey doesn't take all day. I've stopped going to parties, to my teammates dismay, but they don't seem as fun lately.

Is this what growing up means? Nothing is fun anymore?

If it is, I want to stay young forever.

The campus is bustling with activity as I walk across the quad toward my parked truck. I'm not in the mood to talk to people right now, too tired for human interaction. But a pale beauty with shiny black hair catches my attention and holds it hostage.

Some days I wonder if she knows how pretty she actually is. She has that girl next door vibe going on and it's a huge change from all the girls who try to hang off of me. Evie is the rain in my drought.

She's also caught me staring. Neither of us move as we stare from across the quad. She's wearing high heeled combat boots, black tights, a yellow school girl skirt, a black turtleneck that's tucked in, and her hair is pulled back into a high ponytail, Ariana Grande style. She looks fucking ethereal.

I make the first move as always and approach her. Instead of ignoring me like she normally does she gives me her undivided attention and fuck me if it doesn't feel nice.

"Congratulations on your victories. I'm sure they're well deserved." She has that polite tone that people tend to call a 'customer service voice' and it stings a little.

"Thanks." I wink at her but of course she offers no response to that. I release a sigh as I rub the back of my neck. "Look, I know I shouldn't get my hopes up but I'm hoping that now we are texting we can move forward as friends."

She stares blankly at me causing my heart to plummet. "I can't guarantee anything, I already don't have time for my current friends, all two of them. We can try but you probably will be really disappointed. My first priority will always be school. I told you before that I'm here to make a better future for myself, not make friends and have relationships. As long as you're okay with that then we can try."

I feel the smile growing on my face before I can tamp it down. "Yeah, we'll start slow." An awkward silence falls over us, neither knowing what to say.

"Well, it was nice seeing you, I have to get back to work. I guess I'll, uh, see you later?"

"Oh, sure. Where do you work?" I'm desperate to keep her here, even if it isn't for long.

"I write short stories and upload them on a pay to read website. It pays well enough that I continue." She shuffles her feet in the snow but when the silence continues to drag she turns and leaves. I watch her until she's out of sight before heading the

ON THE SIDELINES

opposite direction to my truck.

    Maybe we aren't a lost cause after all.

7

Evie

This can NOT be happening! It's Thursday and I'm in my last class for the week, creative writing. I've chosen my normal seat in the very back of the class so I can see everything going on in the room, which means I can see the door. The door that Tanner just walked through. He hasn't seen me yet and I'm hoping he doesn't.

Of all the extra curricular courses he could take, he chose the same one as me. Was this on purpose or is my luck just that bad?

If the surprise on his face says anything, it's my bad

luck. When he asked to be friends I figured we could exchange a few texts and that' it. Now that we have a class together that can't happen.

He takes the steps two at a time, his eyes never leaving mine despite all the girls in the class swooning for his attention. One going as far as grabbing his arm as he passes, trying to pull him into the seat next to her. He pulls his arm fee and continues toward me.

"You're in this class?" I nod as he shuffles in front of me so he can take the empty seat on my right. Great, now I'm stuck with him.

"Yup, I'm surprised you are as well. This doesn't seem like your speed." His laughter grabs far too many people's attention.

"You're right, it's not. I'm awful at writing." His eyes sparkle with mischief and I reconsider that this wasn't his master plan after all.

"So why are you taking this class? You could have chosen a course you'd be good at." He shrugs like this surprise isn't wrecking my insides. I've been able to fight my attraction to him for months, it's going to be so much harder now that I have to see him at least once a week.

"I thought about it but I like to be well rounded. I'm hoping if I choose to take this class then I would be forced to try harder than if I had to take it." I don't think he realizes that he didn't actually answer my question.

"Still doesn't explain why this was your choice. There's plenty of English classes that can teach you to write. I'm assuming that's what you're taking this class for?"

"Yeah, I'm here to learn how to write better. I think it'll be more fun if I can use my imagination over learning from a textbook. I'm more of a hands-on learner, if you catch my drift." His eyebrows wiggle seductively. My eyes roll on their own and I decide this is the end of this conversation.

Thankfully, the professor agrees as he starts class.

Tanner stays quite beside me as we listen intently. The first lecture is over far too quickly but we are assigned some 'light' reading of fifty pages. My new buddy groaned loudly when it was assigned. Loud enough the professor heard and called on him to ask why he seemed upset.

Instead of apologizing like a sane person, he stood up and told the professor that he would have taken a normal English class if all he wanted to do was read. We got ten more pages because of him. At least it shut him up.

I'm out of there like a bat out of hell the moment we're dismissed. Unfortunately, I underestimated his leg length as he matches my strides with ease. He doesn't comment on my eagerness to leave, thankfully. I slip between groups of classmates, desperate to put some space between us. Between me and his all consuming presence and cologne.

A few of our classmates try to stop Tanner as we pass them but he completely ignores their existence. He sticks close by me as I maneuver my way through the hoards of people. At some point his hands grab onto my waist and I shoot him a glare over my shoulder. He just shrugs and tightens his grip. "Don't want to get separated."

That's the fucking point! I want to lose you in the crowd!

I almost say it aloud but bite my tongue.

We emerge into the freezing air outside. I'm surprised I wasn't mauled on the way out based on the jealous glares I was getting from almost every girl we passed.

"How about we grab a coffee." He sounds like he's trying not to laugh as I return the glare to a specific girl a few feet away. I'm not the jealous type but I don't appreciate being glared at for talking to someone.

"No thanks, I've gotten enough looks for one day. Plus, thanks to you, we have sixty pages of reading." He at least looks sheepish when I turn around to face him.

"That wasn't the smartest decision I've made, is it?"

"No, now I have more work to complete on top of everything else." His lips pull up in a smile.

"You know what would help you get all that work done? Coffee." I am absolutely dumbfounded by this man. He is relentless. My gaze bores into him.

"It's after noon."

"So?"

"I would like to sleep tonight so coffee is a no go." My phone buzzes in my pocket. I fish it out to see a text from Jimmy. I sigh, having expected this.

> **Psychology guy: I haven't heard anything from you boy toy. What's up with that?**
> **Me: He has my number now.**
> **Psychology guy: Really! I thought you didn't want him to have it.**
> **Me: He's pushy**

I slip my phone back into my pocket as it buzzes again but I don't have the patience to deal with him right now. Or really ever.

"Look, I appreciate the invite but I can't. I have reading for other classes and far too much homework for the first week of school. Not to mention I have a story I need to finish so I can upload it by Sunday. Maybe another time but not right now." I expect some push back but I guess Oli was right, all I have to do is toss him a bone and he'll be happy. Just the idea that there might be another time has him wagging his tail like a puppy.

"Text me, you have my number." He winks at me as he walks away, leaving me to deal with the swarm of girls who are now creeping in from all sides. Of all the people I could have caught the attention of, it had to be one of the school's star athletes.

It's two a.m. and I'm halfway done with the reading for creative writing. I've long since finished my homework for my other English class and my math class which leaves creative writing, geology, and history. I'm well past tired.

At least I finished the homework for both of my Monday classes.

My bed is calling me but I don't have any responsibilities for tomorrow so I *could* write more of my story. I only have about two more chapters before it's finished. Maria is steps away from finding her best friend's mangled body and the suspense is killing me. I want to find out what happens next. Will she die too?

Logic wins out in the end and I decide to crawl into bed instead. I'm out like a light the moment my head touches my pillow. The soft confines of my comforter like a soft hug.

My alarm is going off far too soon but I force myself out of bed. I have a schedule for a reason, if I differ from it then the rest of my day is thrown off. My childhood doctor said I would grow out of it but I never did. One of my professors last semester said it's likely due to OCD and I should see a doctor, if only to get diagnosed. I'm still deciding whether I want to or not.

It's only six a.m. but I shoot off a text to Tanner asking if he still wants to grab coffee. I try to stay away from caffeine as much as possible but I can tell I'm going to need it today. I really need to start going to bed earlier.

I don't anticipate a response from him since it's so early, so I start my morning walk around campus. I'm halfway to my favorite smoothie spot when my phone alerts me to a new message.

Tanner: That sounds amazing
Tanner: Coffee hut?

I send back a thumbs up as I change direction.

He's sitting in a booth when I arrive thirty minutes later. I motion I'll be right there as I walk up to the counter and order my favorite, half mocha half vanilla iced. I don't care how cold it is outside, if I go out to buy coffee it will always be cold. Buying hot coffee should be a crime.

I slide into the booth across from him, holding my coffee like it's my lifeline.

"I was happy to see you're using my number for something not hockey related." He's trying to be cheeky, I know he is. We both know hockey was my excuse to talk to him.

"I thought hockey was supposed to be your life. I figured that's what you would want to talk about." I sip my coffee and despite the cold, nothing has tasted better in a long time. Honestly, I don't remember the last time I had coffee. Probably for the better if I'm staying up so late.

"Yeah, but that doesn't mean that's the only thing I want to talk about." He studies my reaction and the intensity of his gaze unnerves me a little. I visibly shift under his watchful eyes.

"I guess so."

"What made you change your mind about the coffee?"

"I was up way too late and needed a pick me up. I texted you thinking you were still asleep and that you wouldn't respond in time." This time it's my turn to look sheepish. It sounds so much worse when I voice it.

"So, you didn't actually want to get coffee with me. You just offered to be polite?" I can't decipher the emotion in his voice but the hurt on his face makes my stomach drop.

"Well, yes I offered to be polite but I did want to have coffee with you. I just didn't anticipate you being awake. I didn't mean for it to come out that way. I want to spend time with you but-" I stop myself before I make a fool of myself. It's been a while since I've had a normal conversation with a guy. God, it has to have been close to five years now. I've basically been an only child and after the incident with my father, I stopped talking to him and the guys at school stopped talking to me like a person, I was an object for them, something they could take without having repercussions.

"But what? I'm trying to understand what you want, where we stand. Please help me understand." He's begging now and I feel awful. Can I really be just friends with him?

"I don't know how to explain it without telling you things I'm not ready to disclose yet. I don't make friends easily, people scare me, men scare me." I look away from him and focus my attention out the window. Swallowing past the lump in my throat.

Silence descends over our table as he contemplates my words. I'm praying he won't ask too many more questions, it's too early to delve into my childhood trauma.

"I dated this girl named Mia in high school. We met freshman year and I fell for her *hard.* I spent the entire year chasing her, asking her to be my girlfriend at least once a week. The first week of our sophomore year she finally said yes. It was the best day of my life. She made me feel whole." He's talking in a wistful tone, like he's remembering something that brings him a lot of happiness and sadness.

"We were together the entirety of high school until fate tore us apart our junior year." He's looking out the window now too, it's still dark outside so it serves as a mirror. His eyes are on mine, tears glistening in them. "It was the night of Prom, we had agreed to meet at the school because she was driving one of her younger friends.

"No one knew about it at the time, but her friend Stacey moved to our town to get away from an ex. They were passing the local bakery when he saw Stacey smiling and laughing. The camera caught the accident. He hit Mia's car at seventy miles an hour, hitting the passenger seat side. Somehow, he walked away unscathed but Stacey died on the spot.

"Mia managed to call the police before the airbag deployed and suffocated her. She died a slow and painful death and Stacey's deadbeat ex didn't even realize the driver was in the car, didn't realize there was a driver. He left her to suffocate. The police caught him the next night and he's serving life in prison. Mia's dad showed up at the school and took me to the hospital to say goodbye. Even in death, she was the most beautiful woman I had ever seen." The tears have long since fallen but he doesn't wipe them away, letting them stream freely down his face. But it's his soft smile that catches my attention, he's smiling while talking about a horrific event in his life. Will I ever be able to do that?

"Thank you." I don't need to elaborate. He shared a part of him to help me feel more comfortable to share parts of me. "It's not just my story, if she's alright with you knowing my side, I'll tell you one day."

"Of course. I didn't tell you in hopes of you spilling your life to me now. I just want you to know that you're not alone, I'll always be here for you if you need someone to talk to." I didn't know I could feel this way towards someone. My heart feels like it might explode from all the emotions swirling through me.

"Thank you."

8

Evie

I think Tanner is trying to make everyone in class hate him. He has earned us an additional twenty pages of reading today because he can't keep his mouth shut. We only had twenty pages before he opened his big mouth. Two hours and forty minutes later, we leave the lecture hall.

He avoids everyone's eyes on the way out. People aren't glaring at me this week, their viscous eyes are pointed at him. A sick sense of satisfaction weaves its way into my soul.

"I'm hungry." Tanner mumbles. We were already walking

toward the cafe we met in when he starts whining. Over the last week, we've become closer but there's still a huge gap between us. While I'm more comfortable with him, there are still times he scares me. It's not like he does anything wrong, he just has some mannerisms that remind me of high school. I'm trying and for that, I'm proud.

"You're always hungry. I get at least one text from you a day talking about food. I think you have an issue." He feigns hurt, even going as far as clutching at his chest.

"I don't have a problem! I just love food." He dramatically huffs out.

"Fine, you don't have a problem. But, you don't have to complain about hunger when we're on our way to the cafe." I pause, contemplating my next question. "By the way," I look over my shoulder to where he's following me, "are Sean, Oli, and Dillan going to be there?" I can't decide if I want them to be there or not.

"Oli will. Dillan is still passed out from partying too hard last night. And I don't know about Sean, maybe." The cafe comes into view and of course Tanner speeds up, leaving me in his dust. I roll my eyes at his eagerness but I don't stop the smile from spreading. I heard about that party, only because Tanner didn't go. With every party Tanner doesn't attend, people talk more.

He already snagged a table when I walked in and had ordered two waters for us. I take the seat next to him as I definitely would not want to sit next to Oli. Sean maybe but not Oli, he's too rambunctious. I lift the menu to cover my face as I cross my legs.

"So. Tell me more about yourself." When I look up from the menu his gaze is already on me.

"Well, what do you want to know?" I quirk my head.

"About your childhood, if you have any siblings, if you've had any boyfriends and why the relationships didn't work out. Those kinds of things." Well, I'm not talking about my childhood today, so I go with the easier answers. I still haven't talked to Alyssa.

I look back at my menu so I don't have to look at him. "I have one sibling, a half-sister. She's a lot older than me, close to ten years. The courts awarded her mom with full custody so I rarely saw her. She became even more scarce when she turned sixteen and chose to stay with her mom full time with as little time spent with my dad as possible. Dad was understandably upset by that.

"I don't talk to her anymore for reasons you'll find out some other time. As for ex-boyfriends, I have one. Allan dated me when I was in eighth grade. I didn't realize it at the time, but our relationship was extremely toxic. He was a senior in high school and seventeen. I gave him all of my firsts. But in the end he chose someone else. Actually, my sister visited, and he slept with her. I think they're still together. They deserve each other, both ugly pieces of shit." It's hard to keep the venom out of my voice.

Tanner is quiet beside me. The bell over the door chimes, followed by the voices of Oli and Sean. "Hey guys, sorry we're late."

I smile at them. "No worries, we haven't ordered yet. Do you know what you want?" I direct the question at Tanner, but he seems to be frozen to the spot.

"Uh, you okay there buddy?" Oli slides into the booth across from us followed by Sean.

"Your ex is a dick." I sigh as I look back to my menu.

"I'm aware, that's why he's my ex. Do you know what you want to eat?" I try to keep emotion out of my voice. While it's been a few years, it still stings that he chose my blood family over me but he's also a pedophile. I'm better off without him.

"You."

I've never heard silence so loud. A flush creeping up my cheeks.

I know he finds me attractive, but he's never outwardly flirted with me, at least not that I've realized. Though I've been known to be dense.

Not wanting to acknowledge his statement, I pour all of my attention onto the menu. "I'm thinking I want their grilled cheese with a side of fries. What about you two?"

When neither responds I look at them expectantly. Sean breaks first, laughing so hard he starts coughing his lungs out. Oli is still stunned, though now he's watching Sean die.

"Uh, what did we walk into?" My eyes pinball between the two.

I shrug, patting Sean on the back. "Not much, I was just telling Tanner about my sister and my ex-boyfriend." I retract my hand over the table and sit back down. Tanner continues to stare at me, but I refuse to meet his eyes. He's the one who wanted to know. It's not my fault he can't accept the truth, or whatever he's doing in his head right now.

The waitress chooses then to show back up to take our order but Tanner waves her off, saying we need more time. She scurries off to grab two more waters for the newcomers, leaving us to rest in silence.

"So...." Oli starts, "no one wants to talk about Tanner's statement?" Me? Not so much. Tanner, Sean, and Oli? Very much so.

"Yeah, where did that come from? Like, how do you go from bashing her ex to telling her you hope she's on the menu?"

Despite Sean asking him questions, Tanner's eyes burn a hole in the side of my head.

"Why would you choose to tell me about your shitty ex and half-sister but not your childhood?" I take a *long* sip of my water, trying to prolong the inevitable. If it was just us two, I could brush it off, but Sean doesn't let anything go.

An equally long sigh falls from my lips. "Because it's not just my story to tell." I hope they leave it at that and thank the lord when the waiteress returns with the waters and I place my order before one of the guys shoos her away again.

They begrudgingly follow my lead, and it turns out Tanner isn't the only one who can pack it away. Sean orders the biggest breakfast the diner has and adds to it, with extra everything, basically ordering two of it. Oli ordered everything as sides and told the poor waitress to charge him whatever way is easiest. Three hashbrowns, six sausages, eight bacon, four pancakes, and four eggs. Tanner orders the same as Oli with one less side of hashbrowns.

I'm staring at them dumbfounded as the waitress walks away. Where does all that food go?

I poke Tanner's side to see if it giggles, because there is no way it all is muscle. They would have to live in the gym.

"What are you doing?" I stare intently at his side.

"Trying to see where it goes?" Tanner vibrates against my hands as I continue to poke at him.

"Where what goes?" His voice is filled with laughter as his body shakes with it.

"The food. Last time you had a double cheeseburger and three sides of fries! You ate some of mine too! Where does it go?" I poke his stomach. "Is this a black hole?"

He's not the only one laughing now. I turn my scrutiny on the other two. "You guys are no better! Where does it go?" I half shriek, still trying to maintain an appropriate volume level. Not that it matters. The three of them are laughing so loud the entire restaurant can hear them.

It feels like every woman is glaring holes into me, jealousy radiating off of them. I hate the attention, but the boys seem to bask in it. They soak it up like dry ground in a drought.

I feel Tanner's hand play with the fabric of my sweater over my shoulder. His arm a heavy weight on my back. Someone decides that's as much as she can take. A tall blond with a body people would kill for, approaches the table. I can tell the moment the others notice her as well. The table is blanketed in tension so thick you could cut it with a spoon, not a knife, a fucking spoon.

"Is this Mia?" Her voice is calm, but I can hear the strain in it. Tanner's arm around me flexes, his hand now flat on my shoulder.

"No, Brianna. Now leave." Her shoulders stiffen but she remains glued to her spot.

"Tanner, sweetheart. Come on. Don't be like that. Don't act like our history means nothing to you." This time I'm the one who goes stiff under Tanner's touch. Her tone is condescending, but the words hit their mark. A reminder of his past.

"I don't know what history you're talking about. I have turned you down every time you try to force yourself on me. And don't call me sweetheart." I've never heard him angry, now I'm wishing I never learned what he sounds like pissed. Because that's what he is, pissed.

Brianna opens her mouth, but Sean cuts her off. "You're obviously not wanted here, just take your loss and leave." He also sounds upset. How do they know this girl? And why do they hate her?

I watch her mask slip and out comes the bitch they knew was there. But her attention is no longer on them, it's on me. And I'm not liking it one bit. She looks me up and down as best she can with a table covering most of my body, and scoffs.

"You're nothing. If you think they'll stick around, you're wrong. You're just another girl that warms their bed. Just another tight pussy they'll get tired of in a few days. Enjoy it while it lasts. Cause once they're done with you, they'll come crawling back to me." She sashays away, leaving a den of pissed off lions in her wake.

Tanner: Coffee?

I ignore the text like everyone before it. He's been extra pushy after that encounter a week ago. I think he thinks it upset me. He would be right but that doesn't change anything. Last Thursday was a mistake on my part, it should have never happened.

The semester is in full swing now, I don't have the time to be messing around with him. I warned him that he'll be my last priority and he was okay with that, but now he doesn't seem to be. I'm tempted to block his number, but he'll still have mine and could use his friend's phone to text me.

How do I know this? He already did.

He used one of his teammates' phones to text me yesterday

when I didn't respond to him.

I ignored that text as well.

Class starts in an hour, and I'm tempted to skip if only to avoid him but I made a promise to myself that I wouldn't let some guy distract me from what's important. So here I am, getting ready for a class I don't want to be in, sitting next to a guy I don't want to be around.

I finished reading the textbook for that class since Tanner is bound to add extra reading for us. I won't have any reading to do if I've finished the book.

We're supposed to start on short stories today and I'm stoked.

When class starts a little over an hour later, I'm surprised to see Tanner is not there. The two hours go by in a blur, and I leave blissed out with no reading and a three-page story about a young girl learning something new. We're allowed to make it whatever lesson we want, no matter how dark and twisted that may be. Which of course made me extra happy since that falls into my style.

I'm already planning ideas in my head as I walk back to my dorm. My phone buzzed for the millionth time in the past hour but I don't fish it out to look. Whoever is texting me can wait, I'm too hyped to get distracted.

An hour later I'm finishing proofreading my story about the young girl who learned parents don't have to love you, they choose to, and her parents choose not to. My phone is still buzzing occasionally but I've left it on my bed, under blankets to muffle the sound.

I'm in the zone now so I continue on with my latest story. It's taken me longer to publish than I'd like but I did a poll about which genre I should try writing in. Classic romance won out and now I'm struggling.

I'm only halfway through and a week behind. I've had to put a message out apologizing for the delay. Everyone seemed cool with it a few days ago but I'm getting worried that might no longer be the case. Alyssa would tell me I'm being paranoid but I'm worried if I don't publish something soon, I'll lose a lot of my readers.

The typing of my keyboard fills the silence in my room as I let the words flow through me, like I'm a ghost narrating someone's day-to-day life without them knowing.

Sally has confessed her love for Johnny, but he doesn't reciprocate. A few days pass and Johnny realizes his mistake, realizes that he loves her, and spends the next month winning Sally back. I can't be the only one who thinks guys who grovel are hot.

A few hours of writing later I have a story I'm semi-proud of and press publish. It's about ten pages shorter than I'd like but at least it's out. I'll check back in tomorrow to see what people think of it. If it goes over well, I'll try to do more but have them focus more on the dark romance aspect of the genre than this one was.

Powering off my laptop fills me with an indescribable happiness. Knowing I finished and overcame a challenge today makes me so proud of myself that I push the rest of my responsibilities for today to the back of my head and take a nap.

I didn't sleep well last night, and my bed has been calling my name since I crawled out of its confines this morning.

I don't bother changing into my pjs as I climb onto my bed and promptly pass out on top of my covers.

9

Tanner

Evelyn is ignoring me. I don't know why but I'm worried it has to do with Brianna's words last week. What she said was completely uncalled for and not true. But I don't think Evie knows that.

She was quiet for the rest of the meal, hardly taking, not making eye contact. It hurt to see. She's such a happy person and to see her lose the sparkle in her eyes because some bitch can't keep her mouth shut. It pisses me off more that Brianna does.

I tried to invite her for coffee yesterday morning before I had to board the bus for an away game, but I never got a response. All of my other texts go unanswered as well as the one I sent with James' phone.

I know I shouldn't have but I was terrified she blocked me. Turns out she didn't, which makes her avoidance of me hurt that much more.

My bed creaks under my weight as I shift, trying to find a comfortable position. I was able to get my assignment for Creative writing this morning when I got back and now, I'm struggling to think of a 'lesson' this young girl could learn. My groan fills the quiet of the room.

"Yo, we're ordering pizza for dinner. What do you want?" Collins' voice echoes through the small house. The fucker could have come upstairs to ask instead of yelling but that would be too much work for him.

I'm meandering downstairs a few minutes later because unlike him, I don't like yelling across the house. "What are you guys thinking?" They're gathered around the small island in the kitchen when I enter.

We have a small house, but I like to think of it as modest. It's a three bedroom with a den. A decent sized kitchen that feels far too small with all of us in here. I'm standing at the island staring toward the main kitchen. To my right is a small hallway that leads to the front door and closet. Directly behind me is a small half bath for guests. To my left is the spacious living slash dining room but the latter has merged into the former.

A sliding glass door leads to a small-ish backyard. There's a tree and some grass but that's all. We don't tend to spend a lot of time out there. Along the wall behind me is another hall that leads to the garage and laundry room or mudroom, whatever you call it. Maybe both.

On the wall I'm staring at is the main kitchen with a wall of cabinetry and the fridge. The sink is to my right under a window. Next to the fridge is the pantry and next to that is the stairs leading upstairs.

There's a short hall that's next to the stairs that leads to the den. When you go up the stairs, you're met with a loft that serves as a divider for the rooms. My room is the master bedroom. The others put up a fight about it until I very kindly pointed out that we wouldn't have this house if it weren't for me. I'm the one who found it and poached the idea with them.

Well, anyway. The master bedroom is in front of the stairs while the other two you have to walk through the loft to get to their rooms. The doors are in a hall facing each other with a bathroom at the end.

Like I said, it's a modest house for college students. At least for this area it is.

"As much meat as we can put on." Sean's scrolling on his phone, presumably on the pizza places website.

"Nah, pepperoni, sausage, and bacon." Collins is leaning against the island next to me, putting all of his upper body weight onto his arms.

"Why not both? We'll eat it all tonight and you both know it." They both just shrug and that's that. We wait in silence for the pizza to arrive, them doing whatever while I continue to struggle to find a lesson a fictional child needs to learn. I'm not finding anything worthwhile online, so I make the stupid mistake of turning to my friends. "I need to write a short story about a girl who learns a valuable lesson. Any ideas as to what that lesson could be?"

"What about the importance of kindness?"

"Ooh, sharing is caring."

"Nah, that's too generic. Maybe be grateful for what you have."

"Treat others how you want to be treated."

"You can't please everyone all the time."

"Money can't buy happiness."

"You can't always have everything you want."

"Not to take anything for granted."

"Don't judge a book by its cover."

"Always have patience. Life goes at its own speed."

"You have to work hard for what you have."

"Always take accountability for your actions."

"It's not always selfish to put yourself first."

"Change is inevitable."

I can't tell if they actually want to help me or just want to one up each other. They keep going on and on until they veer off topic and it turns into a debate about what soda brand is better, Pepsi or Coke.

At some point the pizza arrives and they take a break just long enough to pay and scarf down one slice before they're at it again. I pile two slices of each onto a plate and leave them to it.

I spend the next hour trying to think of something worth writing about. Eventually I landed on 'it's okay to question authority'.

It's already late when I open a word document, so I type out my prompt, save it and go to bed.

My phone lights up and foolish hope lights up my insides as well, thinking it might be Evelyn. Hoping she's just busy and not actually ignoring me. I asked her earlier what lesson she went with, maybe she's finally getting back to me.

My heart soars when I grab my phone and read the notification.

> **Evie: Parents don't have to love you, they choose to**
> **Me: Cool**
> **Me: I went with how it's a-ok to question authority**
> **Evie: But you play a sport**
> **Me: So?**
> **Evie: Doesn't that mean you kinda HAVE to listen to authority? Like your couch is an authoritative figure, are you saying you don't listen to him?**
> **Me: Nah, I listen, I may be a little stupid from the hits I've taken but I know not to talk back to Coach Henderson**
> **Evie: You're not stupid**
> **Me: Ya think so?**

The conversation ends there but the broad smile stretching my face until it hurts stays until I fall asleep. I don't expect anything when I wake up the next morning at eight but amongst the notifications on my phone is another text from Evelyn.

My smile is back full force as I brush my teeth, take a shower and get dressed for the day. I'm so happy I think it might be contagious.

It's still freezing out and I think snow is on the forecast. It's normal for mid-February but it doesn't suck any less. Though, I have learned Evelyn loves the snow.

> **Evie:** Sorry I fell asleep.
> **Me:** No prob, good morning
> **Evie:** Moring

Today's one of the rare Saturday's we don't have a game, so we all bunker down in the living room to work on assignments. There's another party tonight the guys are going to, so they want responsibilities out of the way. We learned after moving in that it's easier to get things done if we're together and can bounce questions and ideas off of each other. We're mildly dumb to somewhat smart on our own but together, we're a solid C student! Just kidding, that's just me.

I'm halfway through my story when I give up for now. My head is starting to hurt, not to mention my brain. Sean has been piping in every few minutes when he looks over my shoulder, reading what I'm writing and criticizing. I need a break before I throw my computer across the room, or at him.

I glance over Collins' shoulder, but his homework makes my head pound harder. A grunt slips past my lips as I stand and head toward the stairs. Neither notice my absence which is unsurprising. They're both fully immersed in their course work.

I know I could turn in absolute shit for most of my classes and get a passing grade because I'm a starter on the hockey team but that doesn't feel right. Knowing other students are working their asses off just to get a barely passing grade and I could turn in an empty paper and get an A just because I'm an athlete is fucking stupid.

I'm here to get a degree and go pro, not just go pro. I know how likely it is for me to tear my ACL once I'm in the big leagues, so I'm not going in without a backup.

I'm stripping the second I enter my room, leaving a trail of clothing in my wake. My room is pretty basic, a queen bed along the right wall facing a table with my tv on it. Tucked away in the corner on the right wall and on the far wall is my dresser. Next to my tv, closer to the far wall is the doorway into my bathroom and closet. You have to walk through my closet to get to my bathroom, which is exactly what I do.

On the right is a dual vanity with a full mirror. Directly in front of me is a stand-alone clawfoot tub which is big enough to fit me with some room to spare. And to my left is a glass shower that spans the length of the room.

I walk into the shower and turn the nozzle to get the water warming up. Whoever designed this is a genius, you can stand in the glass and turn on the water without getting wet.

When steam starts coming off the water, I sit under the spray, letting the hot water pellet my stiff muscles.

Gradually my shoulders relax. My mind wanders back to Evelyn, like it seems to be doing a lot.

Her big brown eyes flash through my mind. Those plump lips pulling back into a seductive smirk, something I'll begrudgingly admit she has never given me. A soft pink tongue poking out to wet those tortuous lips.

My dick hardens as she saunters up to me, her hips swaying with every step. She is in that damned outfit I love.

Black turtleneck, plaid skirt, black tights, high ponytail, a black cardigan, and those sky-high heeled combat boots. She looks ethereal in my head, with red lipstick and mascara. Pure perfection.

She's noticed my 'little' issue causing her smirk to widen. She's right in front of me now and fuck me if she isn't the most beautiful person I have ever seen. Everyone seems to pale in comparison to her.

When I grab my dick in my hand, wrapping my fingers around it, it's her hand in place of mine. She's the one that starts to slowly stroke me from base to tip.

Her hand strokes me faster, pulling a moan from me. Her smile widens with the sound. She goes faster, desperate to hear it again. Blood rushes through my ears, muffling all the sounds.

My abs tighten until it's painful. Her grip tightens, sweeping pre-cum from my tip and smearing it along my shaft. Suddenly I'm exploding. My vision goes black as my cum paints Evelyn's black turtleneck white.

When I open my eyes again, she's gone. My cum is no longer on her shirt but sprayed across the tiles of my shower wall.

My head falls back on my shoulders as I groan. What am I supposed to do? She drives me crazy just by existing. I want her so badly, in my arms, in my bed, under me. I don't want her only for her body but for her brain. I want her personality.

Fuck. I just want HER.

But she's ignoring me. Well, maybe that's the wrong

word. She'll reply as long as it has to do with school. I know she warned me she'll be like this, but I was hoping she might, I don't know, not be. I said I'd be okay with it, but stupid hope has clawed its way into my head.

I was hoping she would at least try to be my friend, put in an effort. But I can't even be upset because she told me this is how it will be. She told me she hardly has time for her current friends.

I know patience is a virtue, but I don't have THAT much patience in me!

I force myself out of the shower after cleaning up my mess. My towel is wrapped tightly around me as I walk back into my room, an idea sprouting in my head. If she will only talk to me if it pertains to school, then I'll use that to spend time with her.

Before I know it, I've already sent off the text to her.

> **Me: If I ask nicely, would you help me with the assignment? I'm struggling and Seans making fun of every other sentence I write.**

10

Evie

"**M**aybe he really does need help. You said he joined that class because he sucks at writing, right?" I was helping Sasha with her homework when the text came through. Needing her opinion, I showed it to her. I'm starting to regret that now.

"Well, yes." But this is a simple assignment, first of the class.

"So? What's the big deal? You write for a living; it makes logical sense for him to ask for your help." She's right, that's what I'm doing here.

"I guess so." I feel like I've been on an emotional rollercoaster. My heart and head raging a war with each other.

The sound of a key inserting itself into the doorknob catches our attention. Sasha perks up. "We can ask Alyssa." Said girl is opening the door, exhaustion evident in her features. Sash told me she's been spending a LOT of time with her boyfriend. Like more time there than she spends here. Most nights she doesn't come back to the room.

I'm worried. Every time I see her, she's more worn down than the last time.

"Hey." She glances up from her phone, jumping from surprise.

"Evie! Jesus. You startled me." She offers a weary smile while clutching her chest.

"Sorry." My frown deepens the longer her half assed smile stays on her face. It's barely ten in the morning but she's dragging her feet like it's ten at night. She looks seconds away from passing out. "Are you okay?" Emotion flashes through her eyes, emotion she tries to hide,

She plops down next to me on her bed, sagging deep into the mattress. "I don't know Evie." She sighs, her tired pale blue orbs meeting mine. "I really like Jasper but he's getting...." She trails off but she doesn't need to explain further. He's always been a little controlling but lately any of Alyssa's spare time has to be spent with him otherwise he goes ballistic. It's a little scary.

"I feel stupid even asking but why not leave him?" Sasha has turned her chair around to face us, eyes pinballing between us.

"It's not stupid. I want to, I really do, but I'm worried about how he'll react. I've never been afraid he'll hit me, but I am afraid of how bipolar he is. One minute he tells me I'm his everything and that he couldn't live without me, the next I'm a worthless whore that's replaceable." She slowly rises to sitting.

Worry eats away at my insides. She's never worried about him getting physical, but I have. I met his ex a month ago and while she didn't outwardly say it, she hinted that he isn't above 'asserting his dominance' anyway he may see fit too.

"So, let's lighten the mood. Whatcha doing now, maybe I can help." No one stops the attempt to change the subject.

"I'm struggling with my essay. Evie offered to help." Sasha whines out. "It's so annoying."

"Anything you don't understand or don't *want* to understand is annoying to you." My deadpan response earns me a wink from her. "We were also talking about Tanner."

"What about him?"

"He texted me a little while ago asking for help with our assignment for creative writing. He said Sean's laughing at every other sentence he writes." I sigh as I fish my phone out to show her the string of texts from the last few days.

She scrolls through them silently, her face showing no emotion. I know she doesn't like him much. I know she sees him as an entitled jock. Whether she's right or not, that's just how she views him. I can't really blame her.

"Have you told him?" I startle. Tell him? Why would I? She never told me I could. I understand I went through loads of trauma and abuse because of my father but so did she.

"No."

"Why not?"

"Because it's not just *my* story to tell. I didn't want to tell him if you didn't want him to know. I know you don't like him, so I didn't bother to bring it up." She hands me my phone back while releasing a resigned sigh.

"You're right, it's not just your story, it's mine too. And if you want to tell him, I'm alright with that. You're also right about me not liking him that much but I'm not blind. I can see the way he lights up when he sees you. How desperate he is for a moment of your time. He's been chasing you for over half a year." Even Sasha seems surprised. "When you have a history like we do, we have a lot of misplaced fear; and we struggle to trust people even if they have given us no reason not to. Tanner is a great example of that.

"He has given me no reason to mistrust him, and yet I chose to look at his title over the man in front of me. I know now how wrong I was about him. I think he's good for you. And I think when it comes up again you should tell him. While it's not just your story, it's still your past. It still defines you and has shaped you into who you are now. If you think there's something there between you, he deserves to know. If you don't see it going anywhere then don't, the choice is yours. I'll support whatever decision you come to."

I'm speechless. Truthfully, I don't know what I want.

Tanner is amazing. He's everything I used to dream of as a child. He's the type of guy who I used to think was my prince charming, back when I still believed in that stuff. But I don't know if I want to bare my soul to him. At least not yet.

"So, you think I should give him a chance?" My voice is flat to my ears, devoid of emotion.

"Yeah, I do." I look at Sasha for her opinion and see she's just as surprised as me. Alyssa has always taken the first opportunity to bash Tanner and his friends. Granted they act the same as the jocks in high school that raped her. I never understood why but they would always 'choose' her. While a few went for me, most of the boys who hurt me were outcasts. They were the drugged-up kids that thought it was cool to take advantage of people, and I was their favorite toy.

"You like him, don't you?" I zone back into the real world where Sash is staring at me.

"Yeah, I do."

"Okay, so. What's the worst that can happen? He's just like the rest?" I nod. "But the best outcome is he's the best thing to happen to you. You're due for some good karma." I nod again because she's right. But that doesn't stop the worry seeping into my head.

"Thanks guys, I don't know how this started as a conversation about him needing help with homework and turned into you both telling me to give him a chance, but I don't think it matters. But while we're on the topic of relationships. I think you need to leave your boyfriend Alyssa. I fear he may become physical with you." She just nods. I think deep down she knows it too but she's afraid to admit it out loud.

Our conversation takes a turn to schoolwork, and I continue helping Sasha with her homework. Alyssa is quiet but no one pushes for her to talk about her thoughts. We've all had enough of the morbid topics for one day.

I was on my way back to my dorm when I finally text him back.

Me: Yes, I'll help you.
Me: But I need something in return

It's almost six in the evening by the time he gets back to me. It's given me plenty of time to think about what I'm about to ask him. I'll probably regret it but I need to take the chance. It's obvious he has a thing for me and I'm tired of fighting my attraction to him.

Tanner: Should I be worried

I ponder his message for far too long. Because no, he doesn't have anything to worry about. I do. I'm the one about to do something way out of my comfort zone.

Me: No
Taner: You're not being very forthcoming
Tanner: I'm starting to worry

I don't know how he does it, but I can hear his teasing tone through the phone. It's quite impressive.

I don't bother replying to his teasing. I sent him my room number and told him to be here in an hour. After that I power my phone off completely.

I wait with bated breath.

Time seems to have slowed to a crawl. I have started to stress cleaning while I wait. I remade my bed, being sure there isn't a single wrinkle on the fabric. My desk gets the same treatment.

I go through all my drawers, emptying and refilling them in

different ways until I'm happy with how it looks. I dump my pens out onto the desktop and organize them by color. Arranging them along the side of my desk in a rainbow.

When he still hadn't arrived by the time I finished, I moved onto my closet. I refold most of the clothes in my drawers and reorganize how they're placed. I'm halfway through my last drawer when there's a knock on my door. Instead of finishing the few items I have left, I hurriedly stuff them into the drawl and close it. Nerves causing butterflies in my stomach.

When I swing my door open, I'm met with the amazing sight that is Tanner. His dirty blond hair is more tousled than normal. There's a devilish glint in his sage eyes. How someone's eyes can be such a light green will always be a mystery to me, but I do know that they are beautiful.

He's wearing a black hoodie with gray sweatpants. I'm not shy about eating him up with my eyes. He looks incredible. I also notice he didn't bring a laptop or even a notebook.

"So…" he doesn't finish his sentence. Neither do I.

Neither of us make a move to do anything until I hear voices floating down the hall. Suddenly I'm grabbing his wrist and yanking him into my room. I lock the door once it's fully closed then turn to look at him, leaning heavily on the door.

"Are you going to tell me what I'm doing here?" His voice has taken a husky tone to it and it's now that I realize what I'm wearing. Despite it still being winter I'm in a thin camisole and sleep shorts. I'm not wearing a bra and I realize that fact is extremely obvious.

My hair is thrown up in a messy bun and I'm devoid of all makeup. I look like I'm about to go to sleep, even if it's the last thing on my mind.

I take a deep breath, needing to build confidence for what I'm about to say. "I want you."

The words hang in the space between us. I wait for him to say something, anything. But he doesn't. He doesn't move, doesn't speak, I don't think he even blinks. I think I broke him.

Slowly, like he's waking up from a dream, he blinks. Once. Twice. Three times. Then he moves.

His legs eat up the space between us until he has me backed against the door. Both of his hands press into the wood by my head, bracing him. His head lowers until his mouth is inches from mine, but he doesn't close the distance. "Say it again."

"I want you." My voice is stronger this time, more confident. I can see the desire in his eyes.

"Fuck." It's barely a breath that leaves his mouth but it's impossible to miss the strain in his voice. His eyes closed tightly.

"Tanner?" Those beautiful orbs snap open to meet my brown ones. He waits patiently, or semi-patiently for me to continue. "Kiss me."

In the next breath his lips are on mine, devouring me whole. My arms snap around his neck as I arch into his broad chest, seeking relief.

He nips at my bottom lip forcing a gasp to fall from my lips, giving his tongue access to mine. Small noises fill the room, all originating from me. If I could think straight I'd be embarrassed but he frazzled my brain when he acted on my demand.

He swallows every noise like a man staved, barely leaning back enough to breathe before diving back in for more.

He tastes like heaven.

"What do you do to me?" He doesn't give me time to respond, his lips capturing mine again.

I can't tell how long we stay like this, kissing and clawing at each other, trying to get closer. At some point I take his hoodie off only to see he's wearing a long-sleeved shirt.

I must make a disgruntled noise when I see it. He's moved on to my neck where his laugh vibrates my skin.

I tug at the hem until he leans back to allow me to pull it over his head. My eyes greedily take in his sculpted chest. God, he's perfect. He must know what I want since he makes no move to come closer. He stands back and lets me take him in.

I'm a little disappointed to see no tattoos. I've always had a thing for them, but I'll never admit it out loud. Mom would have an aneurysm if I brought home a guy who was covered in them. She's always disapproved of Melissa's father, a girl from high school, because he was inked from head to toe.

A primal need takes over when I see the hunger in his eyes. My lips are on his in less than a second. His hands are on my waist, traveling around the area trying to find purchase. He feels amazing.

My hands are no better. Traveling from his chest to his shoulders until they finally land in his hair. The thick strands of his dirty blond hair are softer than I ever imagined. A soft tug on them rewards me with a low grunt.

Here's a secret. I've never liked French kissing. I've always found the idea disgusting.

Why would anyone want someone else's tongue in their mouth? I mean, come on! Does no one understand hygiene?

Well, I'm now forced to take back all the negative things I've said on the topic. The second Tanners' tongue is in my mouth my brain ceases to work. All of my previous thoughts are reduced to a pleasurable buzz inside my head.

It's unfortunate that it doesn't last long. Soon enough, Tanner no longer exists, in his place is Marcus. The boy who took my faith in people and ripped it to shreds. It's his mouth on mine, his tongue fighting me, his face in front of me.

Panic surges through me, pulling me out of my head. But the damage is already done.

I've already pushed Tanner away. I've already stumbled back until I'm flat against my door. My hands pulling at the strands of my black hair. Tugging until I can't feel the pain anymore.

I don't know when I fell to the floor or when the surprise on Tanner's face shifts to worry. All I know is I just made a huge mistake. And I don't know how to fix it.

My pulse races as he gingerly steps forward. He approaches me like one would approach a wounded animal. When he's nearly a foot away I come to my senses and jump to my feet.

My sudden movement surprises him enough to allow me to switch positions. Now he's the one by the door and I'm by my bed. I know this was my idea. I asked him to come over. But I'm realizing now how stupid that was. How stupid *I* am.

"Sorry, I uh, I think you should go." My voice comes out meek as I hug myself tighter. My eyes stay glued to the ground as I wait for a response. Another mistake because I don't see him approach me. I don't see his hand reach out to touch me.

My fight or flight instincts take over as I attempt to stumble back. Alas, my bed frame is behind me, and I can't move back without crawling onto my bed. Except in my panic, that is exactly what I do.

Soon enough my back is pressed to the wall, my legs pulled up to my chest, my arms wrapped tightly around myself, as I shake like a leaf.

I thought I was over this. I thought I could move on. But obviously I was wrong. This just proves I'm not ready.

My subconscious is well aware Tanner is the one in front of me, but he's not who I see. I see Marcus. I see Jake. I see Chad. I see Alex. I see everyone who has ever hurt or taken advantage of my flash by like crime scene photos.

"Evelyn?"

The man puts his knee on my bed. Tanner, I have to remember it's Tanner.

The mattress shifts under his weight as he kneels in front of me. He doesn't move, doesn't speak, just waits. But my head, my memories, don't realize he's not moving. My eyes squeeze shut as tears spill down my face. I can feel myself shaking as I wait for him to take what I know he wants. Me.

"If-" I hiccup, "If you're going to do it, ju-just d-do it." I don't recognize my own voice, but he does.

"Evelyn." Silence. "Shit, Evelyn. What did I do? How can I help you? What's going on?" More silence.

He sounds far away. But the sound of his crying is loud and clear. I'm not the only one who's scared right now. I'm scared of him, and he's scared for me.

I keep repeating that to myself like a mantra until my breathing evens out and my tears stop.

When I meet his eyes all I see is pure terror. Guilt hits me like a brick. He doesn't deserve this. He doesn't deserve me scaring him. He deserves more than I can give him.

"Please leave. I want to be alone."

I keep my gaze anywhere but at him as I wait for him to leave. Except he doesn't. He doesn't even move a muscle.

"Tanner. Leave." I shakily point to the door, but it does no good. He stays plated on my bed, watching me. "Please."

"No."

My eyes fly to his, widening from shock. "W-what?"

"I'm not leaving."

When I see the determination in his eyes, the hard set of his mouth, I know won't. I want to tell him off, force him to leave. But my throat is dry, and all the fight has left me. It's late and all I want to do is sleep. So, I admit defeat and let him stay.

As if he's moving in slow motion, he lifts me up just enough to pull my comforter down and for us to settle under. I don't fight him when he tugs me close and cuddles me. And I don't fight sleep when it takes me away.

I know we'll talk about this later. We'll have to. I just had a breakdown over a kiss. He's going to have questions and I'm going to have to give answers. Whether I'm ready to or not.

11

Tanner

It's still dark out. Pitch black to be exact. Which is why the insistent and annoying ringing of an alarm blaring in my ear is all the more disorienting.

I let out a long groan when the noise doesn't cease. A sigh follows. Finally, I open my eyes which further confuses me. Something is not right but I can't put my finger on it.

I slap around my bed until my hand comes in contact with my phone. I turn the alarm off and see the time is five a.m. Though that's not the only thing I see.

The background isn't Sean and I as freshman, instead it's the back of two girls. They're sitting shoulder to shoulder as they stare into the sunset. Both of the girls have extremely long hair. One has pitch black hair that cascades down her back in loose waves. The other has box braids in a ponytail.

I'm embarrassed to admit I stared at the photo for five minutes before realizing I'm looking at Evie and her friend Alyssa.

Speak of the devil and she shall arrive.

The door creaks open and Evie tiptoes inside. She startles when our eyes meet. Confusion creases her beautiful puffy face. Wait. Her face shouldn't be puffy.

Last night's events came rushing back to me. Which explains why I'm in her dorm room.

"You're, uh, up early." She sounds nervous, but can I really blame her? She practically begged me to leave last night, and I refused to. A twinge of guilt forms in my gut.

"Yeah, it seems you have an alarm set." Her mouth forms an O.

"Sorry, I forgot about that." She crawls over me, back into the corner where she slept. "I didn't realize it was five already. I would have taken my phone with me if I had." I just shrug in response.

"It's not a big deal." I turn to my side to allow for a better view of her. God, she's perfect. At some point she put her hair up so now it's in a massive messy bun. Adorably cute.

I reach out to tuck a loose strand behind her ear. A smile pulls at her lips with the gesture. Her hand comes up to cover mine, keeping it in place.

My eyes flick between hers and her lips, which her tongue

pokes out to wet. I notice she's doing the same. I take the silent invitation and lock our lips. She tastes just as good as she did last night, like cherry candy just now with a hint of salt.

I reluctantly pull away. She pouts when she realizes I'm not leaning back in. "Why did you stop?" Her voice has a breathy note to it and it takes all of my self-control to not lean back in.

"We need to talk about what happened last night." The panic in her eyes pains me to see but this is something I can't ignore. She broke down, had a panic attack because of the kiss we shared. My heart tightening at the memory.

Since I want to share more, I need to know why she freaked out and how to stop it in the future.

"Yeah, we do." She moves so she sits up, leaning against the wall. I follow suit, sitting up opposite of her.

"Was it something I did?"

She shakes her head. "No, you didn't do anything wrong." She searches my face for a few moments before releasing a sigh. "Is this something you want?" She motions to the space between us.

"Yes." No hesitation.

"Ok." I wait for her to continue, allowing the silence to stretch on. "It started the summer before freshman year of high school. Alyssa was staying over like she often did, and my father made another one of his odd comments about how we are a strange duo. We're not that similar, never have been. But I didn't realize until that night he was saying that to justify his future actions."

She pauses to take a deep breath. "It was late, around eleven. Mom was asleep and I thought dad was as well. We were having trouble sleeping and Alyssa decided she wanted some water. She left to grab both of us a glass. We've been friends forever and we both know each other's houses like the back of our hands so while she did that, I was cueing up a movie on the small tv my mom bought me for my birthday.

"I heard a crash in the kitchen. It wasn't until then that I realized how long she had been gone. She'd been grabbing water for almost twenty minutes. So, I went to check on her. I figured she was just getting snacks and stuff. It was that time of the month for both of us, so we were abnormally hungry. But when I walked into the kitchen, I saw she wasn't alone." Tears are streaming down her face, but she doesn't swipe them away and neither do I.

"Dad was on top of her, pinning her to the ground. I didn't understand what I was seeing at first. I mean I knew what sex was, I had already given my virginity to my first boyfriend the year prior. But I couldn't wrap my head around what was happening until Alyssa's eyes met mine. She was terrified and crying. That's when I saw it. The blood on the ground and her sleep short around her ankles.

"As soon as it registered in my brain that my father was inside my friend, I started screaming. Obviously, that caught my father's attention. He yelled at me to shut up, he said if I didn't, I would be next." My hands are white from how hard I'm clutching at the blankets below me. I've been mad before but never have I felt this emotion. I'm beyond pissed that the man who was supposed to take care of Evie threatened to rape her while he raped her friend. What a shitbag.

"Well, I didn't stop, and I eventually woke up my mom. Her scream woke up our neighbors. By the time the police arrived my mom had managed to pry my dad off Alyssa and was beating him with a wooden spoon. The sheriff pulled my mom off him, and the question began." She finally meets my eyes. There is absolutely no emotion on her face or in her voice.

"Instead of doing their job, the police in our small town lectured us, the victims, about how serious it was. I remember the sheriff asking Alyssa if she really wanted to 'ruin' my father's life with the 'accusation'. My mom blew up on him, screaming about how it isn't an accusation. Alyssa went through it and both mom and I were witnesses. But by the time the police left, no report was filed. They refused to file a report against my father.

"Mom obviously got a divorce and dad moved across the state. But the boys at school knew by that point that there would be no consequences if they were to follow in my father's footsteps." I'm shaking by this point. Not only did her dickhead of a father get away with his crime but he showed others they could as well. "Not all of them did but there were a handful that took advantage of the knowledge."

"How many?" She averts her gaze once again, but I can't blame her. I sound murderous, exactly how I feel.

"For me, five. For Alyssa, three." The sound of the blood rushing through my ears is the only thing I can hear. I'm already thinking of different ways to bring Evie and Alyssa justice. Collins family has a lot of connection in the justice system on top of having a lot of money. A plan forms in my head but I need Evie's permission before I go through with it.

"Can I help?"

"What do you mean? There's nothing to be done. It was years ago now." She shrinks into herself. My heart hurts for her, seeing her like this.

"You've met Collins, right?" She looks at me curiously.

"Briefly, why?"

"His family is big in the justice system; I think they might be able to get you and Alyssa the justice you should have gotten a long time ago. I know this is a big ask but, can I tell him and see if he can do something?" She perks up, hope shining in her features.

"Do you really think he could help?"

"I don't think it would do any harm in asking." She moves faster than I can react, pouncing from her spot on her bed into my arms. She is beaming at me when her lips connect with mine. The kiss doesn't last long but I can't complain when she peppers kisses around my entire face and down my neck. "Can I assume you're okay with the idea?"

"I am but I need to talk to Alyssa first. She'll be up at around ten, I'll ask her then." She kisses my neck and cheeks a few more times. "Thank you. Really, this means a lot."

"Of course, Princess. Anything for you."

"Did you just call me Princess?"

"Is that alright?" I nervously search her features for any indication of how she feels.

"Oh, it's more than okay. Baby." She gives me a cheeky smile before kissing me again. Damn, I could get used to this.

12

Evie

As I thought, Alyssa was willing to give it a shot. What's the worst that can happen? Nothing comes from it? No one gets prosecuted? Well, that's what already happened so it's worth a shot.

Tanner had morning skate that day and had left my room at six thirty to head home to grab his things. We'd plans for him to come pick me up so we can head to his place later around five this evening. He still needs help with his creative writing assignment and apparently, I'm still the only person he knows that's good at writing.

I sent him a text an hour after I talked to Alyssa to give him permission to talk to his roommate Collins about my father. His response was a thumbs up.

"Do you really think this guy can really do anything?" Sasha types away on her laptop, briefly glancing at me. It's now Tuesday and still nothing has come about in response.

"I don't know." I shrug. "Maybe."

"Well, Tanner seems to think he can help so I'm willing to try." I've been cuddled up next to Alyssa for the last few hours as we discussed our options. The topic had been heavy in the air since I asked her opinion.

"I guess. But aren't you worried there could be some retaliation? What happens if your father pushes back, or any of the other guys push back? Are you ready for the possibility of having to see them again, deal with them in person?"

"Sasha, I know you're trying to help but I've thought about this already. The worst possibility is they all walk free just like they have been for years now." We've been going back and forth like this a while now. I'm starting to lose my patience with her.

"Sorry, sorry. I'm just worried for you both. I care for you deeply and really don't want to see anything bad happen to you guys." She sets her laptop aside before sliding off her bed.

I scootch over to give her space to climb next to me. Her arms wrap around me while she squeezes my shoulders. "I know. Thank you."

"I'm hungry. Let's get food." Sasha and I laugh at Alyssa topic changer.

"Yeah, let's get food." I slide off the bed and pull them both with me.

We end up at the diner across campus. Each of us have a milkshake and fries. I have a strawberry, Alyssa has vanilla, and Sasha has her chocolate.

It's surprisingly empty for a Tuesday. I feel bad for our waitress, we're her only table and no one has walked in since us. I can tell she's desperately trying to find something else to do but it seems everything that needs to be done is already done.

I've never worked as a server, but Sasha has a friend who is one and she tells me this is normal. There tends to be a lot of fluctuations between guest counts, and it's expected. It doesn't ease my thoughts unfortunately. I'm well aware of the amount of people who depend on guest count and the number of tables they get to survive.

"Maybe we should order something else. I just got paid yesterday." Sasha sighs for what must be the millionth time, completely fed up with me.

"It's not your responsibility to single-handedly keep a server afloat. I'm sure she's had plenty of tables before us and will have more after. It's still fairly early."

"Yeah, you're right." My phone buzzes on the table in front of me.

"I think your man is trying to get your attention."

"I told you already Alyssa, he's not my man. We're not official yet." I wish we were, but I dumped a lot of information on him the other day. I need time to process and so does he.

I'm still a little in shock at how well he took the information. I could tell when I was recounting my past trauma that he was mad. He was white fisting my bedspread. But never in my wildest dreams did I expect him to try to come up with a solution to a problem I had given up on.

I knew he was a good man, but he proved himself to be better than I ever thought he could be.

I realized after that conversation that he was a man, not a boy. He may act childish sometimes and immature. But when I really needed him, he came through. He took my fears about him and squashed them without ever knowing they were there.

"Why not? It's obvious you two like each other. Why not make it official so other bitches know he's taken. I just *know* those puck bunnies are still trying to get a bite of him despite his lack of interest." Sasha's right, I've watched women practically throw themselves at Tanner all year. That's part of the reason I kept my distance. I didn't want to be the center of attention in my first semester in college.

"We both need time to digest the heavy conversation we had at five am the other morning. I'm still stunned I was able to spit it out. I'm sure he's still processing all of the information I dumped on him. Just give it time." I flip my phone over to reveal five new messages from him and smile at his latest one.

> **Tanner: I told him**
> **Tanner: He was pissed but said he'd see what he can do**
> **Tanner: Since the police never let any of you file any reports it may be hard to bring them to justice**
> **Tanner: I miss you**
> **Tanner: Where are you? I want to see you**
> **Me: I'm at the diner where we met.**

Tanner: On my way

"Tanners on his way. Apparently, he can't wait three more hours until our study session."

"Girl, you've got that man wrapped around your little finger." Yeah, I guess I do. The bell above the door chimes. Before I can turn around to see who it is, Sasha makes a face. "It's Ella. What a bitch." I have to choke back my giggle.

"Be nice. We haven't had any problems with her this semester." That gets me looks from both of my friends. Both of which believe I should file a formal complaint against her for the way she has treated and bullied me.

"God no, she's walking this way." Alyssa glares at Ella until she stops at the edge of the table.

"Evie, can I talk to you?" Her entourage stayed at the host stand waiting to be seated.

"Sure." She looks at Sasha who decided to answer for me.

"Alone." I look between her and my friends a few times before deciding to relent.

"Yeah, okay." I shimmy out of the booth and approach the bar a few feet away. "What's up?" I tilt my head and wait for the barrage that usually comes.

"Do you know someone named Marcus?"

"Uh, I'm not sure. Do you have a last name?" I have a bad feeling, a really bad feeling.

"Yeah, give me a sec. I saved it in my phone." She swipes through different apps until she finds what she's looking for. "Here it is. Marcus Flocken." My heart plummets to my feet.

I use the counter behind me as stabilization as the world spins around me. I feel like I'm going to be sick. To Ella's credit, she sees my reaction and seems unnerved by it.

"I take it you know him?" All I can muster is a nod which almost forces my stomach content to evacuate my body. "He uh, contacted me a few days ago. He replied to a post where I was complaining about things, you happen to have been one of them." I know what post she's talking about, I saw it. I was only briefly mentioned and the part about me wasn't really about me, it was about Josh.

"He privately messaged me asking about you. He said he knew you from high school. I didn't realize at the time that I never gave out your full name, just Evelyn. I kind of figured he went here and that's how he knew who I was referring to. But this morning he sent a few messages that made me second guess everything." She's watching me closely, everything about her right now seems regretful and concerned. "Evelyn, where are you from? Where did you go to high school?"

"Montana. In the Northwestern corner, seventy-two miles from the Canadian border." I don't know how I managed to get the information out but I know I needed to. Ella needs to realize that I'm not from here, which means Marcus isn't either. How did he even find Ella? Find her post? It's statistically unlikely, like super unlikely.

"That's a long way away, isn't it?"

"A little over two thousand miles."

"I'm sorry. I didn't know."

"Ella, what did he say?"

She shifts uncomfortably but instead of responding, she hands me her phone which is open to their conversation.

MFlock876: Thanks, I've been looking for her for a

> while now
>
> **MFlock876:** We have some unfinished business
>
> **Ella_Rossa_79:** How do you know her?
>
> **MFlock876:** We fooled around in high school
>
> **MFlock876:** I can't believe she went to the East Coast
>
> **Ella_Rossa_79:** Wait, you don't go here?
>
> **MFlock876:** Nope
>
> **Ella_Rossa_79:** How do you know we're talking about the same person?
>
> **MFlock876:** Evelyn Campbell
>
> **MFlock876:** I know my Evie
>
> **MFlock876:** Jake is gonna be ecstatic that I've finally found her
>
> **MFlock876:** If you see her tell her we're on our way

Is the floor moving? I feel like the floor is moving. Ella's phone isn't in my hand anymore, does she have it?

"Evie?" Who said my name? Is it Tanner? It sounds like Tanner. "What the fuck did you do?" Oh, he's mad. That's not good. I want to tell him I'm okay but I'm clearly not.

"I didn't mean to. He contacted me. If I knew he didn't go here I wouldn't have offered any information."

"Who contacted you?" That's someone new, Oliver maybe.

"A guy named Marcus. He said he knew Evelyn." Ella sounds like she's panicking.

"Evie, sweetheart. I'm here. Please open your eyes." Tanner here, that much I'm certain of. His hands are on my face.

I crack my eyes open only to be met with his sage ones. My panic subsides only slightly but it's enough to start thinking clearly again, kind of clearly.

"Evie, who is Marcus." Tanner makes sure I can't move my head so I'm always looking at him. But it doesn't matter, I can't say it. I won't.

"Ella, what did you say to her?" It's Alyssa. She doesn't sound mad, she sounds scared.

"Here, just read it. It will be faster." A few moments pass of silence.

"He contacted you? He knew who she was from a post?"

"Yeah. I don't know how but he did. Who is he? What did he do?" I see Alyssa's head pop over Tanner's shoulder. She's just as freaked out as I am, I can see it in her eyes. He tormented both of us.

"Tanner." She sounds calm. How does she sound calm right now? "He was the first one after her father."

I see the moment the information registers. His jaw tightens, his biceps flex, his eyes promise violence. "What did he do?"

"He says he's coming here, with Jake." He glances at her quickly.

"Who is Jake?"

"The second." Oliver is asking questions to everyone around us but the poor dude isn't getting any response.

"Oliver." Tanner moves aside to let me see Oli. I can tell He's not happy I'm addressing his friend before him, but Tanner knows what's going on, Oli doesn't. "He's a bad person, both of them are. They have done some really bad things."

The world has stopped spinning, I still feel nauseous but I'm a lot better now. I take advantage and step into Tanner. I never wanted to rely on a guy before but I'm extremely thankful I can rely on Tanner.

I see my waitress standing at the edge of our little gathering and ask her for our check. She rushes off only to return with the bill. Before I can take it, Oli has it in his hands and is following her to the register. "Ella," she looks to me, "if you know what's good for you, block him, immediately."

"Come on, you're coming to my place, all of you." Ella apologies again as she backs away and rejoins her group. I don't hold her responsible; she had no way of knowing.

It isn't until I'm climbing into the middle seat in Tanner's truck that I realize I didn't grab my belongings. When I try to go back for them, Sasha just holds them up for me as she climbs into the backseat.

Alyssa takes the middle in the back and Oli sits next to her. I realized then that I don't need to be in the middle up here, but I really don't want to move, and Tanner hasn't told me to. So, I buckle up and get comfy for the ride to his off-campus house ten minutes away.

13

Tanner

The drive home is quiet, really quiet. The radio is off, and no one speaks. I can't decipher my emotions. I'm mad. I'm worried. I'm upset. But it doesn't matter what I am, all that matters right now is Evie. She was so pale, brown eyes squeezed shut, shaking like a leaf.

She pressed right up next to me while I drove. Close enough to feel me but not to close that I can't control my truck with ease. I have my right arm draped around her back so I can rub soothing circles on her shoulder. Her presence alone calming me.

I had sent a text to Collins to make sure he's home. I had pulled him aside after practice Sunday and told him about Evie and her past. If someone from said past is trying to track her down, and has succeeded, he'll know what to do.

Thankfully he's in the living room when we all file in. So is Sean who I assume Collins wrangled up.

"What's going on? Hey Oli."

"Hey." Sean and Oli nod their heads in greeting.

I guild Evie to the couch and have her sit down. Alyssa sits on her left and I take her right. Sasha, Alyssa's roommate settles on the arm of the couch next to Alyssa. Oli decides to remain standing along with Collins, but Sean takes a seat in one of our armchairs.

"This is about what I talked to you about Collins." His jaw tenses in response. The situation the two women by my side were put in pisses him off just as much as it does me.

"Am I the only one lost here?" Sean looks around at everyone expectantly.

"Nah, they haven't told me shit. Other than some bad guys were in contact with Evie's old roommate Ella."

"The fuck does that mean?"

"It means exactly what he said." I don't mean to snap at the two, but I do anyway. If they keep talking, we'll never get anywhere. "Evie, Alyssa," I turn my attention to my right where the two girls sit, "it's up to you guys. It's your past."

They exchange looks. Whatever passes between them is quick, but Alyssa speaks up. "Evie's dad isn't a good man. He did a despicable thing and got away with it. Because of that some guys at school learned they could get away with it as well. The guy that contacted Ella is one of those guys. He has connections that secured him a lot of date rape drugs. Drugs he and his friends used on Evie and I. Marcus mentioned Jake, one of those friends. I don't know how but they now know that Evie goes to school here and seem to have decided to take a road trip. The earliest they could be here is Tuesday, it's like a thirty-five-hour trip by car." It's silent for a few minutes.

"Am I correct in assuming these guys drugged and took advantage of both of you?" Oli takes a step closer to the girls, I presume he means it in a protective manner, but it comes off more predatory.

"Yes, they are two of them." Evie mumbles beside me. If the room wasn't silent, I don't think anyone would have heard her.

"Of them? How fucking many?" Collins puts a hand on Sean's shoulder to keep him seated.

"Including Evie's father there were four."

"Because of my father there were five."

I watch as the information ping-pongs around in their head before settling in. Thankfully they leave that information be, latching onto something else. "So, what do we do?"

"How do we stop these assholes?"

Finally, Collins joins the conversation. "I talked to my dad after our conversation. Turns out one of his partners has connections in Montana. I'm waiting to hear back but since the police refused to do their fucking jobs, the only 'proof' we have that it happened is the calls they responded to."

"What do you mean they refused to do their jobs?" Oli looks between the women including Sasha into his question.

"They refused to file a report. They didn't even take a recorded statement." All eyes turn to Sasha. I figured she knew but I didn't ask in case she didn't.

"Isn't that illegal?" Oli looks at Collins.

"No, not technically anyways."

"What the fuck is that supposed to mean?"

"It is up to the police officer. If they believe the matter to be civil, they do not 'need' to file it." You wouldn't know it by looking at him, but Collins is from a family of lawyers and police officers.

"That's fucking stupid." I nod my agreement.

"Well, there's nothing we can do about it now. But we can do something to stop it from happening again." Evie clutches at my arm drawing my attention to her. She still looks scared, but she calmed down a lot in the last hour.

"I agree. Sasha, you and Alyssa share a room, right?" They both nod. "Evie, who is your roommate?" She looks at Collins before looking back at me.

"Uh, I don't have a roommate."

"You're staying here." Three voices echo at once. At least everyone is in agreement.

"Are you sure that's alright?"

"Evie, sweetie, you basically live alone. There is no way in Hell that we are letting you go back to your room when we know two God awful people are looking for you. You are staying here." Her brown eyes stare deeply into mine.

"Okay." She nods like she's made up her mind. "What about Sasha and Alyssa?"

Sean stands and walks toward the front closet only to return with a metal baseball bat. "From the sounds of it, they aren't looking for Alyssa, only you, and they don't know she goes here. So, until that changes, here's a baseball bat. Aim for the balls." A shit eating grin spreads across his face as he hands Alyssa the weapon.

"I'll see if I can talk to the dean first thing tomorrow. He's more likely to listen when it comes from me, unfortunately." Collins uncle is friends with the dean so he's right, if the dean was to listen to anyone it would be Collins.

Evie tugs on my sleeve until I look at her. "Can you take me to my dorm so I can pack for the next little while?"

"Yeah, let's go."

14

Evie

It's been two weeks of me living with Tanner. He's great, so is Sean and Collins, but I really want my own space back. I feel like I'm going crazy.

The dean has been made aware of the problem with Marcus and Jake and has doubled security around campus. All of the members of faculty have been given updated photos of both of them and have been given instructions to contact campus security if they see either of them.

A few days ago, Collins' dad got back to him about his partner's connections. Turns out there was a report about *all* of the incidents, but none of them were filed.

Mrs. Paterson is a kind old lady who works for the local police in Libby. She has a close friend active in the field who had her document every encounter. Her friend hated that they couldn't file a report because their superiors told them not to. So she asked Mrs. Paterson to make the reports but not file them, that way there was proof that something happened.

So, there has been documentation of every incident from my father to the last time anyone touched us. I can't describe the weight that has been taken off of my chest when I learned of this. It's like I can breathe again.

When this is all done, I am going to thank Mrs. Paterson and her mysterious friend. If it weren't for them then there wouldn't be a case against everyone involved, including the police who refused to follow protocol and take action against rapists.

I'm not quite sure what all can be done now since it's been five years for my dad and two for everyone else, but I've been told they will get prosecuted.

It's Thursday and Tanner and I are in creative writing. The professor is going over something in the textbook. He's halfway through his sentence when he sees something in the hallway.

Hushed conversations arise when he pauses and locks the door. He holds up his hand in a give-me-a-moment gesture. He calls someone and proceeds to have a hushed conversation with whoever is on the other line.

"All right class!" He retakes his position by the whiteboard. "It has been brought to my attention there is someone lurking by my classroom door that should not be here. Until security can handle this person, everyone is to remain *inside* the room."

Hands start flying up left and right. He calls on someone a few seats away from me. "Are you implying there is someone dangerous in the hall right now?"

"Good question. Not necessarily. The person outside bears a shocking resemblance to a person I have been told to keep an eye out for. As far as I am aware this person is not dangerous in the sense that they may attack. I have not been given the exact reason why I need to inform security of his presence, but I know it is important that everyone stays calm and seated."

He motions for the rest of the hands to go down and continues his lecture. I try to stay focused but it's hard when I'm pretty sure I know who's on the other side of the door.

Tanner nudges me as he shows me his phone where there's a conversation open.

> **Collins: Someone who fits Jake Schelve's description has been taken to the dean**
> **Collins: I've been informed that it is indeed Jake Schelve**
> **Collins: Security is on their way to who they believe is Marcus Flocken**
> **Collins: STAY IN THE CLASSROOM!**
> **Collins: MARCUS IS OUTSIDE YOUR LECTURE HALL!**

"Well, it's a good thing the door is locked." I don't know how I'm so calm, maybe it has to do with the two weeks I have had to cope with the knowledge they were on their way.

"Want to know what's even better?" He's smiling ear to ear,

showing off his dimples.

"What's better?"

"Logan was able to get a warrant out for their arrest an hour ago." Logan is Collins' father.

"How did he manage that?"

"He was able to access all the unfiled police reports and brought them to the attention of the local police. There was enough evidence to issue a warrant for their arrest. Along with the fact that all of this happened in Montana where the Stature of Limitations for rape is ten years." It takes me longer than I'd like to admit to understand where he's going with this.

"Does that mean-" I trail off, not wanting to get my hopes up.

"Every person who has raped you and Alyssa now have warrants out for their arrest across the United States." I had faith in Tanner, don't get me wrong. What I didn't have faith in is the US Justice system.

I've never felt so light, so free. Knowing everyone who hurt me can be tried for their crimes. Everyone who hurt Alyssa. I'm so happy I almost don't hear the commotion outside.

Yelling and screaming is wafting into the classroom. It's hard to make out what is being said but someone is NOT happy. The longer the person yells the more I hear their voice. The voice that without a doubt belongs to Marcus.

The hall goes silent along with everyone in the room. Ever wonder how to make two hundred college students be quiet? Tell them there is a wanted person outside and then proceed to have that person start yelling.

The door rattles from the force of Marcus being thrown against it. A loud struggle ensues and continues for the next ten or so minutes. Eventually the police arrive and tase him.

The class is let out abruptly, well as soon as we were given the go ahead to leave.

Tanner keeps me close as we make our way to the quad where everyone is waiting for us. At some point Dillian and Josh were informed of what was going on and they offered their assistance if it was needed.

The moment I see Alyssa, I break out of Tanner's hold and race into her arms, almost tackling her in the process. We're both smiling ear to ear. We stay like this, embracing each other and rocking on our feet until Sasha joins us, this time her embrace does take us to the ground.

None of us are naive. We know the battle has just begun, but the thought that our rapist may get punished for their actions is thrilling.

We're giggling as we stand up. Tanner's arms wrap around me from behind and I lean into the embrace. We haven't made things official, but we might as well be.

During my first week in his home, he slept in the den. Eventually I got fed up and tried and failed to get him to sleep in his room. I'm not quite sure where his thought process came from, but he assumed I wouldn't want to share a bed with him. I know, stupid right? I mean, we've already slept in the same bed for Christ's sake!

When he refused to come upstairs, I went down. I waited until he was asleep and quietly made my way downstairs into the den. They have a *very* uncomfortable pull-out couch in there.

I crawled under the covers and curled up next to him. Granted I woke up in his bed the next morning with a grouchy Tanner chastising me, but it was worth it when he came to bed that night in his own room with me.

Nothing happened past cuddling but it was nice to sleep next to him. I never thought I had trouble sleeping but maybe I should have. I slept *so* much better in his arms than I have in years.

"I'm proud of you." His breathy whisper causes shivers to rake my body.

"Yeah? Why?" I look up at him from under heavy eyelids.

"You knew one of your old abusers was mere feet away and yet you were calmer than a cucumber." More giggles erupt from me at his analogy. One thing I learned in these last two weeks? Tanner can effortlessly lighten any mood, no matter how depressed it has gotten.

"I knew I was safe."

"You did, did you?"

"Yeah," I turn around in his arms so he's embracing me. "I knew you would never let him hurt me while you were there, so there was nothing to fear." His signature smile makes an appearance. All white teeth and a hint of mischief.

I know I've already said this, and I will continue to do so because Tanner is the type of man that no one doubts he's a man but he likes to act like a boy. It's odd to say because I've never met a male I could easily call a man, they were all boys, no matter their age. A boy doesn't become a man just by getting older. Being a man has to do with mindset and accountability and a bunch of other things.

Tanner is most definitely a man.

I snake one arm around his back under his grip on me and the other around his neck. I use my grip on his neck to pull his head down to mine to kiss that stupid grin off his face. Oh, who am I kidding? I love that stupid grin of his. It's all him.

A collective groan rises from our friends once they notice

what's going on. One of Tanner's hands leaves my side for a moment before returning with a tighter grip. I presume he flipped them off.

"Would you two get a room and fuck already? The tension is suffocating." I pull away to a disappointed huff from Tanner to laugh at Sasha's whining. I shoot her a shut-up look, to which she laughs at.

"How do *you* know we haven't done it yet?" I raise a questioning eyebrow at her.

"Girl, you and I both know you would have told us if you had. You don't keep secrets from us." Touche.

A snicker rises from Sean and Oli who are standing behind Sasha. When I meet their gaze Sean wiggles his eyebrows suggestively. I take a page from Tanner's book and flip him off. He fakes being hurt by clutching his chest, but his shit eating grin gives away how he truly feels.

"So," Josh pipes in. I've talked to him a few times, but I can't say we're close. I thought Tanner was full of himself when I met him, but Josh takes that to a whole new level. "Are you two a thing now?"

Before I have a chance to respond, Tanner lowers his head into my neck so his lips can brush my ear. "It's up to you. You already know what I want. Are you ready?"

I turn my head as best I can with his giant head blocking me. His green eyes sparkle as they watch me. "I thought you'd never ask." A smile breaks out across his face.

Tanner has always been attractive but when he smiles, he's fucking devastating.

"Do we get an answer or are you going to continue to ignore us?"

"Oh, shut up Josh. Let them have their moment." Out of the corner of my eye I see Dillan smack Josh on his shoulder.

"Nah, we're together." Tanner's words are barely above a whisper. I think he meant them only for me to hear but Josh had stumbled close enough to hear thanks to Dillan smacking him.

"Oooo, Tanner has a girlfriend." He announces the news to our group in a sing-song voice, also gaining the attention of a few people passing by.

It takes a few minutes but eventually we're able to shift the conversation to something else. Since almost all the guys here play hockey, no one should be surprised that that's what the conversation turned to.

I promise I try to pay attention. I really do. But my fluttering heart makes it near impossible to focus on anything but it.

I have a boyfriend. A boyfriend who is insanely attractive and kind and a million other things I thought I would never find in the same guy. After the shit that happened in high school, I thought I would never be able to give my trust to someone else. Yet here I am, quickly falling for the last person I ever thought I'd care about.

15

Tanner

I'm more than a little disappointed when Evie moves her stuff back into her dorm room. I understand that she's paying for the room and all of her belongings are there, but I still wish she'd stay a while longer.

The police have officially charged Marcus and Jake with drug possession and multiple counts of rape. While Marcus chose to plead innocent, Jake learned that if he pleaded guilty and turned against Marcus, he'd have a lighter sentence.

While I'm happy one of them is willing to take accountability for their actions, I'm not happy it's only because he wants a shorter sentence.

"Dude! Come on! We're going to be late!" Collins shouts from what I assume is the front door. Snapping out of my thoughts I quickly grab my bag and race downstairs. He's right, we have to leave now otherwise we risk pissing Coach off.

We're leaving today for a week-long stint of away games, and no one wants to deal with a cranky Coach for that long.

A minute later we are all piled into my truck and on the way to the arena where we were told to meet.

When we arrive, I'm thankful to see we aren't the last to arrive. We aren't the first but at least we won't be the ones to incur Coaches wrath. Most of the team has already filed onto the bus so we drop our possessions off in the compartment on the bus before climbing aboard and claiming our seats.

The bus is taking us to their airport where we'll fly to Maine to play the University of Maine. Then we'll fly to Boston to play Harvard. After we beat them, we'll take on the University of Michigan in their home rink. Next, we fly to Minnesota to play St. Cloud State University. Finally, we go to Missouri to play the Lions at Lindenwood.

If we win three of the five, we'll go on to the semi-finals for the frozen four. It sucks we'll be on the road for a week and a half but once we go on to get our automatic bid, we'll be playing at home for the rest of the tournament. At least we should be.

I can't wait to ask Evie to come watch me play wearing my jersey. She hasn't come to a game yet, but now that we are officially dating, she knows it's only a matter of time.

We argued for an hour yesterday about the best sport, *which* she refused to change her answer. The little heathen still thinks baseball is better! The nerve of her! You can't be dating a hockey player and not like hockey, that's ludicrous.

Three hours later and we're stuffed like sardines on a plane that is taxing the runway. We're all still in our suits that we are forced to wear but once we're up in the air we can change.

A few of the Freshmen near the back of the plane haven't stopped complaining about the dress wear since they were told it was a requirement now that they go to a D1 college.

The flight attendants scurry to the back of the plane. One of them brushes my shoulder as she passes, batting her eyelashes at me. Collins laughs beside me at my obvious discomfort. I'm used to women trying to throw themselves at me but when our team flight attendants do it, I've always felt uncomfortable.

It's one thing for women my age to flirt with me, it's a whole nother when someone the age of my mom does it.

"She totally wants you in her tonight." Collins chuckles.

"Not happening. The one person I want to be in tonight is Evie." Dillan is on the other side of the isle obviously eavesdropping.

"She's got you good, huh?"

"What the fuck is that supposed to mean?"

"Dude. We haven't made it off the ground and you're already talking about her. That girl has you wrapped around her little finger." A smirk rises on my lips at how true that statement is.

"And I'm happy to be."

Suddenly, my head gets pulled back when the plane speeds up, the change in velocity catching me by surprise. I've been flying most of my life and still the change in speed catches me off guard.

The plane takes off. I can see out of Collins window as the ground slowly disappears below us.

We flatten out in the air about thirty minutes later, or at least what feels like thirty minutes. Flight attendants start their round on the plane starting at the front with the coaching staff.

The woman from earlier is quickly making her way to my isle, her eyes occasionally flicking up to mine.

I try my best to ignore her. Unfortunately, that's not enough of a hint.

She leans over me to talk to Collins, pushing her breasts into my face. "Is there anything I can get you, sir?"

"No thanks." She turns her attention to me. A sultry gaze in her eyes. She leans back but barely.

"What about you? Anything I can do for you?" Her lashes flutter as she attempts a seductive smile. I almost laugh in her face at how desperate she's coming off. There is nothing about this woman that makes me want her.

I prefer the innocent smile gracing Evie's lips over this seductress. I prefer the big brown eyes full of hope versus the devilish glint in hers. Don't get me wrong, I'd love to see Evie looking at me like this woman is, but we haven't made it that far yet.

A court date is supposed to be chosen soon and the last thing on her mind is having sex while she sends her rapists away.

"No." My sharp tone jolts her back, her smile flattering slightly with her surprise.

"Are you sure? I'd love to help you with anything you may need." This woman places her hand on my shoulder, squeezing it. I've avoided learning her name since I don't want to know who she is. But it's difficult when she's pushing her chest with her nametag in my face.

"I'm positive." A frown mars her bright red lips.

She opens those lips, about to say something when Dillan decides to take pity on me. "He has a girlfriend." The flight attendant ever so slightly turns so she can look at Dillan. "I'm well aware there are men out there, women too, that those words don't mean anything to, but Tanner isn't one to cheat."

She says silent, still leaning over me, still pushing her boobs into my face. It's been long enough, and I've told her no far too many times. I grab her shoulder, which catches her attention.

She must think something else is going to happen since she shoots Dillan a triumphant smile. A smile that falls as fast as it comes when I use my grasp to push her back into the aisle and away from me.

"You heard my teammate. I have a girlfriend and she's so much hotter than you. There's no way in Hell I'm going to cheat on her and throw away the most amazing woman I have ever met." Someone clears their throat behind the woman. I peer around her to see a different flight attendant. "Perfect timing Ashleigh. This woman is harassing me. Can you do something about that?"

We don't have the same flight crew each flight, but Ashleigh is still on most of our flights. I've known her my entire college career. She's an older lady, around fifty. Sweet as can be. But she's fiercely loyal and doesn't like when other people try something with those she cares about. I'm lucky enough to be one of those people.

Her normal curly bob is perfectly styled. At some point last year she decided to lean into her new white hair and dyed her hair completely white. She looks good and I make sure to tell her every time I see her.

When I first met her she was probably five-foot-seven but now she's closer to five-foot-four. Her uniform is looser than the one her coworkers wear but she's not trying to show off to anyone. She has her amazing husband and three kids. I heard she may be expecting a grandchild soon.

Her makeup matches the rest of the crew, hers is just more toned down. All but her lipstick. She's always loved her red lipstick.

"Shanon, how many times do I have to tell you to leave the passengers alone?" Her deep voice is gravely from many years of smoking.

Shanon rolls her eyes before turning her back to Ashleigh and walking to the back of the plane. I watch her go and stop to talk to the last row. I can tell she is flirting with them but so can Ashleigh.

"I'll deal with her, don't worry. Now what is this I hear about you finally having a girlfriend?" Dillan groans while Collins laughs when I waste no time in telling her everything about Evie. What? I'm a man obsessed.

We're sitting in the locker room at Michigan State while Coach gives us a pep talk. We won against both the University of Maine and Harvard. We only need one more win to secure our spot but that won't stop us from trying to win every game we play.

We need to be on the ice in five minutes. Coach releases us

to do our pre-game rituals which everyone who has one breaks away to do. I never used to be one of them but now I am. Though my pre-game ritual looks a little different than theirs.

I grab my phone from my locker to text Evie, she rarely answers before I go on the ice but that's okay, I know when I come back I'll find a text waiting for me. When my phone powers on I'm surprised to find a text already waiting for me.

> **Evie: Good luck out there! I know you guys will win and you'll take us to the frozen four. That is the tournament for college hockey, right? Well, whatever it's called, you'll take us to it. I miss you, come back soon.**

I know I look stupid, grinning down at my phone like an idiot but I can't help it. She's trying to learn about the game that I love. My heart swells with an emotion I don't want to think too far into right now.

> **Me: Yes it's the frozen four**
> **Me: I'm about to head to the ice**
> **Me: I miss you too**

I put my phone away as the team lines up to head out on the ice. I take my spot near the back of the line.

It's time to win and prove my girl right.

16

Evie

I've been back in my dorm for a week now and I'd be lying if I said I didn't miss sleeping in Tanner's bed. If I'm being honest, if he didn't have a stint of away games I would have stayed in his house with him for a while longer. His bed is loads comfier and larger.

Everyone who was involved with drug distribution and everyone who raped both Alyssa and I have been officially served.

I know Tanner is upset that Jake took a plea deal but without it, a lot of people involved would have walked free. Not only that but with one saying it happened and willing to say exactly what happened, it's no longer our word against theirs.

It's looking more and more like we will get justice for the awful things that happened to us.

I just got off the phone with the local police where they informed me that Jake would like to talk to me. I'm waiting until Tanner's game is over so I can talk to him about this. I want to talk to him; I want to know why he did what he did but I'm scared.

The clock ticks over to another minute as I pace my room waiting for the text that will let me know when Tanner's game ends. I think they're playing St Cloud right now. They won the game against Michigan 5-2. I'm a little ashamed to admit that I've never been to a hockey game even though I'm dating a hockey player.

God that sounds odd. Me. Dating.

I never thought I'd find someone who would help me overcome my past, especially not so soon after leaving Montana.

A knock on my door brings me attention away from my head.

Alyssa barrels into my room the second the door is open wide enough to let her in. She flops onto my bed face down while I close my door and lock it. She doesn't say anything, doesn't move either.

"Are you okay Alyssa?"

A low groan rumbles my bed as her only response. I can't stop the chuckle that escapes me. The small sound earns me a piercing glare from my best friend.

"What's the matter Al?"

"You're using Sasha's nickname now?"

"Maybe, just seeing how it tastes on my tongue." I shrug nonchalantly. Something is obviously wrong, but her deflecting won't help today. "What's going on?"

She gingerly pulls herself into a sitting position, leaning heavily against the wall. "I broke up with Jasper." I have to strain to hear her small whisper.

"Did you say what I think you just said?" Her glassy eyes raise to meet my brown one and she nods.

"He was mad that I never told him about my past. He said if he knew we would have never gotten together. After all, he doesn't want a whore for a girlfriend. His words, not mine. So, I broke up with him." I know I should be sad but I'm over the moon she finally dropped that asshat.

I fling myself around her, squeezing her tightly into a hug. "I'm so proud of you. You don't deserve that shit in your life." She laughs half-heartedly into my shoulder while she hides her face in my neck.

"For once, I think I actually believe you." A silence falls over the room as we hug. It's Sunday so neither of us have plans, I had hoped to spend the day writing. The popularity of my stories has skyrocketed and I'm thinking about possibly writing more of a book than a short story and see how that goes.

"Do you want to stay here for a while?" She nods against me. I won't mention it but my shoulder is dry as a bone. She hasn't shed a single tear since she came in here. "Alright, you know that's fine with me but I'm going to let go now. I'm going to write for a little while. Stay here as long as you need." She nods again before I release her and grab my laptop.

I plop myself down next to her with my phone in easy reach.

She curls herself into the corner with her phone tucked up next to her as well.

We stay like this for hours. Me writing and her sleeping.

I've been quietly texting back and forth with Tanner and I haven't failed to notice her phone lighting up as well. I don't know if it's Jasper, but I hope it's not. I haven't mentioned their breakup to my boyfriend since she never gave me permission too, but I have been tempted to bitch about what a douche he is.

> **Me: So, the sheriff called**

I let the statement hang. I want to see his reaction before pushing farther.

> **Tanner: Is everything alright?**
> **Tanner: Why'd he call?**

I really wanted to tell him while talking on a call, but I don't want to wake Alyssa up and this isn't something she needs to hear right now.

> **Me: Jake wants to talk to me**
> **Tanner: WTF!**
> **Tanner: Why does he want to talk to you?**
> **Me: I don't know**
> **Me: I haven't decided if I'm going or not**
> **Tanner: Do you want to?**
> **Me: Kind of?**
> **Me: I have questions only he can answer**

Me: But I'm scared to know the answer

My phone lights up with a call from him, which I quickly decline.

Me: Alyssa is over and she's asleep
Me: I don't want to wake her up.
Tanner: I'll be quiet
Tanner: Just please answer

This time when my phone lights up, I answer. It's not a facetime call so I can't see his face but hearing his voice is enough right now.

"You have every right to be scared. What that boy did to you is despicable. But you're also allowed to want answers. I fly in on Wednesday, if you want, I'll go with you." His voice is soft, quiet.

"I'd appreciate that. Thank you." I look over my shoulder at the still sleeping Alyssa. "How'd your game go?"

"Great, we won."

"That's wonderful. What was the final score?'

"2 to 0. We wiped the floor with them. We fly to Missouri tomorrow for our game against Linwood on Tuesday. Then we'll take a redeye flight home. We'll land around three am Wednesday." I smile. He answered all of my next questions without me having to ask.

"Do you want me to pick you up from the airport?"

"Nah, I drove. But I'll come right over once I drop Sean and Collins off at home."

"Or" I let the word hang for a second, "I could stay the night at your place Tuesday."

"Are you suggesting that I could have my girlfriend in my bed when I get back?"

"Yes."

"I'd love that." I can hear the smile in his voice as he says that. God, I miss him. He's only been gone a week and I already feel like a needy girlfriend.

Fuck it. "I miss you. I wish you were here." I don't care if he thinks I'm needy. These last few years I haven't had someone to lean on other than my best friend who was going through the same things as I was. It feels nice to have someone to lean on.

"Me too, baby. Me too. Only three more days."

We stay on the phone as I return to writing, making sure to stay quiet so we don't wake up Alyssa.

It's getting late by the time she finally stirs. "What time is it?"

"Eleven."

Silence.

"Why didn't you wake me?"

"You seemed like you could use some sleep," I shrug.

"But you get up early, I'm keeping you up." I finally look away from my laptop to see her staring at me.

"No, Tanner is doing a great job at that." She looks around the room, her brows scrunching together.

"You said I wasn't keeping you up!" His voice filters through the room from where my phone still rests next to me. Her eyes finally spotting it, clearing her confusion.

"The last time you asked me was hours ago. I have a morning class tomorrow. You should know this."

There's blubbering down the line before it goes quiet.

Alyssa laughs for the first time today and the sound is like music to my ears. "I'll let you get some sleep."

"You can stay here." A soft smile touches my lips, but she just shakes her head as she slides off my bed and starts grabbing her things. "Alright, I'll be down the hall if you need me."

She chuckles lightly. "Technically, you're up two floors and down the hall. But thank you. For everything."

"Of course, you're my best friend. Would I really be your friend if I wasn't there for you when you needed it." I put my computer to the side and walk Alyssa to my door where I lean against the frame. I reach my arm out to rub her sleeve. "I know I've already said this but, I'm proud of you. That guy was a real dick. You deserve better, loads better." She just nods as she walks away, down the hall into the elevator.

I lock my door on my way back to snuggle into my bed. Tanner's still on the phone, humming a soft melody. I lean my laptop against the side of my bed, I'll deal with that in the morning.

I've made it through four chapters which is quite the feat. I've always been told I'm a fast reader and I guess that transferred over to writing as well. At least if I have the motivation.

The humming continues as I plug my phone in and place it next to my head. If he can't be here at least I can have him on the phone.

"Tanner?" I mumble sleepily.

The humming pauses just long enough for him to respond. "Yes baby?"

"Will you stay?"

A soft laugh, "I'm not going anywhere."

"Good" A yawn escapes me as my eyes flutter close. The last

ON THE SIDELINES

thing I hear before I fall asleep is Tanner singing softly to single ladies by Beyonce. Typical.

17

Tanner

I'm bouncing off the walls while I impatiently wait for Sean to get off the plane. I sat next to Collins, so I was able to drag him off the plane and we were the first ones off. I only kind of feel bad since Sean is taking so long but I want to get home. There was a photo waiting for me once I turned my phone off airplane mode. Evie is sitting in my bed, wearing my clothes, smiling at the camera. She sent it with the caption 'Can't wait to see you *winking face emoji*'.

Collins sways on his feet as the next wave of our teammate's files down the stairs onto the runway. We landed late, it's almost four in the morning and everyone is feeling it.

The plane was close to silent the entire flight since most of us were asleep.

It takes a few more minutes before Sean makes it to us. "Sorry Tanner, I tried to get off earlier, but I got stuck."

"It's alright, let's head home."

The house is dark when we walk in. There's shifting on the couch that catches our attention while taking off our shoes. "Evie sweetheart, is that you?"

A soft groan fills the space. "I never want to hear you call me that again Tanner." Alyssa's voice comes from the couch before a lamp turns on. "Sorry, Evie said it would be okay if I stayed the night."

Sean's hockey bag thuds to the floor as he walks into the kitchen. "Yeah, that's fine. The den would be better though, It's like its own bedroom without a door."

"Oh, thanks." She looks around at us cautiously. "Did Evelyn tell you what happened?" She directs the question to me but continues to look between the three of us.

"Nope," I follow Sean into the kitchen where I'm reminded that we have no food. "Pizza anyone?" I get a chorus of yeses, so I go about finding a place that's open at this time. "She said if you wanted me to know you would tell me yourself." I glance at her just in time to see a small smile quirk her lips.

"Of course she said that. She's the best." She falls silent for a few moments, debating something. "Can I stay here for a little while?"

The three of us share a confused look. Before any of us can respond Evie comes barreling down the stairs and jumps on me.

Her legs wind tightly around my waist while her arms squeeze my neck. "I missed you." Her voice is a quiet breath against my ear.

"I missed you too." I feel her smile against my neck where she is currently burrowing her nose.

"Can Alyssa stay awhile?" She pulls back to look me in the eye. "I'll stay too if it helps."

Sean looks to me so I look to Collins, Collins flips us both off. "Yeah, I see no issue with that. Can we ask why though?"

Alyssa glances at Evie before releasing a long-drawn-out sigh. "I broke up with my boyfriend Jasper a few days ago." She looks up at me. "That's why I was sleeping in Evie's room the other day. Well, when I got back to my room that night, I checked my phone and saw a bunch of messages from him. I figured they were empty threats. He's always been all bark and no bite. But two days ago, he started showing up at my dorm and banging on the door, yelling to let him in.

"Sasha called the campus police on him a few times, but he just kept showing up. Evie mentioned she was coming here last night and offered for me to come with, so I accepted. Sasha told me that it would be better if I wasn't in the dorm for the next few days. Or until he calms down."

"Why did you guys break up? I thought you were happy together." Sean seems to voice all of our thoughts. Last I knew they were getting along great and seemed incredibly happy with one another.

"We weren't happy. He was." She shakes her head slowly. "He wanted control over everything to do with me. Then when Marcus and Jake showed up, he lost that control. It made him really angry. He called me a lot of really awful things and said if he had known we would have never been together. He said he didn't want a whore as a girlfriend, so I broke up with him. He left a lot of messages saying he was sorry and that he responded poorly. But I was asleep when they came through. When I didn't respond the messages changed.

"He was no longer sorry, he was pissed. He threatened me, threatened to come to my dorm and not leave until I talked to him. I didn't think that was so bad until they kept coming. Eventually he started threatening to put me in the hospital and when that didn't work, he threatened Sasha." She goes quiet but somehow, I know she's not done. "He told me he'd hurt Evie, now knowing her past said he'd rape her and a whole bunch of other awful things. In his words, 'it wouldn't matter since others already used her.'"

The world feels like it stopped spinning. When I look down at the beauty in my arms, she doesn't seem surprised by the information. My arms tighten around her, desperate to keep her safe.

"Both of you are staying here. If Sasha ever feels unsafe, she's welcome as well. We'll figure out a place for her to sleep when the time comes." A beautiful smile lights up Evie's face.

"Thank you." A lump in my throat stops my response. Will these girls ever get a break?

⛸

The girls fell asleep on the couch before the pizza arrived and slept right through the three of us loudly eating. They must have been exhausted. Sean carried Alyssa into the den while Collins got the pull-out couch ready for her. Not once did she wake up.

Evie also slept right through me carrying her up to my room and the shower I took.

I slip on a pair of sweatpants before walking back into my room. I don't know where Evie and I stand on that front. She's made a few sexual jokes but there's never any heat behind them. I don't want to make her uncomfortable by walking around my room naked while she's here.

She's still laying in my bed but she's awake. She follows me with her eyes as I walk around to the unoccupied side and lay down next to her.

"I'm sorry." My forehead creases as I stare at her.

"Why?" She shies away from my gaze.

"Because every time things seem to be going good, something from my past or my friends throws a wrench in it." Her honey eyes slowly rise to meet mine, glossy from her unshed tears.

"Baby, I know those aren't your fault. I would never blame you for the actions of someone else." Tears slowly fall from her eyes, which she tries to no avail to blink away. I use the back of my thumb to swipe them away before kissing her wet cheeks.

"Thank you." She cuddles into my chest, swinging a leg over my chest. We stay like that until we fall asleep. Neither of us have a morning class today so we can sleep in. Thank God for black out curtains.

18

Evie

Is it too soon to say that I love this man? Because I do, with everything I have.

He's proven far more times than I wish to count that he wants me, no matter what the future may hold. He's heard the horrors of my past and grew angry on my behalf. He's housed me when said past has clashed with the present and again when a deranged man has threatened my safety.

I've come to terms with the depth of my feelings over the last few days. We have almost a month left in this semester and the longer I take these classes, the less I care about them. I still don't know what I want to do with my life, the only thing I'm good at that could possibly become a career is writing but that comes with its own challenges.

I'm still trying to write a short book instead of stories and I think I'm almost halfway done. I'm ten chapters in but my audience on the writing app I use is getting restless.

I've had people privately message me asking why I haven't posted in two weeks, and I feel bad that this is taking me so long. I know I have no reason to feel this way, but it doesn't change the fact that I do.

I folded and posted the rough draft of a story I was working on just to get something out there. I posted it as a free story and asked for readers' opinions on where this story should go. That was this morning.

It's currently Monday, the start of spring break despite snow still resting on the ground.

Tanner has a game tonight that I'm going to with Sasha and Alyssa. Three days ago, Sasha showed up at the house asking if she could stay here.

Jasper had somehow gotten a key to their room and was waiting for Alyssa inside. But Sasha was the one to enter not Al. She hasn't told anyone what happened between them but whatever it was, was enough for her to show up shaken and terrified.

Sean and Collins have been good sports about the whole thing. Alyssa feels horrible about living in their space, but they keep assuring her that it's not a big deal.

These men have such big hearts it's unreal how lucky I got.

On the topic of luck, I definitely feel it when I turn over in bed and cuddle into Tanner. He's sound asleep and an idea blossoms in my head.

When he mentioned it he was joking, well he said he was half joking. The other day he said if I ever wanted to wake him up with a blowjob he wouldn't complain. I haven't done anything sexual that I actually wanted to do in years. But for the first time in a long time, I want to.

With shaky confidence, I slowly peel the comforter off of us as I situate myself between his legs. He's wearing a pair of sweats which do nothing to hide his morning wood.

I've never seen his size, nor have I felt it so I have no idea what to expect when I pull his pants down.

I laugh to myself when I learn he's decided to forgo boxers. That laugh dies quickly though when his length comes into view.

He's big.

Like really big.

Insanely big.

There's no way that will ever fit in me. And yet, I still want to try. I glance up to see he's still asleep, or he's really good at pretending.

Steeling my nerves I take a deep breath and go for it.

I grip his base loosely, my fingers almost closing around him. I lower my head until it's right there. Oh God, it's really big.

My tongue pokes out to taste him. He's salty but surprisingly good. I taste him again until I lick him like a lollipop. I hear his intake of breath when I put my mouth around him and suck down.

"Holy fuck." If I could, I would smile. But since I can't, I just look up at him.

Tanner's watching me with dilated eyes, heavy with lust. His eyes are wide as I slowly start to bob. I'm careful not to take him too deep, afraid of choking and losing air. I must be doing something right if the noises Tanner is making are any indication. Low groans and moans fall from his open lips fueling my own.

"You look incredible, baby. Oh fuck, just like that." I moan around him and attempt to swallow. His hands find their way into my hair, threading through the strands. "Can I?" Control. He wants control. While I'm scared, I nod, letting him have it.

His hands tighten in my hair as he starts to guide me. He pushes me further down that I'm comfortable with, causing me to gag around him. He holds my head down until tears fall. When he yanks me up I'm gasping for breath. "Goddamn." His words cause a smile to rise on my lips which I quickly put back around his cock.

"Oh shit." I take control back. Bobbing my head, my hands taking care of whatever I can't reach.

Tanner's breath becomes choppy as his hips jerk up involuntarily. A few more pups and he spills in my mouth.

I don't swallow yet, instead I lift my head so he can see and stick my tongue out, his seed sliding down and dripping onto his bare chest. "For fucks sake baby, you're killing me.

I smile as I swallow and lean down to lick his chest clean. He releases a shuttered breath which fills me with pride. I did this to him.

"Good morning." I place a chaste kiss to his lips before sliding off the bed and walking into the bathroom. I hear Tanner chuckle behind me as I enter his bathroom so I can brush my teeth.

I also need to take a shower, but breakfast sounds more appealing right now.

I'm in the middle of washing my face, my head bent down when Tanner's hands encircle my waist. "What a wonderful way to wake up. Jesus babe, we should do this more often."

I laugh but silently agree with him.

I stand to my full height while I reach for my moisturizer. Tanner rests his head on my shoulder as he watches me slather product onto my face. He presses a chaste kiss to my neck while peering up at me through hooded eyes.

I offer a small smile through the mirror as I finish. I should've realized that his eyes are his biggest tell, because the second I put my things away, he pounces. My body is being forcefully turned until I can look at him. His arms stay snaked around my waist whilst his eyes search my features for any sign of discomfort.

When he finds none, a predatory smile lifts his lips. Looking at me like that, he looks downright sinful.

"You took care of me, now it's my turn." I put one hand flat on his chest to stop him from leaning in. I can see his confusion. It's not that I *want* to stop, but if he thinks he needs to return the favor then we need to have a serious conversation.

"If you're only doing this because of how I woke you up then don't. I don't want you to think you *have* to do anything."

A cocky smile overtakes his face. "Baby, I don't want to do anything, I need to. I need to taste you on my tongue. See how pretty you are when you come around my fingers. Hear your tortuous moan as I make you come harder than you've ever imagined possible. This isn't some transaction where I 'repay' you." He adds air quotes around repay. He sounds upset, like the idea that I thought he felt obligated physically pains him.

"Okay. I want you." He searches my face one more time

before his lips meet mine with such force, I would have tumbled back had Tanner not been already holding me up.

He nips at my bottom lip, asking for access. Access I gladly give with a moan.

My surroundings become muted around me, my own mewled moans sounding muffled to my ears. What can I hear loud and clear? Tanner's cocky chuckle as he continues to dominate my mouth.

I never knew a kiss could get me so turned on. Turns out I was just kissing the wrong guy.

I pull away reluctantly, needing air but wishing I didn't. "Well fuck me." The words come out as a giggle.

"Don't worry princess, I plan to." He called me that once before and I liked it. But when he accompanies it with such dirty words, I fucking love it.

Unfortunately, before he can make good on his wordless promise, there's a knock at the door. Hesitantly, we pull away from each other. I lean up to place one last kiss to his lips before meandering toward the door where another knock sounds from.

"Yes?" I ask as I swing the door open, making sure to make my tone sugary sweet.

Sean stands on the other side wearing nothing but his boxers. He rubs at his eyes when a sliver of light peeking through the blackout curtains hits him directly in his eyes. "Dillan came over, wants to know if you two aren't busy fucking, if you'd like some breakfast?"

A blush creeps up my cheeks. I didn't think I was that loud. "Fuck you man!" Tanner's still in the bathroom but his voice seems to carry just fine.

"A simple yes or no will suffice." Oh, Sean's grumpy this

morning.

"Has he started cooking yet?" I don't smell food but that doesn't mean it wasn't cooked while I was preoccupied by the sexy hulk of a man currently snuggling into my back.

"Nope, whatcha what?"

"An omelet sounds nice." His lips quirk in a half smile.

"Extra meat on mine, hers veggie." My back rumbles from his voice, for some reason he made it deeper.

"Got it. Be done in fifteen." He drags his feet the entire way down the stairs while he lazily scratches his chest.

I release my hold on the door, preparing to follow him when it's shut in my face. A yelp escapes me when I'm thrown over Tanner's shoulder. He stalks to the bed when he drops me like a rag doll. "What are you doing?"

"Finishing what we started, now lay down and let me take care of you."

I do as he says because why the hell not? Fifteen minutes is more than enough time for some fun.

I situate myself in the middle of the bed with my neck supported by his pillows. Tanner looms over me, hunger making his sage eyes darken from lust. His hands slowly massage my ankles before making their way up.

They leave a burning path in their wake as they climb toward my upper thighs. They continue their accent until he finds the waistband of my legging and stop. "You sure you're okay with this?"

"Yes." My single word is enough to snap his restraint. He roughly tugs my leggings off, leaving my only coverage as my boy short undies.

There's nothing sexy about my undergarments. If I had

known this would happen, I would be wearing the lacy set I bought when we started dating a few weeks ago. It's a strappy and lacy set that looks phenomenal on me. I got them in the closest color to sage as I could find, I wanted it to match his amazing eyes.

I could tell him to stop, the set *is* in my backpack in the corner. But I don't want to and neither does he.

"Soaked, and it's all because of me." He's transfixed, his eyes glued to the juncture on my thighs.

"Always for you." I let out a breathy sigh. "Look, I know you want to take this slow, but I don't. And we're on a time limit. So, if you're done staring, take my panties off and put your head where it belongs."

His laugh is like music to my ears. All throaty and hoarse. Fucking perfection.

"Yes princess." God, do I love it when he calls me that.

His hands are back on my hips, pulling my panties down and exposing me. "Fuck." It's a soft whisper but it's there. "Beautiful." I smile to myself, loving his praises. I watch him stuff my panties into the pocket of his joggers, his gaze never once wavering.

He pries my legs apart, just wide enough for his head to fit between.

He places a soft kiss to the apex of my thighs before diving in like a starved man. I throw my head back on a whimper. His tongue slides up my slit on a leisurely journey to my clit. When he sucks the bud into his mouth my hips buck into him. His chuckle vibrates in the most delicious way.

I'm already on edge, I always am when he's around. He doesn't have to do anything, just him existing turns me on.

He continues his almost torturous pace which has me

withering beneath him in a matter of seconds.

A long-drawn-out moan falls from my parted lips as I climb higher. My eyes are screwed shut but if they weren't I'd be staring at the ceiling. I knew he had experience, I just never thought I'd be happy that he does. But at this moment I'm thanking whatever God wants to listen that he was a player.

My first boyfriend tried this once, and it was awful. Goes to show there's nothing wrong with you, if you can't come it's because you're with the wrong man, or you're with a boy. Not in a predatory way, in a you're both children kind of way.

Tanner sucks my clit back into his mouth and that was the last push I needed. I fall over the cliff into blinding pleasure. I'm faintly aware I'm making a lot of noise, but I can't tell if I'm being loud or not.

Tanner continues his motions until I'm squirming under him, trying to get away. When he finally sits up, his face is glistening with my arousal. He licks his lips while he just stares at me.

I smile, a giggle breaking free. "Holy hell, baby. That felt amazing."

He smiles in response, leaning down until he's lying on me, snuggling into my neck. "Yeah, this morning rocks."

My stomach growls, reminding me that I haven't actually eaten yet. I let out a contented sigh, not ready to move quite yet. Tanner places kisses along the length of my neck and it feels so good. So right.

Just like I know that I love this man, I also know he's it for me. I'm never going to find someone who fits so perfectly into me, into my life. If I believed in soulmates, I think Tanner would be mine.

I'm seconds from falling asleep when my stomach angrily reminds me it's still empty.

"Come on big guy. Time for breakfast." We disentangle ourselves from our little cocoon. While I put my leggings back on, Tanner heads into the bathroom. He returns with my hairbrush, which he so kindly and gently runs through my hair until it's smooth and untangled. He tosses the brush onto his bed as he drags me to the door.

Once it's open, the sweet aroma of eggs floats in and carries us down the steps. Dillan is standing over the stove, plating different servings of a scrambled omelet. He gives me a knowing smirk when he hands me mine to which Tanner smacks him upside the head.

Sean and Collins raise their hands in surrender when we pass them. Unfortunately, my friends aren't so kind.

"Thank God you're finished fucking. I really wasn't looking forward to interrupting."

"Sasha!"

"What? I wasn't. And neither were you Al. Hey! Don't hit me." She gasps. "You bitch!"

"Okay, okay. Settle down. You two can have your little cat fight later. For now, let's eat." We all settle down in the living room as we eat in relative silence. The boy's scarf down their plates in less than a minute, practically inhaling it.

When they all disappear into the kitchen to rinse their plates, Sasha finally speaks up. "So," I wait for her to continue, despite knowing she wants me to offer the information up. She sighs when I remain silently eating. "The second the boys go for their afternoon skate; you're telling us every little dirty secret."

I just shrug in response. "No, I won't." My two friends share a devious smile. I know I'm not getting out of this, but I'd like to pretend for the next few hours that they might forget and I won't be grilled the second the door closes. But the three of us know there's nothing I can say to stop their questions, and nothing can happen that will stop this conversation. Maybe delay it, but not stop it.

19

Evie

I told them everything. Of course I did. I didn't want to spend my entire afternoon fending off their questions. So, the second the door closed, and the lock slid into place, I told them. I didn't even give them a chance to ask.

I mean, let's be honest. I wanted to tell them as badly as they wanted to know. I needed their opinion on the emotions I'm feeling. Whether I should be worried about how quickly they came on or if I should just go with the flow and give in to them.

Their answer was a resounding, give in. So, I have, kind of.

Tanner is getting ready for his game and will be for the next hour, so I have nothing to give in to right now. All I have is the thoughts in my head.

Alyssa announced after breakfast that she's feeling anxious about being in one place for so long despite the radio silence from Jasper. The guys discussed different options and came up with a suitable solution.

Sasha is taking over the den and for the next two weeks Alyssa will be staying with Dillan. The team is two games away from taking home the trophy for the frozen four and as long as they don't lose tonight's game, they don't have to travel anywhere for the rest of the season.

Tanner left his away jersey on his bed for me to wear tonight as well as one of his black hoodies.

I pull on a clean pair of leggings, now only wearing them and a bra. I meander to the mirror where I put on just enough foundation to cover my bags and even out my skin tone. I've always been blessed with clear skin so I try to wear as little makeup as possible. I haven't found a brand that doesn't make me breakout, so I prefer to go bare.

I want to keep my look natural, so I do a light brown eyeshadow look with brown mascara. Pale blush adorns my cheeks and some pink lip gloss that I make sure to stick in my purse, so I don't forget it later.

I slip Tanner's hoodie over my head, watching as it swallows my curves. This is the hoodie that's super tight on him so it's not as loose as some of his other ones, perfect to go under a jersey. Which is exactly what I do, pulling the maroon fabric over my head, making sure to pull the hood out to lay on top of the jersey.

I head back into the bathroom so I can use the mirror to put my hair up in a messy styled bun. Tanner's favorite. Not really.

He says his favorite is my high ponytail that's reminiscent of Ariana Grande's signature look.

I grab my favorite pair of chunky heeled suede ankle boots as I exit the room and head downstairs to where the others wait for me.

We make it to the arena with fifteen minutes to spare. The arena is standing room only, but we don't have to worry about that. We cling to each other as we walk down the crowded stairs toward the ice. We apologize to the people already sitting as we squeeze past them on our way to Tanner's reserved family seats.

At the beginning of the season, Tanner requested three seats, two for his parents and one for me. All that time ago, when I was still ignoring him, he still believed he'd be able to win me over. I've never been so annoyed at him, yet happy for his confidence.

His parents aren't coming to this game, so the three seats are all ours. Now that I think about it, he doesn't talk about his parents, nor do they go to his games despite having great seats.

The team is out on the ice for warm up. Once I've settled in my seat, I look around the rink trying to find him. It takes me a moment to see him behind a group of his teammates but he's there, laughing and having fun.

Like he can feel my eyes on him, he turns, and we lock eyes.

Then he's off like lightning, racing full speed toward me. I think he's going to slow down but nope. He slams into the boards at full speed with the goofiest grin on his face. His hands plastered to what I've been corrected as high-density polyethylene, not plastic. He squishes his face against the not plastic. If I didn't love this man before, I definitely do now.

I never thought I would want a giant goofball for a boyfriend, but I couldn't be happier.

His coach calls him away from me but before he goes, he places a faux kiss to his gloved hand and presses it in front of me. I follow his lead, placing a real kiss to my hand and flattening it over his, the not plastic between us.

His coach calls him again and this time he takes off to where the rest of his team is gathered, making fun of him.

The game starts a few minutes later after Havard takes the ice.

We win the first puck drop, Dillan taking off with it across the ice. It's not long before Harvard takes control and the battle for the puck begins. I have no idea what's going on but that doesn't stop the excitement I feel when our team has the little black flat ball.

Anytime Tanner is on the ice, I'm on the edge of my seat cheering him on.

I don't get why he's only on the ice for a few minutes at a time. When the question started to eat at me, I asked Sasha. She's not the biggest fan of the sport but she grew up with hockey on the tv.

"What they are doing is called shifts. Sometimes they last a long time, sometimes they don't. The game is extremely physical and tough on the body. Tanner is in the first line, which means he's going to be on the ice with a lot of the same guys. That also means he's really good.

"There are four lines but if you are in, say the fourth line, that doesn't necessarily mean you're bad, it might just mean you're on a really good team. But if you're in the first line I think you're more likely to have more time on the ice since you're seen as the best the team has to offer."

"What?" Sasha laughs softly, or I think she does. Her shoulders are shaking but it's too loud in here to be able to hear her.

"Ask Tanner, he'll be able to explain it better."

"I would rather not." I turn my attention back to the ice where Tanner has just joined his teammates.

"Why not?"

"Because if I let him start, he'll never stop." It's not a lie. We argue about sports quite a bit and they tend to last a few hours because Tanner won't let go of the fact that I prefer to watch baseball. It's a whole lot less violent.

The puck is stolen and passed to Tanner where he takes a shot at the net. The puck sails through the air straight to the goalie. I watch it in slow motion as Harvard's goalie raises his hand to block the shot. He's a tad too slow and the crowd erupts as the puck hits the back of the net and the buzzer goes off.

Tanner gets tackled to the ice by his teammates in celebration. When he finally gets back on his feet, he skates over to where I am, the biggest smile on his face as he slaps his hand on the divider. I place my own on top of his, smiling like an idiot, profusely proud of my man.

The game continued and, in the end, we won 2-1. I drag my friends to the players tunnel where Tanner asked me to wait for him. We're not the first there but we are amongst them.

I recognize a few of the other players' girlfriends, girls I've seen from a distance but never actually met. Then there's the mass of girls I've never seen before. There are a few guys sprinkled throughout the crowd, but they are definitely overwhelmed by the sheer number of females. It's a little unnerving.

I'm standing in the middle of the tunnel, tucked away against the wall. The players still haven't come out and it's nearing ten minutes, but I don't know how long post-game stuff takes so I'm not worried.

A group of girls shove their way toward the front of the pack talking loudly about my boyfriend. "Don't worry girls, he'll come to his senses. If Tanner is going home with anyone tonight, it'll be one of us."

"He better. I've been trying to get his attention all year, but he hasn't even spared me a glance. I mean look at me." She jesters down her body. She's tall, around Alyssa's height. Beautiful bronze skin that is very obviously not natural. Long auburn hair cascades down her back landing just above her waist. She's beautiful, there's no doubting that. But for the first time, I realize I'm not worried. Tanner is mine and I'm his. He chose me over this woman which means in his mind I'm more attractive and that's a huge confidence boost for me.

The girls pass us continuing their conversation. Sasha sends me a sidelong glance once she realizes who their topic is. I just shrug, like I said, I'm not worried.

A few minutes later the guys start filing out of the locker room. The tunnel erupts to a near defining level with each new player. Most of them pair off with their partner or a random girl or guy. A few just walk through without sparing the people here a glace.

I know the second they walk out. The level somehow raises even louder. I can barely see them over the head of the other people, but I can see all of them looking around, presumably for my group. Sean has women throwing themselves at him, but he completely ignores them as he pushes his way through the throngs of people.

Oli follows behind him, trying his best to avoid the women grabbing at him. I can see Tanner's head as he wades through the people. Suddenly he stops and looks down. I can see the back of a woman's head, a woman's head with auburn hair. She throws her arms around his neck as she tries to snuggle into him.

In his defense, he tenses up and attempts to step away from her. Something behind him forces him to stop his retreat, then another pair of arms come around from behind him.

I watch this happen for another minute before I can't take it anymore. I shove my way through groups of people who part unhappily. Collins is next to Tanner, trying to get the girls off of him with little success. Dillan approaches behind them, watching the chaos in front of him.

He notices me as I get closer, a brilliant smile lighting up his features. I'm finally close enough to hear what they're saying, and it makes me smile. "Brianna, Alisha, get off of me."

"Come on guys, he doesn't want you to touch him."

More words with the same idea come from their mouths but they fall on deaf ears. I know Sasha and Alyssa are behind me so if need be, I have my friends as back up.

I finally get close enough to touch who I assume is Alisha, the auburn-haired beauty. Without hesitation I grab one of her arms that's around Tanner's neck and rip it off. Her head whips to where I am, she's mad until she gets a good look at me, and the bitch shrugs me off.

She tries to put her arm back on my boyfriend, but I stop her. I step into her, forcing her off of Tanner. She goes to open her mouth but Collins places his hand over her mouth and wraps an arm around her waist so she can't come at me.

I remove Brianna's hands, which she also does not appear to be too happy about but I couldn't care less. Not when Tanner's watching me with hunger in his eyes and the sexy curve of his lips.

I replace their hands with mine. Tanner's hands land on my waist and he uses his grip to lift me up. I wrap my legs around his waist and wrap my arms around his neck. I cover his lips with mine in a possessive kiss that he returns with hunger.

When I pull away, I'm given the perfect view of a seething Brianna. "Hello, I'm Evie, Tanner's girlfriend. Just so we can avoid this confrontation in the future, he's off limits. We're happy together and neither of us are too keen on you putting your hands on him. And if that doesn't deter you, then next time I'll make sure to get the interaction on camera, so I have proof when I go to the police with sexual harassment." A smile of pure sugar graces my face as Tanner chuckles under me.

Collins releases an angry Alisha who scoffs and pushes him away. They both glare at me as they walk away. The other two in their group follow behind without a backwards glance.

I try to slide down my boyfriend's body, but his arms tighten around me. "Nu-uh, you aren't going anywhere."

"But I can walk on my own." My protests fall on deaf ears as he starts walking toward the exit.

"I know." I sigh, giving up for the time being. This isn't worth the fight.

He finally sets me down once we reach his truck. My feet only touch the ground for a few seconds before I'm lifted back up into his truck.

Us girls drove Sean's car so the other two are driving back

with him and Collins so Tanner and I could have some time alone.

He's quiet as he pulls out of the parking lot and onto the road. The radio plays softly, the only sound in the cab. I'm scared to break the silence; I can't tell if he's upset about what I said. For all I know those girls were his friends and I just made an unnecessary enemy that I will have to see often.

I shift nervously in my seat when we turn onto an unfamiliar road. I've lived here for almost a year, and I have yet to explore the town that surrounds the campus.

He keeps driving, eyes never straying from the road. Ten minutes of tortuous silence later he pulls into the parking lot of a family-owned diner I've been dying to try. A smile lifts my lips because I've mentioned that more than a few times to him. Actually, I've talked about it so much that he's taken to shutting me up with a kiss when the conversation comes up.

"Come on, let's get some food in you." My smile widens when I see him hop out of the truck and literally run around to open my door for me.

"Thank you. This is really sweet."

"Well, you don't shut up about how cute this place is and I figured after that confrontation, you deserve a reward." He hides a cheeky smile behind his hand when he scratches his jaw.

"You're not mad?" He looks at me questioningly. "I just acted without thought. You were quiet the entire way here, so I assumed you were mad at me." He laughs, loud and boisterous.

"No, I'm not mad. I hate those girls. I've turned them down every time they approach me, but they never seem to get the idea that I don't want them."

"Oh, good. Well not that they don't listen to you but that

you're not mad at me." I chuckle softly. "Okay, let's get food. I'm hungry so you must be starving."

20

Tanner

My girl hums happily next to me as she digs into her Belgian waffle with strawberries and powdered sugar. She got a meal with it, but I don't think she'll get to the rest.

I've offered to eat it since I'm still hungry and she's not, but she threatened my balls if I even thought about eating her leftovers.

We haven't talked much. I think she still believes for some reason that I'm upset with her. I don't understand where those thoughts came from, but they are completely wrong. We've had a run in with Brianna before and she was a bitch to Evie. Did she forget about that?

The only thing I was feeling toward her while she was putting on her little show was lust. It took everything in me not to carry her into one of the supply closets and fuck her until she couldn't walk straight.

I plan on doing just that when we get home. I can't even describe how turned on she made me. Her possessive display was the hottest thing I've ever witnessed.

Our waiter brings over another side of fries for me and Evie rolls her eyes when I waste no time in devouring them. She can't really be annoyed with me. I mean come on, I just played a grueling game of hockey and won. I'm a hungry boy.

She sets her fork down and turns her undivided attention to me. "You're really not mad?"

I force myself to swallow the lump of food in my mouth, she's yelled at me more than enough times now for me to realize she hates it when I talk with my mouth full. "No, why would I be? That was fucking hot."

"They aren't your friends? They seemed really close with you, so I just assumed you guys were friends and I made a big deal out of nothing." She looks down at the table, a rare shyness taking hold of her.

"Princess," I pinch her chin and lift until she's forced to look in my eyes. "They are NOT my friends. I've been turning down their advances since freshman year. They're puck bunnies, chasing the next high with anyone who wears a hockey jersey. At some point it became a game to them, competing with each other to see which one of them would be the first to climb into my bed.

I've spent the last three years telling them no, only for them to come back the next game and try again.

"What you said was nothing I haven't thought about before. I know I had sort of a reputation for sleeping around but I didn't take just anyone to my bed. Most of the time I would spend a few weeks with the same girl before moving on. I've never been a one and done kind of guy. It never felt right to have one-night stands. So no, I'm not mad at you. Actually, I'm extremely impressed and turned on right now. Plus, she was a bitch to you last time, so it was well deserved."

I release her chin when she starts giggling. Seeing her smile so carefree like this does things to my heart. Things I haven't felt since Mia. I missed this. I missed having these feelings and being able to express them with someone. I'm not naive, I know what I'm feeling. I'm quickly falling in love with the raven-haired beauty in front of me and there isn't a damn thing I'm going to do about it.

I called him, Mr. Reynolds, Mia's dad. He answered on the third ring. I've never been so nervous, not even when I was dating his daughter and she wanted us to meet. I honestly never thought I'd have this conversation, but I know it needs to be done.

We play against ASU tomorrow in the frozen four finals, and I invited him to come watch. He was hesitant but ultimately said he would come.

I told him he'd be sitting next to someone that when the game is over, I'd like his opinion on. I didn't explain any further even when he tried to pry. I want his honest opinion on Evie before I tell him who she is.

My dad doesn't talk to me or my brother anymore so when Mia introduced us, he became like a father figure. When my brother and I were trying to impress those girls my senior year of high school, he showed up with my dad. He was the one who made it so I could still go to college. He was the one who helped me through the grief of losing his daughter, my own pops nowhere to be found.

So now that I realize that I'm in love with a new girl, it's only right to have her meet the man who raised my last love.

Evie doesn't know about any of this, I don't want her to be anything but herself when they meet. I did tell her I wanted her sitting in a specific seat. She was confused but brushed it off as a, and I quote, 'weird hockey thing'.

I didn't bother to correct her.

I had called him last night after we got home and I've kind of been avoiding everyone since. Evie has tried to talk to me about what's wrong, but I've brushed her off every time. I'm worried he won't like Evie.

She seemed hurt but I don't know how to broach the topic with her. I've only mentioned Mia once to her and I don't know how to have this conversation without telling her what I'm feeling.

I may be a little stupid sometimes, but I do know it's far too early to tell her I love her. There's no way she'll reciprocate. Plus, with everything going on with her past, now's not the time to bring this up.

She still hasn't decided if she's going to talk to Jake. She says she has until the end of the week to make a decision, that's when he and Marcus will be transferred back to Montana. I don't want to add something else to her plate.

"Tanner?" Evie's timid voice comes from the doorway. I hadn't realized how long I've been standing here, staring at my reflection in my bathroom.

"Yeah baby?"

"We need to talk." My shoulders stiffen. I know what those words mean, they always mean the same thing.

"Okay." I sound defeated but she doesn't point that out. She simply closes the bedroom door and takes a seat on the bed, patting the spot next to her. I slowly join her, not really wanting to have this conversation.

"Look, I know what you said but," she pauses, searching my face for something, "your actions are telling me something else."

My brows crease, this isn't how this conversation normally starts, right?

"I wish you would have told me you were mad instead of lying about it. I know I met one of them before but I didn't know the other three."

"Mad? Baby I'm not mad." She sighs.

"Then why are you avoiding me?" Oh shit. I don't know how to fix this.

"Uh," I scratch at my brow. "It's complicated."

"Then explain it to me."

"I guess I'm just nervous. We've never been this close to a Frozen Four win, I think ever. It's a lot of pressure. Add that to the draft and I'm sort of freaking out." Well, not necessarily a lie, just not the full truth.

"The draft?"

"Yeah, I entered this year. I've had some interest in me this season and if we win then I have a good chance at going pro. But I may have to move a long way away."

"Oh." Her face falls when the realization sets in. "Do you still want this?" She gestures between us. "Want me?"

"Yes." No hesitation. There's nothing I want more than to be with her, stay with her. "When the time comes, we'll figure it out but, until then I just want to live in the moment."

She places a comforting hand over mine. "Okay, as long as we are still something you think is worth fighting for." A sneaky smile pulls at her lips, an idea forming in her beautiful brain. "You want to live in the moment?"

"Yeah?" That smile grows.

"Good." She stands up and steps in front of me. "Lay down." I do as she says but she doesn't follow. She walks over to the door, and I'm worried she's about to leave me here until I hear the sound of the door locking. It takes a moment for my brain to catch up but once it does, I'm happy to oblige her every demand.

She struts back over and straddles my lap. "Tanner?" I hum as I watch her every move like a hawk. "Touch me." Oh shit. Gladly.

I waste no time taking off her shirt and discarding it somewhere on the floor. She's wearing this little sage number that's all lacy and holy shit does it look good on her. It does nothing to hide her pretty rose bud nipples that are currently straining against the fabric.

"God damn baby." A coy smile tilts her lips when she leans down, pressing her perfect tits into my chest.

"Do you like it?" She purrs seductively.

"Oh, hell yeah I do." A sweet giggle passes her lips at the eagerness in my voice.

"Great, I did buy it just for you." Oh, sweet baby Jesus.

She steals the words right out of my mouth when she presses her lips to mine. It starts out sweet and soft but quickly turns ravenous. We're both fighting for control, forcing our way into each other's mouths.

She grips my shirt in her hands, using it to haul me up just enough to rip it over my head. I'm left in basketball shorts while she devours me with her eyes. She slowly rises to her knees and motions to the shorts. "Take these off."

"Demanding." I tisk. She glowers at me, the look icing me to my bone. "Yes ma'am, off they go." I yank them down and accidentally take my boxers with them, but I don't hear any complaints.

Evie slides off of me so I can kick my clothes off. While she's standing, she wiggles out of her skirt and when she straightens, I'm left with a sight that will grace my spank bank for years to come.

Her panties match her bra perfectly, all lace with no coverage. She smirks as she gives me a little twirl and fuck me if she isn't the sexiest little vixen I've ever seen. She is, by the way, the sexiest woman EVER!

"Are you just going to sit there gawking or are you going to help take this off of me?" I stumble over my own two feet as I skyrocket to standing. She laughs at my eagerness, but it quickly turns into a yelp when I manhandle her until she's laying on her back as I tower over her.

She watches me with heated eyes as I prowl toward her. She looks awfully smug right now, I wonder how long that will last once I'm inside her.

I grip the waistband of her panties and pull them down her

legs, throwing them over my shoulder the second there off. She bats her eyelashes at me when my hands snake under her back to where the clasps are. With one hand I unclasp her bra before sliding the straps down her arms. Her bra joins the panties on the floor, leaving her naked and completely exposed to my greedy gaze.

"Fucking perfect." The prettiest blush crawls up her neck at my praise.

"You're not too bad yourself." I chuckle darkly.

I pull one pink bud into my mouth, forcing a gasp from her mouth. "Are you going to let me fuck you?"

"Yes, oh god yes, please do." She's already whimpering below me, the sound like music to my ears.

"Then lay back and be a good girl." She nods quickly, another whimper floating through the air.

I slide down her body, nestling myself between her luscious thighs. She spreads her legs for me, giving me a great view of her pretty pink pussy. She's glistening, already ready for me.

"So wet, so perfect." I sweep my tongue out, tasting her. Her hips buck in response. Her hands gripping my hair trying to pull me closer. "Needy, needy girl." I tisk. She yanks on my hair again and this time I go without resistance, burying my head in heaven.

Her sweet moan pierces the air, a chorus of yeses and oh my gods sprinkled in there as well. I work her higher and higher with my tongue and fingers. She's withering beneath me, grinding her pussy into my face, I love it.

I suck her clit into my mouth as I work another finger in. I'm rewarded with another moan, only louder this time.

"Tanner." My name is a breathy whisper and I think I've found my new favorite way for her to say my name.

I quicken my pace until she can't stay still, twisting and bucking, trying to get away. My free arm snakes around her waist and pins her to the bed. Her moans become louder and breathier until I feel her walls contract around my fingers. She damn near screams my name as she comes apart for me.

It's a good thing the boys are at Dillan's right now. I'm the only person who gets to hear the way Evie sounds when she comes, no one else. She's all mine.

I lick her a few more times as she comes down from her high, her legs shaking around my head. "God, you taste amazing. My new favorite dessert." She giggles as I crawl up her body and snuggle into her neck.

"What are you doing?"

"Cuddling. What does it look like?"

"Oh, it looks like exactly what it is, that's the problem." A light laugh falls from my lips and I lean up to look at her.

"And why is that a problem?"

"Because, I didn't say you were done." A smile splits my face, and she continues. "Grab the condom I know is in your bedside table and get your dick in me, now."

"Bos-sy." But I do as she says cause I'm not stupid, I want this as badly as she does. I think if I ever don't, someone needs to shoot me.

Once the condom is rolled on, I position myself at her entrance. I glance up at her, waiting for her permission to continue. She nods meekly, eyes glued to my length.

I slowly push inside of her, giving her time to adjust before pushing in farther. She whimpers but glowers at me when I still inside her.

I grab Evie's thighs, pushing them toward her chest. The

change in position allows me to go deeper and hit that sweet spot that makes her go wild. I still once I've bottomed out and wait for her to give the go ahead to move. It's torture but I don't want to hurt her.

A few minutes pass before she tentatively grinds on me. When she moans, I know I'm in the clear. I start slow, watching her reaction to everything I do. When her face scrunches in pain, I do something else. When she moans, pleasure overtaking her expression, I continue to do the same thing.

My dick is so hard I have to fight not to come. I want her to get as much pleasure out of this as possible, even if it means it physically pains me.

But I'm only human and I know I won't last much longer so in hopes of getting her right there with me, my thumb finds her clit and rubs the tight bundle of nerves. She moans loudly, spurring me on.

"Harder."

"Are you sure?" I don't want to hurt her.

"Tanner." Her tone is a warning. "If you don't fuck me harder, I'll find someone who will."

"The fuck you will. No one is allowed to touch what's mine. I'll rip their hands off if they even think about it." She gets what she wants. I pull back to the tip and slam into her. Her tits bounce with every thrust, her body slowly sliding up the bed. I have to keep pulling her down to keep her in the same spot.

Her moans get louder and higher, and I can tell she's getting closer. She grips my shoulders, nails biting into the skin there. She's going to leave marks and I couldn't be happier.

I pinch her clit and hit that spot deep in her and she's gone, tumbling over that edge as she drags me with her. I spill into the condom, pumping into her a few more times than necessary before pulling out. I begrudgingly drag myself off her and into the bathroom to grab a washcloth and discard the used condom. When I return to Evie, her breathing has evened out as she sleeps soundly. I clean her up, picking up her clothes and putting them in a pile. I put the washcloth into my laundry basket before returning to her.

I can't wait for tomorrow. I get the girl, the win, and hopefully the blessing of the only father figure left in my life.

I lift Evie into my arms and tuck her under the comforter. I crawl over her and settle behind her, spooning her from behind, her favorite cuddle position.

I can faintly hear the front door open and voices drifting up the stairs but I'm far too tired to go greet my friends. I press my nose into Evie's hair and that's where I fall asleep, with my girl in my arms and a smile on my face.

21

Evie

The man in the seat next to me is watching me. I haven't caught him doing it yet, but I know he is. Call it my intuition, but I know when I'm being watched. I'm fed up by the middle of the second quarter and decide to call him out on it.

"Can I help you with something?" My tone comes out harsher than I mean it too, but this guy is seriously creeping me out.

He looks startled by my voice and nervously glances at me. He examines me like I've just grown a second head. I can't get a read on this guy. He was already here when we got here and sat down, but he didn't seem thrilled to be here. I know he's sitting in Tanner's family seats, just like I am but I have no idea who he is.

"Sorry, that came out harsher than I meant it to. I'm Evelyn, but my friends call me Evie. What's your name?" He continues to watch me silently. It's becoming unnerving. "Look, I know Tanner knows you, otherwise you wouldn't be sitting in his family seats. I just want to know who you are to him."

He watches me for a moment more before finally opening his mouth. "Tanner hasn't mentioned me?"

I quirk my head to the side. "Uh, maybe. I'm not sure. I can't tell you for sure unless I know your name."

He chuckles lightly, a giant weight seemingly lifting off his shoulders. "My name is Jensen. But before I tell you anything else, can I ask what your relation to Tanner is?"

"Tanner is my boyfriend." He jumps back slightly, definitely surprised.

"Pardon?"

"I'm dating Tanner Shaw." I hesitate, I told my friends earlier how I felt about Tanner, needing their minds to help decipher my emotions but somehow, I know this man needs to hear this. "We've been together for a few weeks now but before that he had been trying to convince me to give him a chance all of last semester. I know it seems early and premature to say this, but I love him. I love that man so much it hurts."

A silence descends over the two of us as I give him a chance to process my words. "Let me reintroduce myself," he extends a hand toward me which I take in mine and give a small shake. "I'm Jensen Reynolds, Mia's father."

The first thing I do when I see Tanner is slap him. Maybe not the best reaction but one that warranted nonetheless. At least Jenson laughs when the back of my hands hits Tanner's cheek.

"What was that for?" He pouts, pushing his bottom lip out as he cradles his now red cheek.

"Don't you dare. You know exactly what that was for." He flinches back but at least has the decency to look sorry. Sean casts a glance our way but quickly walks away.

"Son," Jensen clasps a hand to his shoulder, "I'm proud of you, and you deserved that."

I watch as Tanner tries to comprehend what's going on. His eyes pinball between Jensen and I before landing on me.

"I take it you know who one another is." He scratches at the back of his neck, now avoiding eye contact.

"Yeah, imagine my surprise when I learned I introduced myself as your girlfriend to your last girlfriend's dad. Tanner, I was mortified." Jensen chuckles next to me.

"I already told you it's alright. It's been five years since we lost Mia, I would be more concerned if Tanner hadn't even tried to move on." Tanner's eyes glance over to Jensen, taking in his old friend.

"You came."

"Of course I came! You asked me to be here."

"Well, we haven't talked in two years, I didn't know if you still wanted anything to do with me." Jensen's eyes soften.

"Oh son, I always want something to do with you. You've just been busy and so have I. That doesn't mean I don't want to hear from you, see you. I always do and always will. I don't care if it's not biological, you're my son. Have been since my daughter brought you home." He pulls Tanner into a hug. I've never seen Tanner break down so fast.

Tears flow freely down his cheeks; he doesn't even care that hundreds of eyes watch him.

"Let me take you both to dinner, we have a lot to talk about." I smile and I take his hand in mine. I tug on it to get his attention. Once I have it I use my free hand to tug his head down to mine. I place a soft kiss on his lips and smile when he does.

"Congratulations on the win, big man. I think you deserve a reward once we get home."

"Oh, fuck yeah I do!"

"Tanner Mathew Shaw, watch your language!" Jensen's voice booms next to us causing Tanner to jump higher than he ever has before.

"Yes sir." He sounds so obedient right now, it's oldy enduring.

"Oh, come off it kid, I'm just giving you a hard time. You're almost twenty-two, you're allowed to cuss." Jensen and I share a laugh at my boyfriend's expense, one he slowly joins in on.

"Come on, I know the perfect place." He tugs my hand as he starts to wind through the hordes of people wanting to congratulate him on their Frozen Four victory. I link my fingers through Jensen's hand as well so we won't get separated. I don't miss the soft smile he shoots me.

It takes us far longer than I'd like to make it to the parking lot but once we do, it's a straight shot to Tanner's truck.

He picks me up and sets me in the passenger seat while Jensen climbs into the back. Tanner rounds the truck after shutting my door for me. Soon enough we're on the road heading toward the outskirts of the city.

Tanner uses this time to catch up with the man behind me and I couldn't be happier he's rekindling such an important relationship. We pull into a steakhouse that I've seen but never been too.

I stay in my seat after I've unbuckled, knowing the drill by now. If I even try to open my own door in Tanner's presence, he forces me back in, shuts the door just so he can be a gentleman and opens it for me. That goes for all doors by the way, not only car doors.

He helps me down from my spot and the three of us make our way into the packed restaurant. I'm surprised when they say they can seat us right away but that's the plus side to being a small group, I guess.

I slide into the booth first followed by Tanner, Jensen sitting opposite of us. "I'm happy for you buddy. You told me you wanted my opinion of her, well here it is. She reminds me a lot of my daughter, but I guess that shouldn't come as a surprise. She's kind and has a huge heart. She has a great sense of humor and cares for you deeply. Despite her lack of knowledge on the sport you play, she never took her eyes off of you, cheering you on the entire time."

I smile at his kind words. "Thank you, that's very sweet of you." An arm wraps around me, a large hand squeezes my shoulder.

"He's right, you're all those things and more." I feel my cheek heat and I can only imagine how pink I must be right now.

"I approve son, so would Mia."

Tanner sniffles but his bright smile says all he needs to.

The waiter comes over to take our drinks before leaving again in a hurry. We all quiet down as we scan the menu. By the time he returns with our drinks we're ready to order.

"So, there's another reason I brought you guys here. We're celebrating more than just our win tonight."

"What else are we celebrating?" Jensen sounds as confused as I feel.

"The Cheetahs want to sign me." The table falls silent. Tanner looks back and forth between us, not knowing where to look.

"This is great news!" Jensen is the first to react. I wish I could say I'm happy for him, but I don't know where the Cheetahs are. I just got him; I don't want to lose him already.

"Baby?" I snap out of my thoughts to see both sets of eyes on me.

I clear my throat before plastering a smile on my face. "That's wonderful." I know my smile doesn't reach my eyes, but I can't help it, I'm not happy, I'm sad. "What team are the Cheetahs?"

"Columbus Ohio."

"How far away is that from here?" I didn't know it was possible, but his smile widens.

"That's the best part. When I'm not on the road, I'll only be a four-hour drive away." My shoulders sag with relief, four hours isn't that far. Four hours seem doable. "You like the idea a lot more now, don't you?"

There's no point in denying it, it was obvious I was less than thrilled a minute ago. "Yeah, sorry I just don't want to be away from you. But four hours isn't so bad in the grand scheme of things. I can handle that."

The conversation continues, flowing freely. The food arrives and I put all of my attention into my plate. The boys are talking about the logistics of everything, including when he leaves.

"One month from now. They want me at their training camp for the summer. They know they want me, but they need to see where I'd fit best. You'll come with me, won't you?" Silence seconds over the table again but I'm too far into my head to really notice. "Evie?"

My head snaps up, eyes searching around until they land on my boyfriend. "Huh?"

"I was asking if you would join me in Ohio for the summer after school lets out."

My cheeks flush at the idea of spending the entire summer with him. Which is odd considering I've spent more time living with him this semester than I have in my own room. "You want me there?"

His brows scrunch together. "What kind of question is that? Of course I do. If I could drag you with me everywhere I go, I would. I don't want to live a day without you by my side."

I smile, I can't help it. This man always knows how to make me feel wanted. "Yeah, I'll join you. That sounds like a lot of fun."

After dinner Jensen heads back home to his small town an hour away and Tanner and I go back to his house. It's odd to think it won't be his house for much longer, only a month.

The house is empty when we enter. Everyone's probably out partying, celebrating tonight's big win.

I take the leftovers from Tanner's hands and put them away in the fridge. I know, right? There were actually leftovers! It may be his third entree, but we'll ignore that fact.

I hear his back door open and close, but I hesitate. My eyes follow the path to where I can see him sitting on the ground, back to the wall. The next thing I do will change everything.

I take a deep breath to steel my nerves. I raise my head up high and join him outside. I don't bother sitting next to him, I'll end up in his lap anyway so that's where I sit. His arms wrap around me and I lean against him.

We sit in silence for what feels like hours. Tonight's a full moon. It's beautiful, in all its pale glory.

"Are you ready for your reward?" My voice is barely above a whisper, a soft breath in the wind. The only sign Tanner heard me is his answering hum. "Baby, I need a verbal answer." His laugh vibrates my side. I can see him looking at me, so I turn until our noses brush.

"Yes, but you don't have to do that. I'm more than happy to just spend time with you." I gasp, leaning back as far as his arms will let me.

"Naughty boy. How do you know that's what I was going to give you?"

"It's not?" I giggle, leaning back in.

"Yes and no. Yes, because that is most definitely how this night will end. But that's not what I was referring to when I asked."

"Oh, then what's my gift?" I smile and press my lips to him.

"I am, silly boy." He rolls his eyes but kisses me back. I feel his desire to deepen the kiss, but I refrain, wanting to keep it soft and sweet. He groans when he tries to come closer, and I lean back. "Not now. I want to have a moment." He resigns, letting me take the reins.

I press another soft kiss to his lips, then to his cheek. He smiles when I continue to pepper kisses to any exposed piece of skin I can reach.

I press one more to his lips and cage his face between my hands. I stare deeply into his eyes, bouncing between his beautiful sage orbs. I smile, the confession on the tip of my tongue.

"What's got you so smiley?"

"You." He chuckles while attempting to lean forward. I use my grip on his face to hold him back. His eyebrows raise to his hairline, but he doesn't question it, just lets me take him in as he does the same to me. "Tanner?"

"Yeah princess?"

"I love you." The words hang in the space between us as he processes my words. I can see the second they sink in. The most brilliant smile I've ever seen takes up his entire face.

"Say it again."

I happily obliged. "I love you."

"Again."

"I love you Tanner Mathew Shaw."

He slams his lips to mine before following my lead, peppering kisses on my face. "You love me?"

"Yeah baby, I love you."

"Oh, thank fuck." He kisses me again but this time softer, sweeter. "Because I think I've loved you from the moment I saw you."

My laugh floats through the air between us. "You think so."

"No," he shakes his head, "I know so." We're both grinning like idiots but neither of us care. "Evelyn Campbell, I love you. And I can't wait to spend forever with you. Cause now that you've said those three words, you mine, and I don't plan on ever letting you go."

"Good, because I don't plan on going anywhere. You're stuck with me." I kiss him one last time before he hoists me into a position he can hold me that allows him to stand. I giggle the entire wavy up to our room because fuck the idea that this is only his, I plan on moving in tomorrow if he'll let me. "I love you." I whisper again as he lays me down on our bed.

"I love you too."

22

Tanner

Beautiful. Exquisite. A masterpiece.

Evie's raven hair fans out around her as I brace myself above her. I'm elated. She loves me and I love her. There is nothing in this world that can take her from me now. She's mine and I'm hers.

I nuzzle my nose into her neck, inhaling her intoxicating scent. Lavender with a hint of vanilla. Somehow, she smells like happiness. Like everything right in the world.

I feel her smile against my cheek. I bet it looks amazing. I lean back and sure enough, it is. She is by far the most beautiful woman I have ever seen.

Wow, how did I get so lucky?

"What is it?" Her voice is soft, filled with concern.

I shake my head, a smile widening my lips. "Just thinking about how lucky I am to have you as my girlfriend."

"Oh." Her head tilts to the side, causing her hair to fan farther under her head.

"I may also be thinking about how badly I want to fuck you until you can't walk tomorrow." My smile turns into a seductive smile. A brilliant blush climbs up her chest onto her cheeks.

"Well?" My brow furrowed. "What are you waiting for?"

My lips crash onto hers forcing them open to allow me in. Our tongues fight for dominance, neither of us giving up the fight.

Evie's nails scratch my scalp, pulling my hair taught. She swallows my grunt of pain.

I move down her body, nipping and kissing every piece of exposed skin.

Evie whimpers, squirming against my assault on her body. "Tanner." Her breathy whine pulls a smirk to my lips. I love knowing I do this to her. Me, nobody else. I'm the only one who gets her noises.

"Yes princess?"

"Stop teasing." My chuckle rumbles over her belly button where I have moved her clothing to the side to reveal her skin.

"Tisk, impatient." I see a frown stretch her face, completely unimpressed by me. "Fine." I pull her into a sitting position. I slip the maroon fabric of my jersey over her head, albeit reluctantly. My last name looks perfect across her back.

I toss my jersey off to the side before moving onto my

hoodie. I smile knowing she chose to wear my clothes instead of hers. I've been trying to convince her it's alright to wear my clothing, that I prefer she wears my clothing, so everyone knows she's mine. But only recently has she warmed up to the idea.

A black lacy bralette covers her tits, barely hiding her rosy nipples. A tortured groan rumbles out of my chest. "You had this on the entire time?"

She shyly nods, a devious look flashes across her eyes.

"Naughty girl." Her pretty blush darkens. "I love it." My tongue flicks out, pressing against her nipple over the fabric.

I play with her tits over the lace, pulling whimpers and mewled moans from my girl. She squirms under me, wiggling away from my mouth. My hands clap onto her waist, pulling her back down. "Where do you think you're going?"

I shimmy her leggings off to reveal a matching pair of panties, and oh fuck. "Incredible." I breathe out, eyes locked onto the goddess in human form.

She turns her head to the side, avoiding my simmering gaze. I hook my finger under her chin, pulling her eyes back to mine. "I want you to watch as I make you come on my tongue. Every time you look away, I stop." She whimpers and nods, desperate for my touch.

I ditch my suit jacket and unbutton the top few buttons on my white dress shirt. Evie's' eyes darken further with every button I unfasten. I leave the bottom half done up, choosing to slide her lacy panties off instead.

My eyes lock onto my own personal version of heaven. She glistens beneath my overhead light. I glance up, making sure she's watching me. A wicked grin tugs at my lips when our eyes meet.

Her hooded gaze follows mine as I lean down and place a kiss on her pussy. My lips come back glistening. I lick them clean, maintain eye contact. Evie's' breath catches in her throat, brown eyes darkening to a near black.

Continuing to keep eye contact, my tongue peeks out to taste her.

"Delicious."

I finally look away, down to where I want to be. I bury my face between her legs with no plans to come out for breath unless her eyes stray from me.

I occasionally check to see if she's following directions, and every time she is I reward her with a "good girl."

I plunge two fingers into her, fucking her with them until she's withering, and her moans grow louder. Her walls tighten around my finger making it near impossible to move them.

I suck her clit into my mouth, pulling hard enough to cause slight pain but not enough that pleasure can't override the pain.

The moment she comes, her head falls back as she arches her back, her tits being pushed into the air.

I continue to eat her out until she comes down from her high. Sliding up her body, I place a soft kiss to her plush lips. "Hi."

She giggles below me. "Hi."

"I love you."

Another lovely giggle. "I love you too, big guy." She leans up, closing the space between us, fusing her lips with mine. "Now how about you show me how much you love me by fucking me?" God, she shouldn't be allowed to say that in such a sweet voice.

My head drops to her shoulder, a hoarse laugh escaping me. This woman is going to be the death of me.

I must not move fast enough for her since she leans over to

the nightstand and produces a condom from the drawer. She casually hands it to me like she's not slowly killing me.

I take it from her hand. Her hands push on my chest until I raise up so I'm resting on my knees. She sits up, her hands making quick work of the buttons I didn't unfasten earlier.

My shirt slides off my shoulders and flutters to the floor. Her delicate hands work on my belt next, then onto my black dress pants. She works quickly, only leaving me in my boxer briefs.

She leans away from me, pointing at the last piece of fabric on my body. "Off." She demands. Like the lovesick man I am, I obediently listen. She laughs, a beautiful sound. "I know he meant it as a joke, but you really are a golden retriever. Cute, kind, obnoxious, and obedient."

I don't know whether I should be offended or not. Is that a good thing?

She potions with her pointer finger. "Come here." I guess it's a good thing if her smile when I follow her command with no hesitation is any indication.

I crawl over her as she lays back down. My frame covers hers perfectly.

"I'm here." I whisper.

"I can see that." She whispers back. "Now what are you going to do?" Mischief twinkles in her eyes. She knows what I'm going to do and that's exactly what she wants.

I place a long gentle kiss on her lips, then cheek, then temple before returning to her lips.

I lift the condom to my mouth and tear the package with my teeth. She takes the rubber out of the package where it also falls to the floor.

Evie's' eyes track the movement. "You're picking all of this up by the way." My head drops to her shoulder with a laugh. Only Evie would comment about the mess we make during intimacy.

"Yes ma'am." I place a lingering kiss to her pale skin as I line myself up with her pussy.

She gasps as I slowly push in. I don't want to rush this. She's not going to magically be able to take all of me with no pain after one time. I want to make this as pleasurable for her as possible. That means taking my time and letting her make all of the decisions.

I stall inside of her, giving her time to adjust. It takes some time but I do recognize that it's less than last time. She rocks against me, grinding her clit against my pelvis as good as she can. Which isn't very good.

I flip us over so she's on top. She shivers above me, slowly rising and falling. It's slow but I take the time to watch her expression. Every pinch of pain and moan of pleasure is absorbed into my mind. Learning what she does and doesn't like.

This time when she grinds down, her clit rubs against my pelvis, creating friction for her. My ball tingle the longer she uses me for her pleasure, but I hold off, wanting to ride this high for as long as possible.

Her moans rise in volume and tone, becoming higher pitched and breathier. Suddenly, she starts jerking on my dick. I grasp her hips, lifting and bringing her back down, forcing myself to maintain the tempo she chose.

Her walls contract around me as she comes with my name on her tongue. I follow her over the edge, spilling into the condom.

We ride out our high together, rocking into each other until we come back down to Earth.

Evie folds over me, snuggling into my neck as her breathing returns to normal. "My God." Her breath tickles. "Every time is better than the one before."

I don't bother to stop the smug smile, but it does earn me a light slap to my chest.

I pull out of her and set her down in the empty spot beside me. She watches as I stand and wander into the bathroom. I dispose of the condom, grab and wet a washcloth and return to her. She smiles as I clean her up and tuck her under the covers.

I discard the washcloth in the basket, putting all of my clothes and hers in as well. At some point she takes her bralette off and hands it to me to put with everything else. It kills me to clean my room knowing she's laying on my bed naked. But she told me to clean, so I clean.

It takes all of five minutes but that's five minutes too long. Five minutes I could have been cuddling with my girlfriend, but those five minutes means she can focus on us and not on the mess I made.

I climb back into bed, pulling her to lay on top of me.

I put on a movie, a romcom Evie had mentioned she wanted to watch a few days ago. We watch in silence, curled into each other as we watch the main characters fall hopelessly in love with each other, flaws and all.

It's close to midnight by the time the movie ends but I'm not ready to go to bed. I glance over at Evie and find her eyes already on me.

She has this sneaky smile on her lips, like she's planning something. "I'm going to take a shower." She mumbles, her eyes shifting down my body. "Wanna join." Her sweet laugh fills my room when I throw off the blankets and scoop her into my arms, carrying her into the bathroom.

I don't set her down until the water is hot. Before I can follow her under the spray she stops me with a hand to my chest. "What are you doing?"

"Joining you?" My brows scrunch. She asked me to.

"Aren't you forgetting something?" I rack my brain but come up empty.

"No?" She laughs again, that twinkle back in her eyes.

"Baby, go get a condom." Oh. Oh!

"Yeah, I'll uh, I'll go do that." I hook my thumb over my shoulder like she needs a visual representation.

I stumble over my own two feet on my way back to my bedside. She has her back to me when I return. Her long black hair soaked and hanging down her slim back. My eyes eat her up while she doesn't realize I'm here.

I follow the arch in her back down to her perky ass and to her short legs.

"Are you done staring, cause I'd really like you to join me." Her tone is teasing but I know she likes my attention as much as I like giving it to her.

We don't go to bed that night. We go until the sun comes up and into the early morning.

By the time we get some sleep, it's late morning.

23

Tanner

I've spent the last week talking with the managers of the Cheetahs, trying to figure out the logistics of everything. They got back to me this morning about salary and to say I gawked at it would be an understatement.

Sean had to pat my back until I could breathe again. I anticipated a big chunk of change but three million is more than I expected from my first year in the NHL.

I need to check the housing market soon so I can have a place to live in three weeks. I just want to have Evie's opinion on it as well. Since I'm hoping she'll be spending as much time as possible there.

I have a meeting with the dean at the end of the week to discuss options for next year. I won't be able to be in classes but I'm hoping to be able to finish my last year online.

I've done the math, and I don't need to be in any more classes this semester to pass my classes, save for the finals, so I plan on spending my time packing, apartment hunting, and worshiping Evie's body.

Speaking of Evie, the angel herself just walked through the door. She swings her bookbag off her shoulder, setting it on the kitchen island. She looks exhausted. The last few weeks have been stressful for her.

With Jasper's threats and the talk Jake wants to have with her, she hasn't been getting a lot of sleep. Jake leaves in two days and has upped his efforts to talk to my girl. She's been receiving multiple calls from the sheriff's office per day trying to get her to come down and talk to him. At first she was going to, now she refuses to.

She doesn't like how pushy he's gotten. Whatever questions she had for him no longer holds her attention so neither does he.

As for Jasper, no one has seen him in almost two weeks. The calls and texts have stopped so Sasha has moved back into the dorm, but Alyssa has decided to stay with Dillan and Oli.

Evie told me the other day that she didn't actually fear that Jasper would try something, she just took the opportunity to move back in with me because she likes sleeping next to me.

"Are you okay?" My eyes glance up to hers. She's watching me intently, trying to get a read on me.

"Yeah, why wouldn't I be?" She sighs, leaning heavily on the counter.

"Because you just got recruited to play hockey professionally. That's a lot of fame that came all at once. And you have this faraway look in your eyes that tells me you're lost in your head. So let me in and let's get lost together. What's going on?"

"I was just thinking about how we need to find an apartment. Which means we need to go up this weekend to look. Does that work for you?" She rounds the islands, wrapping her arms around my chest. She guides my head down to meet hers, placing a gentle kiss to my lips.

"That sounds wonderful." I lift her arms up to wrap them around my neck, my own arms wrapping around her waist. Sean clears his throat next to us, alerting us to his presence. Evie looks over to where he stands, a sweet smile tilting her lips. "Hi, didn't see you there."

"Great, so I'm chopped liver."

Evie gasps, "what? No! I was just distracted by this hunk of a man." Sean laughs, shaking his head.

"I'm going upstairs." He promptly retreats to his room leaving Evie and I laughing in the kitchen.

"I feel bad. He didn't have to leave." Evie giggles some more giving way to her real emotion, amusement.

"Nah, he'll be fine. I'm sure he's used to it by this point. If he's not, then he'll only have to endure it for another three weeks." Evie's eyes shift back to me, an unreadable expression in them. "What's wrong?"

She shakes her head, a curtain of raven hair flowing around her shoulders from the action. "Nothing big. It's just the closer the timeline gets the more it becomes real."

A pang of hurt hits me right in the chest. I knew this would be hard, but I didn't realize how it would make her feel. I mean, I've thought about it, but we've never actually talked about it.

"I'm right here. I'll always be right here. Even when I'm gone, I'll always be there for you. We'll make it work. It's only a four-hour drive, which is insanely lucky. Most new recruits don't get to stay near their loved ones." She sighs as she snuggles into my neck, her hot breath fanning the skin there.

"I know. Jensen told me how lucky we got with your placement, but that doesn't make the idea of long distance any less daunting." I lean away from her to study her features.

"When did you and Jensen talk about this. You've only met once."

She makes an O with her mouth. "We exchanged numbers during your game." Silence descends as my brain works to understand what I'm hearing. It seems I was worried for nothing, they not only get along great, but they are already confiding in each other.

"That's great, I'm glad you two like each other." She leans up on the balls of her feet and places a soft kiss to my lips. She pulls away when I try to lean in. A pout forms on my lips when I try to kiss her and she pulls away again. "Let me kiss you goddammit."

Her laugh reverberates through the kitchen, the melodic sound calming my nerves. "Sorry baby. I'm just tired and hungry and I don't really feel like going farther than a sweet kiss."

My pout melts off my face as I press a kiss to her forehead. "That's okay. I get it. What do you want for lunch? I don't know what we have here but I'm sure I can scrounge something together."

"Thank you. Is there any lunch meat? A sandwich sounds

incredible right now." I turn away from her and riffle through the fridge. I pull out one package of cheese and some pepperoni.

"Uh, I can order a sandwich." I bashfully glance over my shoulder.

"No, I don't want to spend more money, we've been eating out a lot." She's right but I like spending money on her. I work for an old friend's dad at his small construction company over the summers so I can have spending money throughout the year and for rent. My scholarship covers school as long as I keep my grades up and continue to play for their team.

Now that I've been signed money won't be a problem, but I know she won't see it like that. I see my money as hers, but she sees my money as mine and hers as hers and as of right now I know that won't change.

She squeezes past me to look through what food we have. She starts pulling out ingredients for a salad. "Do you want one?"

I lean back against the island, "nah, I'm okay."

I watch as she makes her salad and pour an absurd amount of dressing onto it, this way next time she wants one I can make it for her. She grabs a fork and starts to walk upstairs. I follow behind, making sure to grab her bookbag and carry it up for her.

Just because I'm not entertaining my classes for the rest of the semester doesn't mean she's not.

She plops down on the bed as she eats her meal. I set her bag down at my desk. Her eyes follow my every move as I make my way around the room, tidying up. I made a bit of a mess this morning while I was getting ready. I never realized how messy I was until Evie came into my life and showed me.

My laundry basket is full of both mine and her clothes and it needs to be cleaned desperately, so I excuse myself from the room to go start a load of laundry. I remember being a child and hearing my parents argue over what they called the division of labor, and I never understood it. If it needs to be done and you see it, if you have time you should do it.

Chores shouldn't be only one partner's problem. As a kid I didn't understand why my dad didn't want to help my mom around the house. I always thought if you loved the person you're with you should want to help them as much as possible. You should want to make their life easier.

It wasn't until a few years ago that I realized my dad doesn't actually love my mom, he settled for her when he got her pregnant. It was heartbreaking to learn my mom has endured a loveless marriage so I could live a normal life. She put up with his shit my entire childhood so I would have a father.

Now that I'm an adult I figured divorce would be in their future, but my mom hasn't mentioned anything. I'm worried she doesn't realize what a wonderful person she is because my dad tells her otherwise. She deserves the world, but she won't go chase the world she deserves.

I know it's not my place to tell her to leave my father, but I really wish she would.

I put all of the blacks and navy-colored clothes into the washer with the detergent and fabric softener and press start.

I hear Evie descend the stairs and meet her in the kitchen as she rinses her dishes. I crowd into her from behind, kissing the length of her neck. "Tanner." She giggles.

"Hmmm, yes Princess."

"That tickles." She continues to giggle as I nudge my nose into the crook of her neck.

"Oh, does it?" I kiss her some more causing her to giggle

again.

"Yes." She pants breathlessly.

She shivers when I retreat, hugging herself like she's cold. I take the dishes from her hands and place them into the empty dishwasher. "Come on, I'll go draw you a bath so you can relax. It's been a long day."

"Okay."

While Evie's in the hot bath I pull up different apartments in Columbus Ohio. I'm not sure if I want to rent or buy so I'll have to get Evie's opinion. It'll probably be better to rent until I know where I'm going to end up long term.

I browse the housing market while I wait for her to come out of the bathroom. I've learned she's very particular about layouts and finishes. I don't know why; they don't make a difference to me, but she'll hopefully be living with me part time when she can. Maybe I'll be able to do the same in my off season, come live with her while she's in school. I'll run that by her too, see how she feels about it.

An apartment catches my eye. It's a two bed two bath apartment in downtown Columbus. It has a modern galley kitchen that overlooks the living room. It has stainless steel appliances with a light granite countertop and white cabinets. The living room is fairly small but will be plenty for two people. There's a balcony with brick flooring, again it's not large but it would be more than enough.

The rooms are small, there's no getting around that but the bathrooms are gorgeous. The spare bathroom has a single vanity that matches the kitchen. Next to it is the toilet and then there's a standing shower. The shower has glass doors with black fixtures.

The main bath is a little different. A single vanity sits across from the standing shower. A large tub sits next to the shower, big enough to fit me but not enough to fit us both. The toilet is next to the vanity and on the back wall is a door to the laundry room. The finishings match the spare bathroom so the whole apartment seems pulled together.

In the master bedroom you walk into the room and are immediately greeted with a blank wall that serves as a little hallway into the main room. Looking to the left, there's a large window on the far wall. On the wall that would be opposite the bed is a walk-in closet. The wall opposite the window has the doorway to the bathroom.

The spare bathroom is shown as an office with a sliding barn door. We could definitely make it into a bedroom, but Evie works from home right now, so I like the idea of her having an office to work from. It doesn't have a walk-in closet, but it does have a decent sized one which would be perfect for extra clothes, linins and shoes.

It's two thousand a month for rent with the possibility of being closer to twenty-five hundred a month.

I hear the tub drain and Evie walking around. It takes a few minutes for her to come out in her pajamas despite it still being midday, but this is her subtle way of saying she isn't leaving the house again today.

"Come here." I pat the bed next to me as she eagerly crawls under the covers next to me. "What do you think of this place?" I pass her my laptop and let her scroll through the photos.

"It's pretty." I wait for her to say anything else as she scrolls through the photos again. "I like it. Do you want to tour it this weekend?"

"If you want to, yes."

"Ok," she mumbles quietly. "I'll schedule a time for someone to take us on a tour of the building and apartment." She clicks on a few things. "Done. Have you found any other ones?"

"Yeah." I take the laptop back and show her the handful of other apartments I found that I liked. Out of the seven apartments we agree to tour four of them. Evie sets up time for all of them while we figure out where we're going to stay while we're up there.

She finds a nice hotel that isn't too expensive, and I call to place a reservation for this weekend. At some point Evie starts yawning and by the time I hang up she's asleep. It's three in the afternoon but I'm not tired so I carefully slide out of bed and go downstairs where Collins and Sean are talking in the living room.

"Hey guys."

"Hey," Sean looks up as I walk in. "We're about to play some Call of Duty Zombies, you want to play?"

"Sure, Evie's asleep so let's try to keep it down. She's had a long week between school, work, and the Jake stuff." I take the empty spot in between my buddies as they pass me a controller.

"How's she holding up?" Collins turns on the console.

"Pretty good given everything that's going on. We're driving up to Columbus this weekend to look at apartments and she seems okay with it. She's not excited by any means but I can't really blame her." Collins pulls up the game and gets Zombies set up.

"Does anyone know if Sasha is staying with us or with Dillan?" I look at Sean while he speaks, but his attention is straight ahead.

"Uh, I think I heard her talking about going back to the dorms." Collins perks up, confused.

"Oh, I hope she doesn't think she's a burden here." Sean and Collins continue their conversation as the game starts.

"I don't think she does but she's independent and tells me on a daily basis how she misses her own space." Somehow, I die to the first wave and Collins snickers. "Dude, this is the easiest the game gets."

"Shut up," I mumble as Sean revives me.

We play until it's time for dinner and Evie makes her way down to where we are. She has her laptop with her which she plugs in and takes the seat next to Sean. She types away while we die and fail at killing fictional zombies. I can tell when she's watching us because she'll occasionally laugh when one or all of us die. At some point Collins orders Chinese despite Evie telling him we have food here at that we spend a lot on fast food.

"Yeah, I know but I'm going grocery shopping tomorrow and I don't feel like scrounging a meal together." She huffs but leaves it be. We all know there's enough food here to feed all of us, but I agree with Collins, I don't want to cook, and Sean can't cook. That leaves Collins and Evie and since Collins doesn't want to cook, we're eating out because none of us would expect Evie to cook for the three of us, that's a lot of food.

Thankfully she drops it and seems happy enough when the food arrives. The three of us continue to play while she watches. It's really nice, sitting here, enjoying each other company without any issues. Not that we have a lot of issues but it's still nice when everyone gets along.

"How's your book coming along." Evie looks surprised when Sean asks her and it isn't until she looks to me that I realize it's because she never told him, I did. I offer her a sheepish smile, but she doesn't look mad.

"Tanner told you?"

"Told me? Nah. Bragged to me? One hundred percent." Her smile grows wide as her eyes shift to mine. Collins laughs next to me, probably because of how often I talk about my girl. "Dude, did you seriously just die again?" Oh shit. Yes, yes, I did.

"Babe, I thought you were good at this game?" Silence.

"So did I." Laughter erupts in the room as Collins revives me again.

The night wears on and I continue dying. Evie has gone back to writing and my buddies have stopped reviving me during rounds as a punishment for dying so soon. What a bunch of jerks.

It isn't until well past midnight that we call it a night. Evie had a class at one and Sean and Collins have one at ten. As I cuddle Evie in our bed my mind wanders to what the next few years are going to be like. What if she gets tired of the long distance? What if I get traded to a team across the country? What if we grow apart and break up? No, I can't let that happen. We're going to be together until we die, and when we both end up in heaven, I'll marry her again.

We'll be together until the end of time.

24

Evie

The drive to the city was long but doable, I guess. I'm struggling with the idea that one of us will have to make this trip just to see each other but we'll figure it out, we have to. I refuse to let this be a failed relationship.

We checked into the hotel an hour ago with plans to go out to eat. We have two tours scheduled for tomorrow and the other two are on Sunday with plenty of time to explore the city in between them.

I zip up my combat boots almost ready to leave. Tanner's

singing in the bathroom while he does whatever he's doing in there. I think he's shaving but I haven't checked since he kicked me out of the bathroom so he could use it.

Thankfully it's summer and the weather has warmed up significantly. I grab my purse and take a seat on the bed as I wait.

"Where are we going so, I can pull it up on the map."

"Rosemerry's." I type it into google maps and look at all of the ways we could take. I don't know how the traffic is here, so I click on the fastest and pray that we won't get caught in traffic.

He emerges from the bathroom in a button down and slacks. He's freshly shaven and smells incredible.

"What cologne are you wearing?" I stand and approach him, meeting him halfway. I mess with the collar on his shirt, needing to touch him in some way.

"It's new, do you like it?"

"I love it." His cheeky grin tells me he likes my answer. I kiss the smugness away or try to at least because when I pull back it's still there.

"God, I love you." My belly flutters with butterflies. I love it when he does this. He tells me how he feels and looks at me like I'm the most beautiful person he's ever seen. He knows how to make me feel special because somehow, I know I'm the only girl who has ever gotten this look from him.

"I love you too." But those words don't encompass even half of what I feel for him.

"And I love those heels. Jesus babe, those are fucking hot." A giggle slips past as I look down at my shoes.

"I'll keep that in mind for the future."

"Oh, please do."

"Come on, if we don't leave now, we won't leave at all." That cheeky smile makes a comeback.

"That doesn't sound too bad." I roll my eyes as I step out of his arms, putting necessary distance between us so I can think with my head and not other body parts.

"Maybe, but I'm hungry." I put my phone in my purse and walk to the door. Tanner watches me, more specifically he watches my ass. "Tanner?"

"Hmm?"

"Dinner?"

"Yeah, dinner." His gaze never leaves my ass.

"Baby? Dinner comes before dessert. Let's go get dinner so we can have dessert later." Without breaking eye contact, he walks over to me.

I link our hands together and tug him out of the room. At some point he moves his attention North and becomes immersed in the conversation I've been trying to have with him.

"A girl on the platform I post my stories on reached out and asked if I would be willing to edit some of her books part time. It pays well so I'm thinking I might take her up on the offer. She's a well-known author on the platform and has published seven books. She posts them on the platform and leaves them up for three months then she publishes them."

"Is that something you might want to do for a career?"

"I don't know. I told her I've only edited my own work and she said that was fine. Her previous editor has decided to be a stay-at-home mother. She has a newborn and doesn't think she'll have the time to do everything that needs to be done. I told her I'd get back to her in a few days." The elevator opens to the main lobby, and we exit, heading toward the parking lot.

"That sounds exciting." He unlocks his truck, helping me

inside.

I wait until he's situated in the driver's seat to continue. "It is. If this pans out, I could finish college with the same degree I'm working toward now and can work from home. Which means I can work from anywhere in the world." I watch as the information sinks in.

"Wait, does that mean what I think it means?"

"I would be able to move to whatever city you play in and could in theory go to some of your away games." He pulls out on the main road as I plug my phone into the radio so Siri can tell him where to go.

"I don't want to be biased but I love that idea." I laugh.

"I wonder why." He chuckles, clicking the blinker to signal he needs to merge into the right lane.

"Are there any apartments you're looking forward to looking at while we're here?" I think for a moment, they're all basically the same. Clean, modern, and sleek.

"Not any in particular. But I am excited to see if any of them feel like a space we can grow together in." We turn onto a new road and Siri tells us we have three miles and then our destination will be on our right.

"I know this isn't easy. We just got together and now we're about to put a huge amount of stress onto our relationship. Thank you for keeping an open mind and being willing to try this."

"Tanner, you don't need to thank me for wanting to make this work. I want this as much as you do. I won't go down without a fight, so you better be prepared to be stuck with me for as long as you will have me. I know this is going to be tough, but I also know it'll be worth it. I know you're worth it." His hand slides off the gear shift and makes a new home on my upper thigh. He squeezes me in a silent thank you. I cover his hand with mine, squeezing back.

He turns into the packed parking lot, and we fall silent so he can focus on finding us a spot. We get lucky when a car pulls out of a space a few feet ahead of us and we're able to snag the now empty spot.

Tanner kills the engine and hops out before rounding the truck to my door. He helps me down from the seat, making sure I don't fall.

"Thank you."

"Of course, my Goddess." I freeze, my head turning to him so fast my neck pings with fantom pain.

"You think I'm a Goddess." A sly smile stretches his lips as his hand grasps my chin.

"No Princess, you're my personal heaven." I didn't know my heart could feel so full but every time I think I can't fall for him anymore he says stuff like that.

A giddy smile overtakes my face and refuses to leave the entire diner. It stays in place all the way back to the hotel. It's still in place as Tanner shows me exactly what those words mean when he worships my body and tells me he loves me every chance he gets.

I fall asleep happier than I've been in a long time.

The sun streaming through the open blinds wakes me up. A heavy arm draped over my waist makes it difficult to move as I try to wiggle out of his grasps so I can go to the bathroom.

I grab my phone on my way out of the main room and check the notifications. There's nothing important besides a text reminder about the earlier of the two tours in three hours.

I turn the shower on to heat up as I brush my teeth and my hair before putting it up in a clip so it won't get wet. I peak my head out the door to see Tanner still passed out. I select a playlist and press play, soft music filling the small space as I step under the spray of water.

My shower is short but much needed. With my fluffy towel wrapped tightly around me I walk into the bedroom and call room service to order breakfast.

While I wait for the food to arrive, I get ready for the day. I French braid my hair, one braid down my back. I put some mascara on and curl my lashes. Some lip gloss and eyebrow jell later, and I'm done.

There's a knock on the door so I throw a robe on over my towel and answer it. The girl pushes the cart inside and tells me to leave it outside the door when we finish, someone will come by to pick it up later.

I push the cart further into the room where Tanner still sleeps.

I leave it in the center of the room and climb on top of my handsome boyfriend. I straddle his hips and lean down so I'm lying on top of him.

"Baby. Breakfast is here."

An unintelligible groan rumbles from his chest but he doesn't move.

"Baby, food." Another groan. "Come on baby. You need to get up." He stirs but doesn't open his eyes. I move his hands to my waist. It takes a moment but once he realizes what he's feeling his eyes pop open.

"Hmmm, I like this sight." I smile as I grip his face and kiss him.

"Foods here, come eat it while it's warm."

"I'd rather eat you." I sigh as I climb off of him.

"I know but if I let you start, we wouldn't get to the first apartment in time. So come eat." He slides off the bed and heads into the bathroom. While he can't see me, I slip my towel off, so I'm left in my robe and separate the food.

"Smells amazing." He exits the bathroom, scratching his bare chest.

"It does. I got you a meat omelet with white toast, hashbrowns, and a side of bacon." I hand him the plate with the omelet on it first and a set of silverware.

"Thank you." A chaste kiss later we're settled down and eating in silence. I got myself a crepe with hashbrowns and an egg sunny side up. I finish before him and continue to get ready.

Black ripped skinny jeans, brown cropped tank top, beige high-top sneakers and a brown patchwork cropped jean jacket. Chucky black sunglasses and my tiny black backpack later I'm ready. Tanner heads back into the bathroom for a quick shower while I push the cart outside.

Twenty minutes later we're climbing into the truck to go to the first apartment. Tanner's wearing a navy green T-shirt with black ripped jeans and black tennis shoes.

We pick up coffee on the way to the tour and thankfully make it on time.

The building manager greets us when we walk in and shows us the building. By the time we make it to the apartment I've already decided I don't like this place. The manager keeps sending me lewd glances that Tanner definitely sees. With every look his temper becomes shorter and shorter.

The manager shows us the bedroom which feels like a shoebox it's so small.

When Tanner has his back turned Aaron, the manager, places a hand on my lower back, dangerously close to my butt. His onion breath fans across my ear as he leans into whisper. "Those jeans look great on you, but I bet they'd look better on my office floor."

I step away from him as fast as I can. Without another word I grab Tanner and drag him out of the tiny apartment. He looks confused but I'll tell him later.

Aaron follows closely behind, and I feel his gaze hot on my ass. "So, what do we think of the property?" I send a quick look to Tanner which he thankfully understands.

"We'll keep it in mind, but this is the first of many we're looking at." He tucks me under his arm away from Aaron's unwavering gaze. "We'll let you get back to work, have a nice day."

Tanner quickly escorts me out, making sure his body is always blocking mine.

I don't say anything until we're in the truck driving away. "That apartment is a hard no."

"I agree but what happened back there?"

"When you were looking in the bathroom, he touched my lower back and told me my jeans would look better on his office floor." Tanner's jaw ticks but he fumes in silence. "So, where do you want to go? Anything you want to see?"

"Just the arena I'll be playing in. I should have made a list of places, but I forgot."

"Well, let's go there then." We drive in silence for ten minutes before I can't take it anymore. "Are you okay."

"I'm pissed. The fucking nerve of him to put his hands on you. Especially when I was feet away. The fucking disrespect. I want to go back and clobber the fucker but that won't change what happened. I'm trying my best to remember that."

"I know this isn't what you want to hear, but I'm used to it and eventually you will be too." Tanner pulls off to the side of the road into a parallel parking space and throws the truck in park. He turns to me fuming.

"I will never get used to that and neither should you. That shit isn't okay, and it will never not piss me off when someone thinks they're allowed to touch you wherever they want without your consent. Trust me, I may not physically hurt him, but he will not get away with that unscathed." His jaw ticks again as his sage eyes burn with uncontrolled anger.

"Baby? What are you going to do?"

"Well, I'll start by getting him fired and we'll go from there. If he's married, I'll make sure his wife knows but if he's not then the internet will know what a piece of shit human he is."

As I stare into his eyes I have a realization, I'm completely safe with him. If I didn't know this before his anger towards a random man for making me uncomfortable is a great indication. Tanner will do everything in his power to keep me safe, even at the expense of his career.

Before I can blink them away, tears fall. He swipes them away as the fall, occasionally kissing them away.

I don't know how long we sit here in silence with me crying and him watching me with love in his eyes. Finally, the tears stop.

"Tanner?"

ON THE SIDELINES

"Yes Princess?"

"I love you."

"I love you too."

25

Tanner

The day becomes marginally better as it wears on. My mood hasn't improved but can you blame me? The audacity of that man!

We toured the second apartment; it was the first one I showed Evie. It was just as nice in person and the building manager was much nicer. Evie had relaxed by the time we went into the building and even struck up a conversation with him.

He told her about his wife and kids while we looked around the small apartment. It's definitely a contender.

"Tanner?" I look to my right where Evie's waiting by my truck door.

"Sorry." I open it and help her up. She watches me curiously as I round the hood and take my seat behind the wheel.

"Are you sure you're okay? You seem a little distracted." Well, I haven't tried to hide it. I can't get that interaction out of my mind. What he did doesn't piss me off as much as my clueless ass two feet away does.

My girl was being hit on and was forced to sit still while she was incredibly uncomfortable, and I didn't even realize. I saw some of his looks, but I figured they'd go no further. Obviously, I was mistaken.

"Not really." She watches me as I pull out into traffic.

"I get that it upsets you, but you can't let one interaction ruin your entire day." I grumble a little but thankfully she doesn't chastise me for it. "When we get back to the hotel why don't we go down to the restaurant and have a nice meal?"

"Okay." When I don't offer anymore Evie sighs and turns the radio on. She clicks a few things on her phone and the cab is filled with Indie Rock. It takes us twenty minutes to get back to the hotel and she's quiet the entire time. I upset her; I know I did. She doesn't like it when I'm quietly seething. She's told me it's better to express my emotions and I know it is, but I don't think she wants to know the things I want to do to that man. The blinding rage I felt when I found out he disrespected her. I wanted to go back inside and break his hand so he couldn't put it on her again without her consent.

Evie doesn't like violence, so I'm trying to save her from my less than kind thoughts. What I failed to realize is that on the ride back she's been stewing in her own thoughts and now she's not just upset, she's pissed.

She doesn't wait for me to open her door; she's jumping out the moment the trucks in park. She ignores me the entire ride up to the room. She tries to slam the door in my face, but I catch it before it closes.

"Baby? I'm sorry, okay. I know you don't like it when I bottle things up and don't tell you what I'm feeling." She whips around, brown eyes ablaze.

"If you know that then why do you continue to do it!" She storms up to me, stopping mere inches from my face. "This, us," she motions to the space between us, "won't work if you don't talk to me."

Shame settles in my stomach. "I know." My voice is barely above a whisper.

Her eyes soften and she places a calming hand on my check. "I'm not mad that you feel things, Tanner. I'm mad that you don't trust me enough to tell what those things are."

My gaze lifts to her as I struggle for words. "I trust you; I do."

"Really? Because when you do this, hide away. It sure doesn't feel like trust, it feels like running, like hiding."

I shake my head as much as her hand on my check allows. "That's not it. I promise that's not the reason. The thoughts I'm having, I know you won't like, you won't approve of."

"Just because I might not like them doesn't mean I don't want to hear them. I want every part of you, even the not so pretty parts. You're mine and I'm yours. All of our nice and mean, pretty and ugly, clam and violent parts. Don't hide those thoughts from me when they help me understand where your head is at. Those thoughts help me know you better. When I know what makes you tick, I know you as you. We become one person, not separate beings."

I take a deep breath, needing a small pause to build confidence. "When you told me he touched you it took everything in me not to march back into that building and break his hand. I wanted to make him hurt, make him bleed, for thinking even for a second that he had any right to touch you, to touch what's mine. I wanted to make it hurt so he would learn. I wanted, no needed to leave a physical reminder before I ruined his career, his marriage."

She stays silent as I talk, soaking in every word as it comes out of my mouth.

"You wanted to protect me." Now she's the quiet one.

"I wanted to avenge you." In the next breath her lips are on mine, her body pressed tightly against me. I could feel every one of her soft curves. I pull away to search her face. "You're not mad?"

She tilts her head in the cutest way possible. "Why would I be?"

"Because I wanted to cause harm to someone, and you don't believe in violence being the best option."

"You're right, I don't believe it should even be an option." Her kind eyes stare up at me.

"But you're not upset?"

"No, I'm not. You want to know why?" I nod my head quickly, extremely confused. "Because the violence you felt wasn't because that's who you are. You felt it because you wanted to help me, to protect me. You felt it because the idea that someone would hurt me, touch me, made you so upset that you needed and outlet. The important thing is that you didn't act on those thoughts." I push my head into her palm, grateful she knows this without my dumb ass having to attempt to explain it to her.

"Thank you."

"Of course, baby. Now let's go have dinner, I'm starving." I follow behind her because I'm hungry too. I'm always hungry. She goes to the bathroom before we go back downstairs.

The restaurant isn't packed but there's quite a bit of people here. We're put on a waitlist for twenty minutes and I leave my number for them to call when our table is ready. We don't have anything better to do so go out to the deck that overlooks the public pool.

There're a few families swimming and hanging out but it's still a little cold to be swimming in my opinion.

"It's such a nice day out." Evie sighs next to me, leaning on the wooden rail.

"It is. The sun is a nice change after the cloudy weather we've been having."

"Yeah, but it would have been great if it had rained. I love the rain. The mist, the fresh air, perfect for cuddles on the couch with a window open." I smile as I watch her stare dreamily into the blue sky.

Rainy day cuddles, gonna have to remember that one.

My phone buzzes in my back pocket. When I fish it out and answer, the hostess at the restaurant informs me our table is ready. It's only been about ten minutes but at least they're running early and not late.

With her hand in mine, Evie and I head to our table. She glances over her shoulder and smiles when she sees me already looking at her. As if I could look away.

The things I want to do to her race through my head. Thoughts that should be kept to the bedroom flood my subconscious as I pull her chair out for her. While she's getting situated, I swipe her hair over her shoulder, so it doesn't get caught behind her.

As I take my seat the server walks up and takes our drink orders, me a Dr Pepper, Evie a strawberry lemonade.

"Do you have a favorite?" I snap out of my thoughts to see Evie staring at me expectantly.

"Huh?"

She sighs, unimpressed by my behavior today, though I can't blame her. "Which apartment was your favorite?"

"Well, that's easy to answer, the second."

"If the building manager for the first was a better person, would you have chosen that one?" It was a nice apartment, but I don't think I could see myself living there on my own, let alone with Evie.

"Nah, it was pretty small, not that the other one was big, but I felt like I couldn't turn around in there without hitting something, either the wall, you, or that dickhead."

"It did make me feel a little claustrophobic." The server returns with our drinks and takes our order and scurries off again. "I'm excited to see the apartment tomorrow morning, it looked pretty spacious online but so did the first one, we'll see." She shrugs as she takes a sip of her lemonade.

We make idle chatter while we wait for the food to come out. As much as we try, emotions are still running high, and our fight earlier still rests heavy on our table. We've talked about it but that doesn't mean those emotions just go away.

The silence is deafening as we eat, and I can't take it. "For the future, what would you say the best way to handle that situation would have been?" I know we've already talked about it, but the silence is killing me.

"I don't know Tanner." She sighs, setting her fork down. "There really isn't any good way to handle it. During the interaction, you dealt with it how I would have asked you too, but bottling up your emotion's afterwords, in doing so pushing me away. That's what I have an issue with. I understand you're going into a career that's extremely violent, and people will try to piss you off. It's up to you to regulate those emotions, but I'll always just be one call away so you can talk to me about it. Today it felt like all you cared about was how the interaction affected you, I felt like I wasn't even in the equation for you. That can't keep happening. We're a team and we both need to remember that. I'm not dealing with these creepy men alone and you're not the only one to hate their wandering hands."

Evie falls quiet again while I process what she just told me. She's right, of course. I had acted like my reaction was the only one to matter but she also took matters in her own hands when she pulled us out of there. There wasn't a better option at the time but it's how we handled it after that caused the problems.

"You're right, it didn't even cross my mind that you would have your own reaction to deal with. I'm sorry. From now on we'll do our best to keep the communication open and I'll try not to simmer in my anger without talking to you about it."

"Thank you, that's all I could ask for. And I'll do better to express what I'm feeling. If I had just told you while we were there that he was making me uncomfortable, we could have left before something happened, instead I forgot that you were on my side and hid what I was thinking and feeling."

We both have a long way to go before we perfect this, if we ever do. But acknowledging the issue is the first step. As long as we continue to take that first step, the second and third will follow. They may not be easy, but they are necessary.

26

Tanner

It took a week but finally I was able to sign the paperwork saying I'm the new tenant. Evie and I settled on the second apartment we looked at and I can start to move in at the end of the week. Perfect timing really.

The school year is about to end, and the summer training starts a week from Monday.

I have three finals left until my junior year of college is finished and Evie has two until her freshman year is done.

Actually, according to the time, in about fifteen minutes

she'll just have one left, creative writing.

I want to wait for her to come home but if I do that, I'll be late for my final and if I'm late, I can't take it.

I'm slipping my shoes on, keys in hand when my phone buzzes in my back pocket. Fishing it out I see Jensen's name flashing across my screen with an incoming call. My lips pull into a smile, I missed this. Random calls just to catch up. He's been doing it again. We started these after Mia passed as a way to help calm the pain.

We would talk about things during the day that made us happy, things that made us sad, things that surprised us, so on and so forth.

I click the green button to answer the call, putting it on speaker phone so I can tie my shoes.

"What's up old man?"

"Watch it boy, I may be getting older, but I can still beat you in wrestling any day." A chuckle slips past.

He could, he used to wrestle from junior high until his sophomore year of college when someone used an illegal move on him and gave him the injury that took him out of the sport.

"I'm sure but I can't imagine Evelyn would be happy with either of us if we did."

"Are you kidding? That girl would be front row cheering me on."

"You! Nah, she's my girl so she'd be cheering for me."

We go back and forth until I climb into my truck and my phone connects to my Bluetooth.

"I hate to cut this short but if this call is just to catch up then I'll have to call you back later. I'm about to leave to go take a final." My seatbelt clicks as I shoulder check to make sure no one is behind me before backing out of the driveway.

"Well, there was a reason to my call. Your mother stopped by today." He lets the sentence hang in the air. I'm not surprised, mom used to go to Jensen's all the time when she needed a break from my dad. They became close friends while Mia and I were dating.

"Okay?"

"She is talking about leaving your father." Also not surprising, long overdue in my opinion. "She hasn't fully decided yet but I wanted to give you a heads up."

Something isn't making since. "Why did you call and not her?" The line goes silent as I pull onto the main road.

"Your mother fears you father may have bugged her phone. They haven't been getting along recently and she's sent some texts to friends and a few phone calls have been exchanged while your father was out of the house. The other day he cornered her and questioned why she would tell her friends lies about him while he quoted her private conversations."

Well, that's fucking new. I know my father isn't a good man but going that far is extreme, even for him.

"There's one more thing."

I release a sigh, gearing up for whatever has him sounding so reserved. "Hit me."

"The police were called to their home over the weekend on a domestic disturbance. A neighbor called about yelling. When the police arrived, your mom didn't say it, but it was fairly obvious your father had gotten physical. The police report states fresh bruises but without a statement from your mother, they don't have a case."

I've always suspected that he got physical after I move to

college, but it was never confirmed.

Anger pulses through my veins as I white knuckle my steering wheel. "I hope she leaves that fucker."

"Now Son. I know your upset, but he is still your father."

A humorless laugh falls from my lips. "Is he? Last time I checked the only thing he's done that's remotely fatherly is donate his sperm to my mother." Harsh I know, but I won't take it back. He was never present during my childhood. He was never there for my ups and downs. And he sure as shit wasn't there for me when I lost my girlfriend. Some father he was.

"Tanner." His tone takes a sharp edge to it.

"I know, I know. But something I've learned recently, blood doesn't make a family, love and friendship do. So yeah, he may be my blood, but he is not my family, you are."

"Your right, I will always be here for you, your brother, and your mother. You gotta be close to your campus now so good luck on your final, I know you'll pass. We'll talk more later."

"See ya, old man." The line goes dead right as I pull into a parking spot. I cut the engine but stayed seated. I groan into my hands as I rub them down my face. I exit before I do something stupid and miss my test. I need to pass this test to graduate next year.

I send a text to Evie telling her I'll see her at home, and I know she did well on her exam. She replies right as I walk into the lecture hall.

Evie: Thanks baby. You'll do great. Can't wait to see you at home. Got a special surprise for you.

I smile before powering my phone completely off and

stuffing it in my back pocket. I choose my normal seat and wait for the rest of my class.

The test gets handed out and I make sure to read every question carefully and answer as correctly as I can. Any questions I don't know I skip with plans to come back later if I have time.

For the most part it's pretty easy, I can answer most questions quickly but by the time I finish the last question I have five I have to go back to. It's a simple history test but these have to do with specific times and I'm not great with those.

I go back to the first question and reread it:

What was Archduke Franz Ferdihands' lifespan?

A) Born April of 1860, Died July 1915

B) Born August 1865, Died January 1910

C) Born March 1862, Died October 1913

D) Born December 1863, Died June 1914

I study the answers. The previous question was why he was important. I think his death was a cause for World War one or something to do with the first world war so it's not B. I know when world war one was but I'm struggling to remember the exact date, stress probably.

1913 seems to soon so I eliminate that on so I'm left with A and D. World war one started in July, so I'm tempted to choose that one but if his death is what started the war then maybe he dies in June.

I go back and forth between the two until I land on D and move on. If it's wrong, oh well.

I flip a few pages until I find the second question:

What years did Edward VII reign?

A) 20 January 1936 – 11 December 1936

B) 26 June 1830 – 20 June 1837

C) 22 January 1901 – 6 May 1910

D) 25 October 1760 – 29 January 1820

Was he before or after Queen Victoria? There are two rules before and two after. I think he was after, either her son or grandson so B and D are out.

Queen Victoria ruled until the 1900's so if he was her son then C would make since. A is throwing me off. I know one of the Edwards' was abdicated but was it the VII? But if he was the grandson the timeline wouldn't make since to be A so I pick C and move on.

The third question is on the next page:

How old was William Shakespeare when he passed?

A) 50 years ago

B) 52 years ago

C) 49 years ago

D) 55 years ago

He died in the 1600's so what was their average lifespan? I look at the answers and realize that question is sort of irrelevant as the ages are withing 6 years.

I think 49 is too young and 55 might be too old. So, he was either 50 or 52 when he passed.

Well, if 49 is too young wouldn't 50 also be too young? It only a year older and I don't think he died on a multiple of ten, why? I have no idea; I just don't think he did. So B it is.

I find the fourth question and read through it:

The Anglo-Zanzibar War is the shortest war ever recorded. How long did it last for?

A) 1 day

B) 7 hours

C) 40 minutes

D) 3 days

This must have been discussed in the last few classes because I didn't learn this. I've never even heard of this war.

Based on the times I'm left to assume it was less than 3 days since it's a pretty big-time jump. Not great reasoning but whatever.

I think 40 minutes is far too short, so I eliminate that one now I have A or B. Both are short for a war and since I didn't learn this, I guess A and move on.

The last question is on the last page, also one I don't remember learning about:

What century did Genghis Kahn live in?

A) 12th century

B) 13th century

C) 14th century

D) 15th century

At my wits end I guess C and take my test to the front to turn in. As long as I get a C then I'll pass.

My brain is thoroughly fried as I exit the lecture hall and head to my truck. Evie should be home and that alone keeps me going. The idea that I can snuggle into her lap sounds incredible while she scratches my head.

The drive home goes by in a blur, I was spaced out for most of it which I know is unsafe, but I couldn't force myself to stay focused on anything. The door opens on my way up the pathway and Dillan walks out.

"What's up buddy? How'd your test go?"

"Okay, I think. I didn't know you were dropping by." I pull him into a one-armed hug.

"Neither did I until Collins asked if I wanted to hang after our final. I'm just leaving." He goes to step around me but stops, seemingly remembering something. "I think Alyssa's stopping by later. I think I heard her mention it earlier."

"Cool, thanks for the head up. See you later dude."

I walk into the house and see Collins wrapping up cords for the PlayStation controllers. I nod to him and take the stairs two at a time. Sean's probably still in class so the house is mostly empty. Not really with both Evie and Collins here but Collins probably will head out soon. I heard from a little birdie he has a date tonight.

My door is cracked when I reach it. I push it open to a spotless room which means the polaroid on my bed stands out. I close the door behind me and approach the photo. My jaw drops to the floor at what I see.

It's Evie wearing a red lingerie set. Red thigh highs clipped to a ruffled garter belt. A scrap of red fabric covering my heaven. A lacy see through red bralette doing nothing to hide her rosy nipples that appear to be pebbled. And a chocker with what looks to be a leash attached to it.

My dick perks up the longer I stare. I hear movement behind me before arms wrap around my midsection. The first thing I notice is red nails that match the exact color of the lace. Pointy and glossy, hot as fuck.

"Hi baby." Evie purrs in my ear.

"Holy fuck Evie." She giggles behind me but makes no move to come in front of me. "When you said surprise, this was not what I had in mind."

She circles me then, stopping when she in front of me, sitting leisurely at the edge of the bed. "Do you like it? Sasha and I went shopping yesterday and I found this little thing. Thought it might look good on your floor. What do you think?"

My mouth opens and closes, floundering like a fish. All ability of coherent thought has left my body. Staring at the seductress in front of me is all I can do. I can't move, can't think, can't breathe, and I sure as shit can't look away.

A slow smile spread across her face as she watches me fail at speaking. "I'll take it you like it."

Finally, words find their way into my mouth. "Like it? No, no baby. Love it? Fuck yeah."

Her smile grows ever larger. "Good. Now be a good boy and come take it off of me."

27

Evie

I feel beautiful.

I knew I looked good when I was putting this on but when Tanner looks at me this way, speechless. I feel like the most beautiful girl ever.

I wait for him to approach but he's still dumbfounded. "Tanner." My voice is a gentle reminder.

"Yeah?" God, he's so cute when he's like this.

"Come here." His feet remain rooted to the floor. "Tanner." He mumbles an unintelligible response. "Now."

He finally spurs into action, taking the step that eliminates the space between us. Though he doesn't touch me, just stares. I sigh, I know I look hot, but the point was to get him moving, not whatever this is. I think his final fried his brain cells.

I push to standing, molding my body against his. He blinks but still doesn't move. I wrap my arms around his neck, yanking his head down in the process so I can slant my mouth against his.

It takes a second but he responses. The kiss goes from soft to starved in a few seconds and the next thing I know I'm on my back, splayed out on Tanner's bed as he hovers over me.

"God damn baby. You look-" his words taper off as he searches for the right one. "Incredible."

"Thank you." With my arms still around his neck I pull him back down, needing another kiss.

I never knew someone could get addicted to kissing but here I am, addicted to the feeling of Tanners mouth on mine. Going even a few days without a kiss makes me feel like I'm going through withdrawal. How are we going to do long distance when I'm addicted to him like an addict is to meth?

I pull him closer, needing to feel his body against mine. Needing to feel how perfect we fit together. Who knows how we're going to do this. I guess we'll just have to figure it out together because being apart isn't an option, not anymore.

He trails kisses down my neck until he reaches the spot where my neck meets my shoulder and bits down, drawing a low moan groan my throat. He was so proud of himself when he found that spot last month, now he abuses it.

His tongue pokes out to soothe the ache but it's only temporary. His hands find their way around my neck and suddenly a pressure is released as my choker is pulled away and discarded somewhere on the floor.

I open my mouth, but Tanner beat me to it. "I know, I know. I'll pick it up later." I smile against his hair.

Another bite, this time on the skin just above my left breast forcing me back into the moments as a whimper falls from my mouth. The fucker smiles against my skin like he's proud of himself.

His teeth scrap the lacy fabric of my bralette as I squirm under him, both under stimulated and over. My skin feels like molten lava is running just under it. Every touch, every kiss feels like not enough and too much against my heated overly sensitive skin.

He makes no move to remove any more fabric, instead moving onto my stomach where he places more open-mouthed kisses. At the rate he's going he's bound to leave marks.

I open my mouth to tell to stop teasing me but he bites down just above my belly button forcing a squeak out instead.

"Your skin is so soft, so perfect, a blank canvas for me to leave my mark on so everyone knows your mine." My face heats when I see him looking up at me, his chin resting just above my naval.

Holy fuck, his cheeks are rosy, sage eyes dilated making them seem darker, hair a fluffy mess from my nail that I hadn't noticed were running through it, puffy lips from our kissing and his sucking. We haven't hardly done anything, and he already looks freshly fucked. I can't imagine I look much better.

An unspoken word passes through us and he's moving up again, kissing me gently. Despite what I led on, what I'm wearing is not the surprise, though I had imagined using it on him, not me. Suddenly the idea doesn't sound so bad. I search his eyes until a resigned sigh tumbled from my lips.

"Top drawer of your dresser, the left one." He leans up staring at me with scrunched eyebrows.

"Your drawer? What about it?"

"There's a bag in it, can you bring it out here?" He pushes himself into a kneeling position.

"It can't wait, I was in the middle of something." I smile, laughing lightly because yeah, he was.

I shake my head. "No. What's in the bag is your real surprise." He stares at me quizzically.

"I thought you were my surprise." I lean up on my elbows while shaking me head, locks of black hair fanning around me in the process.

"I'm you present, not surprise." He stares at me silently for a moment. I sigh again, wow I'm doing that a lot today. I gesture to the back of my head where the top half of my hair is being held back by a red bow. "I'm wearing a bow and everything."

Slowly, like he's moving through molasses, he stands and walks into the closet. He returns a minute later with a gift bag in his hands. "Come on, open it." He does, pulling out fluffy hand cuffs and black rope, both from a sex shop so neither should hurt too bad.

His eyes flicker between the objects in his hands to me before eventually settling on me where I'm now sitting on my knees.

I shrug like it's not a big deal, even though it is. "I thought it might be fun to experiment. The original plan was to use them on you but if you want, you can tie me down." The last words come out on a whisper, so quiet I don't think he heard them.

The bed dips as Tanner crawls on it, toward me. "What did

you say?"

"Uh, the plan was..." he shakes his head, stopping me.

"No, the last part."

"Oh, you uh, you can use them on me instead if you want." A gentle hand lifts my head to meet his.

"Here." He hands me the rope then the handcuff. "You wanted to tie me down, so let's do it."

My brows furrow as I watch him stand and discards his shirt. His black jeans follow shortly after, leaving him in the light pink boxer briefs I bought his last week. They were supposed to be a joke since he only wears dark grey and black, but he loves them, and I love that he doesn't care if they're a 'girly' color.

He scoops me up only to set me on my feet at the end of the bed. He confidently takes my place, stretching his arms toward the headboard for me to either cuff him or tie him to.

I blink, dumbfounded with how little resistance he gave. I was sure, for some reason, he would protest. From what I gathered the girl is usually restrained.

"What's wrong princess, don't want to tie your handsome prince down?" His teasing tone pushes me into motion, I quickly take the tag off the cuffs, I'm regretting only buying one pair, I should have listened to Sasha when she said it makes sense to buy two, one for each hand.

Though, I have an idea on how to fix that. I crawl onto the bed, straddling Tanner. I lean over, purposely pushing my tits into his face as I grasp his hands. The cuffs have black fuzz around them so they won't be cold and shouldn't dig in.

I gather his hands in mine and cuff them together. My eyes briefly meet with Tanners heated gaze, but I'm not done so I lean up and reach behind me where the rope sits by Tanner's thigh. I unravel the rope slowly, trying to draw out the action.

I see Tanner watching every move I make as nerves settle in my tummy. I didn't buy a long rope so it's only about three feet. I find the middle and wrap it around the cuffs a few times before leaning up on my knees and tying the rope to the headboard.

Tanner tests his restraints, grunting when they don't offer much give.

"It's not too tight, is it?"

He tugs at them again with the same result. "Nah, just wasn't expecting this is all."

It's then that it occurs to me I have Tanner powerless below me, I hold all the power and a thrill runs down my spine.

I slide off the bed and leisurely walk into the bathroom. Tanner makes noises of complaint but I ignore him. I double check my hair looks okay and my makeup isn't smeared before adding another layer to my red lipstick.

I grab a lighter from one of the drawers, the one I use to light the candles, and walk back into the room. I spot the polaroid I took on the floor and pick it up.

I've made it very clear that these types of photos won't last here. Yes, I'll take them, but I'm too scared of them getting into the wrong hands. So he's aware I'll never send him any and he's not allowed to take any.

I light the flame and hold the photo to it until it catches fire. I hold it as it slowly burns down until the flame almost touches my hand. I snuff out the fire, now all that's left of the photo is a white edge.

"That's better." Tanner chuckles from his spot on the bed.

"I guess it was naive to hope to keep that for a few days."

"Yes, yes it was." I set the lighter down on the closest surface which happens to be the desk and take a set toward the bed.

My arms reach behind my to the clasps of my bra and unclip it. The fabric falls to the floor, bearing my tits to Tanner, relishing in the fact that he can only watch and not touch.

High on a power trip, my hands crawl up my body until I squeeze my tits and play with my nipples. Pinching and rolling them between my fingers as small sounds fall from me. I see Tanner test his restraints again to no luck.

I smile at his attempt as I drop my tits. Next, I unclip my thigh-highs from the garter belt. Instead of taking them off, I slip my panties down my legs and step out of them and reconnect my garter to the red stockings.

A loud groan reverberates through the room as Tanner watches helplessly. I spot my chocker and an idea comes to mind, I quickly pick it up off the floor and fasten it back around my neck.

"Fuck baby. Come here, please." Tanner's tone has a hint of desperate need but it's not enough. I've heard him beg for something he really wants and he's not at that point yet.

I shake my head, crawling on the bed but staying at his thighs. I grab onto his boxers and pull them down, revealing all of him to me.

His cock pops free and I lick my lips. I pull his boxers off all the way before taking my place back on his thighs. One of my hands braces me on his lower abdomen while the other wraps around his length, tugging lightly.

A soft curse followed by a loan moan. I swipe at his mushroom head, spearing a bead of precum that had gathered there. I try to move my hand but there's not enough lubricant. I debate spitting into my hand but that wouldn't drive him as crazy as my mouth on him would.

My lips stretch around him as I slide down his length, using my tongue to spread my saliva. I can tell Tanner's trying his best to hold back his noises but that won't do, I want to hear exactly what I do to him.

I bob a few times before lifting myself off him, but before I do I make sure to scrap my teeth on my way up. Finally, a moan falls from my princes' lips.

"There, that's better." I replace my mouth with my hands and start to work his length. My hand slides much easier now. I tug on my way up again, tightening my grip as my hand slides down his cock to the base. Tanner's face is screwed up with tortured pleasure.

Using my balance on his stomach, I lean forward and kiss the edge of his mouth, moving back before he can fully connect our lips.

"Do you want to come?"

A gurgled moan as I swipe his tip.

"Yes or no baby."

"Noo-oo-o." Hmm, I thought he would want to.

"Why not baby?" His eyes that had been screwed shut snap open to look at me.

"Because I want to, to come, oh fuck, in you." My stomach flutters from the desperation in his voice. The unrestrained need and desire for me.

I kiss him once again before I lean away and take my hand off his dick. He makes a sound of displeasure deep in his throat but says nothing, hope shining in his eyes.

"Are you going to be a good boy and let me come first?" He nods his head vigorously. "I need to hear you say it baby. Yes, or no? Are you going to let me come first?"

"Always."

"Good boy." I rise on my knees and crawl over him. My hand wraps around his dick, working the skin there as I grab the condom I left on the nightstand. I hold it in front of his mouth. "Open it."

He grabs ahold of the foil between his teeth and pulls until it rips. He spits out a corner onto the sheets and I make a mental note that they'll need to be washed later.

I take the condom out and roll it over his length, setting the empty wrapper back on his nightstand.

"Have you been a good boy? Do you deserve this?" I don't know where this confidence is coming from but I'm loving it, and Tanner seems too as well.

"Yes."

I line him up with my opening and slide down an inch and hover. He tries to buck up but a hand on his chest stops him, I tisk and shake my head.

The need to drop all the way is strong but I'm trying to tease him, drive him crazy.

I drop another inch, using all my self-restraint to stop instead of going farther. I feel so full and empty at the same time. My body is begging for more, but my brain is telling me to hold off, a few more seconds. Just a few more seconds.

That's all I last, a groan from Tanner and a half assed attempt to buck up breaks me. With my hands braced on his abdomen, I drop all the way, taking all of him at once. I gasp at the sudden fullness while Tanner throws his head back attempting to hide his moan.

I lean down, molding my chest to his as he cocks his head to mine. The kiss is supposed to be soft, but Tanner has other ideas.

Even without his hands he dominates my mouth. I whimper into the kiss as I start to rock, my clits scraping his pelvis with every movement. It's a delicious form of torture that I never want to end.

With one final kiss I lean up and throw my hair over my shoulder. I lift up until he's barely inside of me and slam myself back down. I shudder as I continue. A low pressure builds deep in my stomach but it's not fast enough.

I put all my weight on one hand and move the other down to where we're connected and rub circles over my clit. My moans drown out Tanners as they get louder in pitch and volume.

With one final drop I'm coming apart on top of him, struggling to keep a tempo as oversensitivity takes hold.

I'm faintly aware Tanner hasn't come yet, but I can't keep moving. I slump forward against him as I catch my breath. I shudder as I reach above my head to release Tanner.

I didn't think this through since the moment he had his hands back I'm being flipped on my back with him towering over me.

He slams back into me, forcing a chocked moan from my lips. He sets a punishing pace, using my body for his pleasure and holy fuck does it feel good.

His hold on my waist is bruising and I hope they leave marks. Fucked up, maybe. But I don't care. I want a visual reminder of this tomorrow and for the next week. One hand leaves my waist and starts to play with my clit.

Pleasure racks through my body, it's too much but his hold doesn't leave me any room to move.

"Don't." Tanner voice is strained. "You can take it; I know you can." I nod, mewled moans pushing their way out of my throat, my eyes close involuntarily. "God, you take my cock so good. Such a good girl. Are you going to come again? Paint my cock with the pretty shades of you release?"

All thought has left my head, all I can do is nod as my second orgasm comes barreling through me.

"Good girl, just like that." As he fucks me through it a new sensation follows, it feels like a bubble about to pop.

"Tan-n-ner." I try to warn him but I'm not fast enough. With his thumb still on my clit and his cock pounding into me, I squirt all over him and the sheets.

"Oh, fuck baby. Did you just?" Too embarrassed for words I just nod. "That's so fucking hot." My eyes snap open to see his already staring at me. I'm at a loss for words as I watch him come, spilling into the condom.

He slumps forward, all of his body weight resting on me.

"God damn baby, that was-" he lifts his head. "We need to do that again, though I wouldn't mind tying you up next time."

Before I can respond he kisses me and stands on shaky legs. Oh God, I did that to him. A warmth spread through my body as that thought settles in. I did that, I made it hard for him to walk. A sense of pride flows through me, I didn't know it was possible to make a guys legs shake after sex and I'm damn glad I learned it is.

I hear the faucet to the bathtub start running and what sounds like Tanner going through the cupboard under the sink. He walks back into the room a minute later to grab the lighter than leaves again.

While he does whatever he's doing I untie the rope from the bed and wrap it into a ball. I open the drawer of the nightstand and put the cuffs and rope in there.

When I go to stand Tanner comes back into the room.

"What are you doing?" I look at him as he comes to stand behind me, his head resting on my shoulder with his arms wrapped tightly around my waist.

"I was going to strip the sheets." His chuckle vibrates my body. He pulls my hair to the side and for the second time in the last hour Tanner takes my chocker off. This time he sets it on the bed.

I watch his hands travel down my body to where they unclip my stockings.

"Sit." I do as he says, turning to face his as I sit on the edge of the bed. He kneels before me, sliding my thigh-highs off and setting them with my chocker. He then pulls my garter down to my hips before pushing me down to lay. I go willingly, allowing him to pull the garter off of me.

He keeps his hand braced on my stomach, not letting me sit up. He places several kisses on my thighs before reluctantly pulling away. As I sit up his arm snakes around my waist and he pulls me into his arms as he stands and carries me into the bathroom where the tub is half full and slowly filling with bubbles.

He kisses my temple as he slides me into the warm water. "I'll be back, I'm going to go throw the sheets in the wash." He's gone in the next breath. The water is still running so I let it fill up a bit more before turning it off and relaxing.

At some point I must have fallen asleep because I'm woken up an hour or so later by Tanner lifting me from the tub and drying me off. I keep my eyes firmly shut as he carries me to the bed and lays me on the fresh sheet, still warm from the dryer.

I hear the tub drain and the scent of snuffed out candles waft in from the bathroom. A few minutes later Tanner joins me in bed.

"A few more minutes then we need to get up." With his body wrapped around mine I fall back asleep.

I don't know how long we nap for but way too soon there's movement outside of the room and an alarm is going off. I do my best to ignore it but when Tanner crawls out of bed, taking my warmth with him, I know it's time to get up.

28

Tanner

I roll out of bed, careful not to wake Evelyn as the bed shifts. I shut my alarm off with a soft groan. Dragging my hand down my face I shuffle to the bathroom to take a piss.

We've only been asleep for a few hours, staying up late into the night tends to be disorienting, it can sometimes feel like days.

There's movement outside my door which alerts me to Seans presence. I debate putting a shirt on before leaving my room. I'm wearing sweatpants so I'm covered but if there's people over, do I really want to leave my room shirtless?

I listen for a moment before saying fuck it. The door closes behind me with a soft click. The morning sun casting long shadows over the loft.

I take the stairs two at a time only to be greeted by an empty kitchen. Theres's noise from the den so I make my way there. Dillan is passed out on the small couch, seconds away from falling off it completely.

I don't remember him coming over last night, but I was out of it after our nap and since Alyssa never came over, Evie didn't want to leave the room.

We stayed in our little happy cocoon all night.

By the time I walk back to the kitchen, Sean's looking in the fridge.

"Morning." I lazily scratch my chest.

Sean jumps, startled. "Damn, didn't think anyone else was awake."

"Just me, another final today." I reach around him to pull the orange juice out. The clock on the stove shows seven thirty-eight, I need to be in class at eight thirty. Then it's back here to pack.

Since the guys are going to stay here through the next year they said Evie can store some of her things here over the summer, whatever she's not taking. She's going back to the dorms to pack with the help of Sasha. I think Alyssa's going to join later after her last final of the year.

"Damn, they're doing it earlier."

"Yeah, my class usually starts when the test is supposed to end. It's the only one doing the testing earlier, it's strange." I shrug as I down my cup of juice. "When did Dillan come over?"

"Dillan came over?" I blink at him.

"Yeah, he's asleep in the den. I figured you invited him over."

Sean glances toward the hallway leading to the den.

"Maybe Collins did." He turns back to the fridge, eyes searching for something.

"Dude, if you haven't found it yet, you're not going to find it." He humph's at me but closes the door.

A creek upstairs draws our eyes up. Another creek followed by soft footfalls. "Morning." Evie's quiet voice floats down the stairs. She lands on the bottom step moments later looking adorably sleepy. She rubs at her eyes while a huge yawn pushes it's way out of her.

"Morning Evelyn." She stops and stares at Sean likes he's grown a second head.

"Huh?"

"I said morning."

"Yeah, but you used my full name."

"Yup."

"Why?"

"Why not? It's your name." She opens her mouth to respond but decides against it. Instead, she gives me a quizzical look. I shrug as she lazily approaches me. She loops her arms around my neck and places a quick kiss to the corner of my lips.

"You're up early, your class isn't until eleven."

"Normally yeah but the test starts at eight thirty." She stops with her hand on the fridge door.

"What? Why?"

I shrug, grabbing a glass down from the cupboard, I set it gently on the counter for her. She pours herself a glass of apple juice. Sean goes to open the fridge again before he stops.

"Why are you up so early?" She directs the question to Sean who stares at the fridge like it has burned him.

"Couldn't sleep." He sighs before walking into the living room. He flops onto the couch. A grunt fills the silence followed by Sean lifting himself up just enough to pull Dillan's keys and the tv remote out from under him.

Evie and I exchange a look but say nothing. I excuse myself to go take a shower while Evie sips her apple juice and scrolls through Tik Tok.

Evie

I scroll aimlessly through my for you page waiting for the text from Sasha saying she's awake and ready to pack.

A video pops up with a short scene from a book. I'm about to scroll when I see who posted it, my new employer.

I'm supposed to start editing her next book as soon as school lets out for the summer. I've already posted to the pay to read website I upload to that the next thing I post may possibly be the last for a really long time.

I'm set to post the short book I've been working on in two days. I finished editing it yesterday and with my last final tomorrow for creative writing, the timing is perfect.

I like the video and continue to waste time on the video app. The shower turns off upstairs, a snore comes from the living room, a grunt from the den.

I rinse my glass out before placing it in the dishwasher. Who knew wasting time was so boring?

My phone buzzes on the counter. I lean across the island, swiping my phone. A text from Sasha awaits me.

Sasha: I'm up
Sasha: Alyssa says she'll join us later
Sasha: She also says she has something to tell us

I look up as Tanner comes down the stairs.

"Can I catch a ride to the school with you?" He looks at me, confusion scrunching his face.

"You know you don't have to ask right? I'll be happy to have you in my truck any chance I can get." We leave the house a few minutes later. The ride to the school is blanketed in comfortable silence. "Are the others packing today or is it just you?"

"I'm not sure. Probably all of us." He pulls into an empty parking spot. Throwing the truck in park Tanner turns to me, pulls me close, and kisses me softly. He pulls back, just enough to look at me.

"God, you're beautiful."

"Thank you." I lean forward with another kiss. "You gotta go or you'll be late."

"Yeah, yeah. I know." He rounds the car to open my door and help me out. As soon as the door is closed, he's running across the quad to make it to his class in time.

The dorms are only a short walk away. On the way I admire the wonderful weather we've been blessed with. Mid-seventies for all of today, sunny but cloudy, and a storm rolling in.

Sasha's waiting for me outside my door. She lights up when I walk out of the elevator. "You ready to do this?"

"I guess, I hope I don't have a roommate next semester. It

was so nice to not have one."

"You hardly were in your room."

"Still, it was nice."

29

Evie

Packing went by a lot quicker than I thought. I know I don't own a lot of things, but I thought I had more than ten boxes. Everything I own is in ten boxes, it's a little sad.

Staring at the now empty room save for the bed that still has my sheets and comforter. Sasha went to get some trash bags that we can store them in for the time being.

It took longer to organize the boxes than it did to pack everything up.

The door swings open behind me and the sound of a trash

bag opening follows Sasha in. "Two hours, pretty good considering your need to have everything in a specific place."

"Well, I want to be able to find things as I unpack them. Makes less of a mess that way." She holds the bag open for me as I gingerly place my pillow cases in, followed by my top sheet then the fitted one. She ties the bag off and sets it with the rest of the boxes. Another bag with my comforter and throw blanket and I'm all packed.

I have to wait for Tanner to move everything but at least it's done. Well, save for what I have at Tanner's place. Probably three or four more boxes of knickknacks and clothes but then I'll be finished.

Looking around the room one last time, I fight back a wave of tears.

"Shall we pack some of your stuff? You're going back home for the summer, right?" I lock the door behind me, and we take the elevator down to her floor. Clearing my throat from the sudden gravel.

"That's the plan. Moms' ecstatic to have another girl in the house, dad is driving her *crazy*." A door at the end of the hall opens as Sasha sticks her key into the lock.

"Evelyn?" A tentative voice calls down the hall. I look to the source to find Ella.

"Yeah?" Sasha makes a noise in the back of her throat but otherwise stays silent. Ella and I aren't friends, but we have come to a truce of sorts after Marcus contacted her. The whole situation really freaked her out.

"I wanted to apologize for everything. I looked up that guy the other day when curiosity got the better of me and saw what he and multiple others were being charged with. I know there's no excuse for the way I treated you but when I first saw you, I was jealous. We're the same age yet you're so pretty that I felt threatened. I came from a high school where I was the most popular, the prettiest and then I walked into my dorm room to see a prettier, smarter girl than me. Then you got Tanner Shaw chasing you, begging for a sliver of your attention. From the outside, you were living the life I wanted, you got the attention I wanted. I always knew that Josh stopping talking to me wasn't your fault. I saw Tanner talk to him from the window that first night. But it still made me irrationally mad that you got the attention of one of the most popular guys in the school. I was so used to high school, I struggled to let go of the way things used to be.

"I hated you because that's how things were done where I'm from. But when he stared texting me, it was an refreshing. We talked for almost two months before you were ever brought up and for once, the mention of you didn't make me mad, it scared me. We had never talked about you before, then I posted that rant and it changed everything. There had been an official post from the school the same day with you in the background with your friends so he must have put two and two together. Then when he knew your full name from what I had thought was just my post, it freaked me out. It was a huge eye opener that not everyone had the same experience and that maybe, just maybe I had been too judgmental off of the bat. Then I saw what he did to you and your friend. I'm sorry I was too caught up in the past to see the future. I know we'll never be friends, but I hope we can at least move past the animosity and maybe on day have something similar to a friendship."

She had slowly approached Sasha and I. She looks so tired

and guilty. But that's not what I'm caught up on. "You didn't like me because I'm pretty?" That had never been a reason I had thought about when I wondered why she disliked me so much that first semester. I almost want to laugh.

"Yeah, I was used to being the only one and then boom, you were there. An only child, the apple of my parent's eye, and then there was another. Like I said, I know it's not an excuse, but I wanted to apologize and at least try to explain." She stopped in front of me looking years older than she did at the beginning of the year.

I don't think there's anything to forgive since she never took anything 'too far.' She didn't bully me, didn't make my life harder, just complained about me being in the same class as her. Yeah, she was a bitch but that's not a crime. Everyone is a little bitchy sometimes.

I offer her my hand with a soft smile. "Thank you. I look forward to next year with you. I'm betting we'll have at least one class together." She gingerly takes my hand and I pull her in for a quick hug. "The first step is always excepting the problem. The second is making it right. Have a great summer, Ella. And if it makes you feel better my first thought about you was how pretty you are." A smile slowly blooms on her face, brilliant and beaming.

"Thank you. I'll see you next year." Someone exits the room she came from, and they leave together. As the elevator closes, Ella smiles at me once more.

"You're way too forgiving." Sasha had made herself comfortable on her bed where she watched the whole interaction.

"Maybe, but some people deserve some leeway." I close the

door on my way in and look around the cramped space. "Now where do you want to start?"

Alyssa walked into an absolute mess. Sasha had emptied her side of the closet and was trying to fold everything in a way that they would fit into her fifteen boxes. Seven were already filled with pens, notebooks, snacks, a few books, chargers, and a small tv.

"Did a hurricane blow through here?" Alyssa drops her bag on the end of her bed, the only free space on the fluffy comforter.

"Hurricane Sasha is leaving her mark on this room, that's for sure." I grumble out. Half an hour ago Sasha told me to go sit in the corner and to let her work. My way worked for me, but she wouldn't even try it. I can guarantee we would be almost done had she listened.

"I can see that." She swipes some piles away to make room for her to sit.

"It's not that bad!" Sasha's head pops out of the closet where she was doing who knows what.

"No, you're right, it could be worse. But that doesn't make it good." Sasha huffs, turning her back to us.

"How'd your test go?" Alyssa leans back against the wall and sighs.

"My brain hurts." I laugh which causes her to chuckle. "It went okay, could be worse." The room goes quiet, the only sound, Sasha trying to pack.

Alyssa looks like she wants to say something but doesn't know how.

"Ahah." Sasha exclaims, pulling a backpack from the closet. It's full of clothes in the matter of seconds.

I sigh, having seen enough I grab her now discarded backpack and unpack it while she's not looking. Refolding everything and placing the clothes strategically allowed for five more shirts and two short to fit. I zip up the bag and with a resigned look, Sasha hands me a box and I start to fold the clothes on the bed. Alyssa helps out after seeing how I'm folding everything. Soon enough she has a bed again and half of the clothes are in one bag and two boxes.

There are more clothes on Sasha's bed but none of us make a move to fold them just yet. A break is needed.

"I have a confession." Alyssa says into the silent room.

Like a dog with a bone, Sasha jumps at the opportunity. "Oooo, spill" She rolls off her bed in her rush to join us on Alyssa's. "I've been dying for some drama." She continues in a sing-song voice.

"Who says it's drama?" I sit up to lean against the wall, ready to defend my bestie from my other bestie.

Sasha gives me a look, somewhere between 'bitch be for real' and 'are you kidding me?' I sigh in resignation as we all cuddle on the twin bed.

"Promise you won't freak out." She directs the question at me and suddenly my excitement turns to worry.

"Alyssa, what did you do?"

She shakes her head. "Promise me."

"Fine, I promise. Now what did you do?"

"I hooked up with Oli." The room is so quiet you could hear a pen drop. It takes me longer to process the information that it does Sasha determined by the high-pitched squeal emitting from her.

"Ohmygod, ohmygod." She jumps off the bed vibrating with energy. "Tell us everything." Her eyes sparkle.

Alyssa looks at me, waiting for my reaction.

"Oli?" She nods. "Really?"

"Yeah." Her voice comes out meek.

"Damn, I thought it would be Sean." A smile breaks free and stretches across her face.

"Why Sean?" I shrug as Sasha squeals again.

"I don't know. I guess I thought he was more your type." She giggles, shaking her head.

"When I first met them, I thought they could be brothers, they look so similar." Her sigh borders on dreamy as she looks out the window. "Jasper showed up two days into me staying at Oli's place, but he wouldn't budge from the door. He told Jasper to go fuck off and that if he really cared for me, he wouldn't have hurt me or threaten to hurt my friends. Dillan heard the commotion and threatened to call the police if he didn't leave. He did, not wanting a police report to ruin his reputation. After, Dillan went to class leaving me and Oli. I thanked him for sticking up for me and one thing led to another. Next thing I know I'm walking up naked in his bed, using his chest as a pillow while he snores softly."

"Was it good?" Sasha jumps back on the bed, shaking the entire frame in the process.

"Oh, he was incredible. He definitely knows what he's doing, and it shows." A shyness overtakes her expression. Sasha's too busy freaking out to notice but I do.

"Are you okay?"

"He asked me out yesterday. And I think I'm going to say

yes." I smile, placing my hand on her shoulder.

"You should. If he makes you happy then you should explore it." My God, Oli? Really?

"Thanks Evie." The conversation dies off as we watch Sasha bouncing off the walls.

An hour later Sasha is all packed, save for the essentials. Alyssa has decided to pack later in the week and Tanner is on his way with Oli and Dillan to grab my stuff.

A month ago, it was decided that Alyssa would stay with Sasha's family for the summer. They aren't heading out until Sunday which happens to be the same day Tanner and I are moving into his new apartment.

This year has flown by, and I've made some incredible friends along the way. I approach the window, looking out to see the guys coming closer. Somehow Tanner seems to know I'm looking at him. He looks up at the window with a brilliant smile and waves.

Can time just stop so I can enjoy this moment forever?

The man I love looking at me like I'm his world while I'm surrounded by my friends. This year couldn't have gone any better.

30

Evie

3 Years later

"The sex is fucking phenomenal, but I think you already know that." Mona giggles from her spot across from me. We're still waiting on Natalia, as always. The three of us were supposed to meet up here almost half an hour ago.

"Well obviously, no one can get a hold of you when you visit him." Mona Simons is a girl I met last year in my advanced writing class. She's majoring in journalism while it's my minor. She wants to be a reporter and has been offered a job at a firm in Vancouver, the side of the city in America.

We hit it off immediately on the first day of classes. I arrived late because my previous class went over. When I entered the lecture hall the only seat left was next to the amazing person in front of me.

I took the only seat remaining, planning on keeping to myself. You tend to do that when your boyfriend of three years is a multi-millionaire who plays for the Columbus Cheetahs. He's made quite a name for himself.

Well, my plan for staying away from people was thrown out the window when Mona turned to me before my butt even hit the seat, introducing herself and declaring I was going to be her new best friend.

We've been inseparable ever since.

"Hey! Look, it's the fat ass from my class!" The irking voice floats through the air, landing right where the perpetrator wanted it to, on Mona. Laughter erupts around the small cafe, all eyes landing on us. Mona tries to shrink in on herself but there's nowhere to go.

"Hey," I place a soothing hand over hers. "Don't listen to that jackass." I raise my voice loud enough for him to hear. "Did you get tired of spending your daddy's money? Is it not getting you laid anymore? I don't blame the girls who leave you, if the only good thing you have to offer is your dad, I'd choose him too." He goes bright red, my words hitting their mark.

Trevor is known around campus as a high spender. He would splurge every chance he got until his dad cut him off, only paying for the basic necessities. The girls that used to hang around him left for someone better, someone richer. Even his girlfriend left him, and to add insult to injury, she's now dating his father.

It's what he gets for being rude. He's one of those guys who thinks women should be a certain size, that size being a six or smaller. Mona isn't one of those girls. She has curves to spare and despite what she seems to think, she's gorgeous.

We've gone shopping enough for me to know her size and I can't believe she thinks that she's 'large'. A size twelve is not large. It's not plus sized. It's beautiful. And one day she's going to find that man that's going to look at her like she hung the moon and worship the ground she walks on.

Trevor stomps, yes, I mean stomps, like a baby, out of the building, his entourage scurrying after like lost puppies. It's a little pathetic if you ask me.

"Thanks Evie."

"There's no need to thank me for being a good friend. He had it coming, and I just happen to be the one to give it to him. He's a dickwad that doesn't have eyes. I mean look at you, you're smart, kind, pretty, and sweet. The ultimate catch." A pretty blush works its way up her tanned skin.

She has light brown curls that fall just past her shoulders. Beautiful Ocean blue eyes that suck you in and make it near impossible to find your way out. Her straight nose points down to full pink lips. All of that wrapped up in a heart shaped face. Like I said, she's fucking pretty.

Add that to her short stature and boys go crazy.

My phone dings on the table between us, a text awaiting me from Natalia. I sigh as I reread it a few times. "Nate says she's stuck at home. Her parents keep adding to her plate before she can head out." I know it's not her fault, but her parents really need to let up. She's twenty-two for heaven's sake! She shouldn't have to ask permission to go somewhere.

I mean I get it; she's living at home for free, the only thing that's asked of her is whatever chores her parents give her for the week. But every time she tells them she's going out; they triple the list and tell her it needs to be done before she leaves the house.

She never argues because you should never bite the hand that feeds you or something.

"Really? That sucks. Does she know how long she's going to be stuck there?" The bell above the door rings, alerting the staff that a new patron has entered the cafe.

"I'm not sure. She didn't say anything else."

"This is ridiculous. We're supposed to be shopping for our graduation outfits right now." Mona moans out.

We graduate on Friday, it's currently Monday and none of us know what we're going to wear. Sasha and Alyssa managed to go shopping sometime last week but the three of us couldn't go, needing to work instead.

Natalia works the night shift at the local diner, Mona has an internship with a news station in the city and I'm working online as an editor for a small-time publishing firm.

I really like it since I can make my own hours, I get paid by the job so as long as it gets done by the deadline, I'm good.

Most nights I keep Natalia company while I work. Nights tend to be really slow unless it's exam season. Then everyone flocks to places like the diner that's open all night so they can study with food.

My phone buzzes in my hand, my attention immediately

going to it in hope Natalia has somehow managed to get away. I feel immensely guilty when I'm disappointed to see Tanner's name on my screen instead.

It's not that I'm unhappy to hear from him. In reality, I'm ecstatic. His team made it to the semifinals this year so there hasn't been much time for us to talk. When we did find the time, it was only for five or so minutes. It gets really lonely.

> **My love: I've been given the go ahead to take the rest of the week off**
> **My love: I'm heading your way in the morning**
> **My love: I should get there after your last exam**
> **My love: Romantic dinner tomorrow night?**

My smile continues to grow with every incoming text. He always knows just what to say.

> **Me: That sounds lovey**
> **Me: I miss you** 🥺
> **Me: I can't wait to see you**

Three dots appear and disappear on the screen a few times before his text finally comes through.

> **My love: The things I'm going to do to you tomorrow night**
> **My love: You won't be able to walk for days** 😈

A blush rises up my cheeks as my face burns. I can feel

Mona's eyes on me, but I refuse to look at her.

> **Me: I look forward to it hot stuff**
> **My love:** 😄
> **My love: God, you're awful at sexting**
> **My love: I love you**
> **Me: Shut up**
> **Me: I love you too** 🩶

Someone clears their throat; my eyes lift and meet with Mona's blue ones. "Oh, don't let me interrupt you two being all lovey dovey." I giggle nervously.

"Sorry." I offer up a sheepish look, but I can tell she's not buying it.

"No, you're not, nor should you be. But seriously, I'm right here. I really don't want to watch you sext your boyfriend. No matter how hot and sexy he may be." I can't stop the triumphant smile that crosses my lips because she's right, my boyfriend is the hottest, sexiest man I've ever laid eyes on, and he's all mine.

"You're right. He is sexy."

Her eye roll is far more dramatic than need be but that's Mona for you, always dramatic. "Of course that's what you hear. You two are two peas in a pod."

The conversation dissolves as we wait for Nate to arrive. An hour later she's finally called to let us know she's on her way.

A few people have approached me about getting Tanner's autograph. In the beginning it was okay, it didn't bother me too much. But three years later it's gotten really old. I get that I'm dating him, but I don't like when people try to use me to get to him.

I'm my own person, and trust me, when we see each other, your damn autograph will be the last thing on my mind. Usually there isn't anything on my mind actually. Our time together tends to be spent naked in the various rooms of his massive apartment. The apartment that will soon become my home.

The closer I get to graduation, the more real my future becomes, the future I never thought I could have.

I've got the man, the friends, and soon I'll be able to move my mom out to wherever we end up. After we put away a lot of people back home, mom has gotten nothing but shit. The community has taken to shunning her. She can't even go into town to get groceries anymore, no one at the store will serve her.

Tanner, bless his heart, was able to convince someone from two towns over to bring her food until she can leave.

It's been two years since they've been put behind bars and in less than six months Jake will be released. I ended up talking to him the day before he was transferred. He wasn't able to answer many of my questions, but he did apologize profusely.

Tanner had come with me and was next to me the whole time. He was exactly what I needed to get through that conversation.

I was surprised when I saw online that he had pleaded guilty and asked for the longest sentence. So was the judge, that's why he still got the shortest. Jake was and still is the only one who showed remorse for his actions.

He had said that being friends with Marcus came with immense pressure to fit in and in doing so he lost himself. He spent most of his time during and after high school on drugs. He even admitted to having no memory of the incidents he was being charged with. Though I'm not sure I believe him. He claims the only reason he knew it happened was thanks to a gloating Marcus.

It doesn't make up for what he did, and I may never be able to forgive him but it gives me some peace that he wasn't in full control of himself the same way I wasn't.

Long tanned arms wrap around my torso, red painted nails on full display. The five of us have decided to get our nails done on Thursday, even made the appointments three weeks ago. But Nate always has her natural nails painted. She said that's how she learned to stop biting her nails and having polish on them is a constant reminder not to bite them when she gets anxious.

Beautiful long blond hair falls over my shoulder. Her chin hooking on my shoulder while her emerald eyes stare at me. "Hi."

"Hey, Nate. Ready to go shopping?"

"Hell yeah." Mona stands to toss her cup in the nearby trash can while Nate and I head up to the counter. I want another fruity lemonade while she wants her coffee. Since she's not allowed to drink any at home, without fail, she always gets one before we go anywhere.

Before she can pay, my card is out and already inserted. She grumbles under her breath about how I *always* pay but that because I have a steadier and bigger income, I also have a super-rich boyfriend who sends me money every month despite my insistence that he doesn't have to and that I would prefer he didn't.

Mona joins us as we set off to the side and wait for our new drinks. Her and Nate fall into easy conversation, mostly complaining about their parents and stuff like that. I met Natalia through Sasha; they became really close friends during freshman year. I'm not proud to say I refused to meet her for almost six months but there was a lot going on in my life during that time.

The trials had just started, and I was basically on "call" as my lawyer called it. I was flying across the country a few times a month and it was really taking a toll on me. I thankfully only needed to testify a handful of times, most of the information that put everyone away came from Jake.

Safe to say Jake is no longer friends with any of those guys anymore and has a pretty big target on his head when he's released from prison. The other people's parents and siblings are NOT happy he helped put their family away for something they still believe wasn't a big deal.

I remember during Marcus's trial his dad threatened me in hopes I would drop all charges. It didn't work and the court security had to drag him out of the courtroom.

I don't care if they do think it's "not a big deal" because it was to me. These boys they tried so desperately to protect took everything from me. My innocence, my childhood, my trust. They had me believing the only reason someone would want me is for my body. Well, they were wrong, Tanner loves me for me. He didn't stay with me for my body, he stayed because he loves all of me. Though he does love my body too, and I love his.

My name is called out followed by our drinks being set on the counter next to us. I grab my strawberry raspberry lemonade while Nate grabs her double fudge mocha latte.

Natalia is gorgeous, inside and out. She's one of the kindest souls I have ever met. After graduation she plans on getting her MBA which requires two more years of schooling. She's moving to Chicago to go to school there, hoping that it's far enough away from her parents she can have a life of her own.

She wants to run a non-profit charity, I don't think she knows what the charity will be for yet but the idea says a lot about her.

As Nate and Mona walk ahead of me, I take a moment to look at her. Tall, five-nine she said, beautiful blond hair that falls past her waist, almost to her butt. Brilliant, tanned skin, like the sun has kissed her. Her heart shaped face is clear of any blemishes. I watched her go through her skin care more times than I can count, so I know she spends a lot of money to keep her skin looking like porcelain.

She has pretty pink puffy lips, I hear a lot of guys want to know if they're as soft as they look. I think talking like that is a little creepy. Long thick eyelashes frame her emerald, green eyes.

She's thin, we wear the same size, a size four. But whereas I'm petite, she's amazonian. If she really wanted to be, she could be a model.

"Evie?"

My eyes flick up to emerald orbs. "Huh?"

Mona giggles, hiding her beautiful smile behind the back of her hand. "What kind of dress do you want? I was thinking long and flowy. Nate wants something a tad bit more form fitting but still loose, like a long slip dress."

"Oh, I was looking into babydoll style. I think it would look really good on me. Plus, easy access for my impatient man." Nate rolls her eyes but the smile on her face gives away what she's truly thinking.

"Good lord girlie. You two are so in love it's a little sickening." Mona nudges her in the side, a playful smile on her lips.

"Oh, be quite Natalia. You're just jealous that she's found her forever while you're still looking."

"Well, duh. Aren't you?" Mona shrugs but her smile does flatter slightly.

"Sometimes, but I don't doubt the right man will come along eventually." Neither do I, Mona will find someone who is just perfect for her. I can't wait for the day she tells me she's found her person, same goes for Nate, and Sasha.

My car comes into view in the student parking lot. I had to get a new one a year ago when mine didn't want to start in the middle of the winter. I had it towed to the local automotive shop, and they couldn't figure out what was wrong with it. It seems like it just quit one day. It's not all that surprising. It was on its last legs when I drove from Montana, so it was only a matter of time.

Tanner was aghast when I pulled up over winter break in a new car. I hadn't told him my other one took a shit because I knew he'd try to pay for my new one, but I had been saving up for a new car anyways. I didn't even have to get a car payment.

Now I drive a cobalt blue jeep. It's my baby.

I jingle my keys as I hop into the driver seat, Nate taking the passenger side while Mona settles into the back seat.

"So, where to first? The mall?" I wait for an answer as I gingerly back out of my assigned parking spot.

"The outlet mall or the indoor, giant mall?" Mona's head pops up between the headrests. She looks between the two of us, eventually landing on Natalia when I don't say anything. I don't really care where we go as long as we leave with dresses.

"Let's go to the indoor mall, there's probably more options there." So that's where we go. It's an hour drive since it's in the next city over and during the drive Nate's mom calls her a total of five times. I don't catch what most of the conversations are about, but they do irk Nate, a lot.

I'm lucky enough to find a spot near the front, next to a Barnes and Noble.

We end up at Christa's. There's every type of dress imaginable in here, save for wedding dresses.

Mona splits off toward the back of the store while Nate beelines for a rack with silky tee-length dresses are hung. I look around but nothing really catches my eye. There are some dresses that might be babydoll style, but the fabric looks awful.

I slowly walk the length of the store and still nothing draws my eye. I've already seen the other two go into the dressing rooms and I'm starting to lose hope that the dress for me is here.

The person who's running the register is watching me and I worry that means she thinks I may steal. But when the sales floor associate approaches me I realize that she just recognizes me as the woman always on the arm of Tanner Shaw.

"Sorry, my boyfriend is a *huge* fan of yours." She giggles as whatever goes through her head. "You look a little lost, do you need any help?"

"Actually, I do. I'm trying to find a dress for my college graduation." Her entire face lights up like she can't believe that I need her help but ecstatic, nonetheless.

"What style are you looking for?"

"I was thinking of a babydoll dress but like those super puff ones. I haven't found any here though." The associate falls silent, thinking.

She turns back to her coworker. "Did we get the newest shipment yet?"

"Uh, let me check." She types away on the store's computer as I follow the girl to the register. "Yeah, it came in yesterday. I can pull up what came in."

"Oh, please do." They go about talking amongst themselves while going through their new stock. "Ooo, that one, click on it." I see Mona exit the dressing rooms with a dress in her arms, the others seemingly disappearing, probably still in the room. She waits by the door for Nate who is still trying on a handful of different options. "What size are you?"

"A size four." More typing, more talking.

"I'll be right back." She scurries off into the backroom leaving me standing here with the other girl who is now back to staring at me. The longer she's gone, the more awkward it becomes. I breathe a sigh of relief when she emerges with three dresses in her hands. "So, I know this one isn't the style you wanted but I think it's similar enough. And these two are both babydoll dresses, just one is puffier than the other."

"Thank you." I take the dresses from her hands and head over to where Mona is still waiting. "You found one?"

"Yeah, isn't it pretty." It's a blood red dress that cinches at the waist and flares out. It's off the shoulder with ruffles for sleeves that look to stop just above the elbows. There's a slit up the left leg, it's beautiful.

"Yeah, it is." She motions to the dresses in my arms and motions to the room she was just in. I enter the small changing room and set my stuff down. I pick up the dress that she said was similar first and hold it up.

It's definitely pretty, that's for sure. It's a pale pink tee-length dress with ruffles that make it a little puffy. I undress so I can slip it on. I twirl in front of the mirror but despite it being pretty, I don't feel like this is the right one.

I pick up the second dress, it's a bright blue true babydoll style. I try this one on but it's the same as the last one, pretty but not for me. The last one is a super puffy pale pink dress decorated with tiny strawberries. I have more faith in this one.

I try it on and it's perfect. It falls to mid-thigh with a waist that pulls in just below my bust. With the puffy sleeves and tulle bottom, I feel like a princess. I twirl in front of the mirror and my smile widens. Tanner is going to love it.

The girls are waiting for me when I leave the room and it seems we all found a dress. Nate is carrying a midnight blue slip dress.

We checkout and leave, going immediately to the food court for lunch. There are texts waiting for me from Tanner.

> **My love: I bet you look sexy right now**
> **My love: Send me a pic, I want to see you**
> **Me: Are you asking for a naughty pic or a pretty pic?**
> **My love: Both?**
> **Me: Nope, you get one or the other**
> **My love: sigh, fine I'll pick**
> **My love: I want a pretty pic**
> **My love: I'll get a naughty one later in person** 😉

I turn around so I can get the others in the picture as well and we all pose. I'm holding up my hand with the sign language sign for I love you, I learned it from Tanner. He learned it from one of his teammates. Mona holds up a slice of pizza and Nate has her arms around both of us.

> **My love:** 🤩

My love: Beautiful
My love: The whole lot of you

I send back a quick thank you and a smiley face before putting my phone away to rejoin the conversation. Today has been fun but I'm ready to get home and crawl under my blankets.

I voice my thoughts and the others agree so we all pile back into my jeep and off we go.

I drop Mona off on campus so she can head back to her dorm and drive fifteen minutes out of town to drop Natalia off at her parents' house. The second she's safe inside I pull away and drive to the off-campus house I share with Sasha and Alyssa.

When I walk in the house is quiet but that's not surprising, they both have a final right now, their last one of their college careers. My last one is tomorrow morning.

I set my stuff down in the kitchen, we got lucky when the guys no longer wanted to rent this place, we took over the lease. Which also means I got the master because neither of the other two wanted to live in the room Tanner and I fooled around in.

My phone buzzes with an incoming call from my boss. I really don't want to answer but I have to, I haven't had work in almost three weeks since I finished the last project so quickly.

My goal is to work privately for upcoming authors but without my degree, that goal isn't easy to accomplish. So, until then, I'm stuck working for a firm that doesn't value its employees.

"Hey Mr. Mcknaw." I push the sugary sweet tone hoping to hide my distaste. He tries to flirt with me every chance possible and it's really unnerving.

"Hello Evie, how are you sweetness?" I cringe at the

nickname. This man is older than my dad, he should not be calling me that.

"I'm alright? Did you call with another project?" And just like that he goes into full work mode. Once I hang up I have a three hundred and seventy page book to edit throughout the next two weeks.

With nothing else to do I climb the stairs and crawl into my bed to take a much-needed nap.

31

Evie

I place my finished test on my professor's desk on my way out. She gives me a small nod in recognition as she continues to grade the test of the first person to finish. I should have my final grade by tonight which is exciting. I know, I know. That's so quick! Well, this professor scheduled the text for today because she didn't have anything else to do and knew she could go one class at a time and have everything graded in time. To all their own I guess, that would be far too much pressure for me.

I check my phone on the way out of the lecture hall. Tanner

messaged an hour ago he was on his way which means I have about two and half to three hours before he arrives.

I plan on using that time to tidy up the house and take a shower. Thankfully I live with clean people, maybe not as big of a clean freak as I am but close, so there's really nothing to do. It should take no longer than an hour and I'll be able to take a much-needed shower.

I've been stiff all week and taking a scolding shower might just be the answer, if not I'll ask Tanner to give me a long, long massage.

I start with the kitchen, running the dishwasher while wiping the counters down. Like I thought, there's not much to do in here so I move onto the living room. I dust and vacuum, refold the blankets and fluff the pillows. The same deal for the den.

When I get to the downstairs bathroom the dishwasher is still running and it says I still have a half an hour before it's done.

This bathroom is hardly used so it stays fairly clean. Again, I know, everything seems to already be clean but like I said, we're a clean bunch. I clean the toilet and wipe down the sink, take out the trash, and sweep and mop.

I move to the stairs, vacuuming them as I go up. The loft is a completely different story. We all slept in here last night so it's *messy*. Pillows and blankets everywhere. Chips and pizza boxes on the coffee table. I cringe at the mess but start cleaning. I bring all the trash down and all the cups, plates, and bowls. I fold all of the blankets and stick them back in the linen closet with the extra pillows that don't belong in someone's room.

I vacuum after wiping down every surface and by the time I get back downstairs the dishwasher is done. I empty it and hand wash all the dishes I just brought down so there's nothing waiting to be done.

I check the time to realize I have half an hour, max an hour before Tanner arrives and I do *not* smell good. I bypass my room, if I have spare time I'll tidy up in here as well, but I desperately need a shower.

I spend nearly the entire thirty minutes under the scaling spray, but the water has done nothing to ease the tension. Looks like I get to ask Tanner to put his hands on me, though I doubt I'll have to ask. I just mention it and he's all over me.

I throw on my favorite hoodie of his and shorts that you can hardly see. Surprisingly, he's still not here but I no longer have the motivation to clean, so I make my way downstairs where the girls have finally gotten home.

"How was your last class?" I take a seat between the two and click on the tv.

"It was okay. I did good on the test, I'm sure of it. But I can't wait to see Tanner. It's been almost three months since we've seen each other in person. I miss him." Sasha bumps my shoulder as Alyssa leans on me.

We stay cuddled up for the next hour waiting for the front door to open, but it never does. I check my phone, but I have no new notifications. I try calling but it goes straight to voicemail. My anxiety spikes the longer there's no word from him. This isn't like Tanner, what if something happened? What if he's hurt? What if-

The door swings open and in walks Tanner. I'm up the second his presence registers in my mind, wrapping myself around him like a koala. I nuzzle my nose into his neck, inhaling deeply. He smells like a bonfire mixed with the day after it rains in the woods.

"Why didn't you answer your phone? I was worried." My voice is muffled by his neck.

"Sorry baby. My phone died halfway here and there was construction, a detour. Traffic was moving at a snail's pace for an hour. I tried to call but that's when I realized my phone had died and of course I just removed the car charger I had." His arms tighten around me, his head dipping into my hair where he inhales. He likes my perfume as much as I like his cologne. Well, it's not all his cologne.

"Are you hungry? I can make you something. A grilled cheese maybe? We don't have a lot of food since our lease ends in two weeks and we're all moving starting Saturday." He sways us for a moment, clutching onto me tightly.

"Yeah, that sounds great. I'm gonna take a shower really quick." He presses a kiss to the top of my head before setting me back on my feet. Before he can walk away, I grab a fistful of his shirt, pulling his face down to mine. Our lips fuse, it's a sweet kiss, a hello.

"Okay," I rest my forehead against his, "you can go take a shower now." He chuckles, his hot breath fanning over my face. Another kiss and he takes the stairs two at a time. "Who else wants some grilled cheese?" Turns out everyone does.

I slip the skintight fabric of my red mini dress over my head. I've taken over the bathroom, leaving Tanner with the bedroom and small mirror I have in there. I do my best to avoid touching my face, so I don't have to redo any of my makeup. I'm not so worried about my hair since I still have to style it.

"Almost ready?" Tanner's voice calls out from the other room.

"Close."

"You said that ten minutes ago." He grumbles out.

"Yeah, and I meant it ten minutes ago. This dress just takes eight minutes to get on." I finally got it situated on my body, now all that's left is to zip it up. "Tanner, baby? Would you be a dear and zip me?"

He appears in the mirror behind me, eyes locked on my ass.

"God damn." He rubs his chin with one hand, the other resting on my hip.

"Baby?"

"Hmm?"

"Can you zip me?"

"Hmm." His hand tightens on my hip but he doesn't make a move to zip me up.

"You're still not zipping me." I'm teasing him. The hunger in his eyes makes my stomach flip.

"I know." My giggles fill the bathroom.

"Baby, that's what I called you in here for."

"I know." Uh oh, I think I broke him.

"So are you going to help me?"

"Totally." Still doesn't move.

Sighing, I move away from him and walk to the bedroom door. I open it a crack, "Sasha, Alyssa! Can one of you zip me?" Tanner makes a noise behind me but again, doesn't move.

Alyssa appears in the doorway and starts laughing at the look on my boyfriend's face. He's staring dumbfounded at my ass, gaze unwavering. "Turn around Evie." I do as she says and watch the disappointment settle on his face when his favorite view is taken away from him.

I feel the zipper sliding up my back, the cool metal a stark contrast to the heat of my skin. Now that I'm facing him, I can see Tanner's eyes freely roam my body, heating my flushed skin as he goes.

It's been far too long, and we both know it.

His sage eyes slowly drag up my body before finding mine. The quirk of his lips causes butterflies to take flight in my tummy. "There you go." Alyssa pats my butt as she steps away and whistles. "Damn girl, you look good. Doesn't she Tanner?"

"Yeah." The word is a breathy whisper that floats through the air and goes straight to the ego Tanner instilled in me. "Magnificent."

Alyssa retreats down the hall with a laugh. A moment later, Sasha's boisterous laughter joins hers.

"I think they're making fun of us." My lips turn up in the sides, creating a small smile.

"Definitely."

"What do you want to do about it?"

"Absolutely nothing." My smile grows as his does.

I'm tempted to say fuck the date and just crawl into bed, dragging him with me. But I have spent *way* too long on my makeup, and getting into this dress is no easy feat. With one last lingering glance, I brush past him so I can finally do my hair.

I slept with braids in last night so it's all wavy, but I want it to be straight. My straightener is already plugged in and heated up. I brush through my hair, sectioning it off into manageable sections.

I'm almost done with the first section when I see Tanner in

the mirror, floating around the doorway, watching me. He has a soft boyish smile on his face, he looks happy.

It takes longer than it should, but I did decide to put on a show. Queuing up songs and dancing to them all the while glancing at my boyfriend who was entranced by me.

By the time we're leaving the house it's close to eight but thankfully we don't have reservations, or that's what Tanner tells me.

He opens the passenger door to his truck for me, helping me in by grabbing my waist and effortlessly lifting me to his seat. His hands linger longer than necessary but neither of us point that out, content to just sit here touching each other.

When my stomach growls, he releases me and slides into the driver seat. He takes me to the steakhouse we went to after the team won the frozen four three years ago, the same night I met Jensen.

He's become a huge part of my life. Tanner doesn't know this but once a month I make the drive to his small town to have dinner with him. We've become really close, so much so it finally feels like I have a father again. I accidentally called him dad last time. When I apologized, he pulled me into his arms and squeezed me so tight I felt like I might pop. Safe to say he likes my new name for him.

When we walk in, the staff goes crazy. Sometimes I forget how famous Tanner is, especially here. He grew up an hour away, played for the local college and went pro only four hours away. This town loves him.

We get sat in a private booth in the far corner. I kind of feel like we're being hidden away, well, not both of us, just me. I've been invisible since we walked in, not just to the staff, but to

Tanner as well. His attention has been pulled in every direction except mine.

I feel selfish for even thinking that, but I can't help how I feel. Tanner wanted to take me out and now it's like I don't even exist.

The whole dinner is like this, nobody paying me any mind, only looking at Tanner. I don't order, Tanner does that for me. I don't speak, the staff take turns coming over to talk to him. I don't hardly eat; Tanner finishes my plate. I don't want to complain but this date sucked.

I don't get my boyfriend's attention, the boyfriend I haven't seen in months. I didn't even get the meal I wanted. I didn't get a chance to speak so there was no way Tanner knew what I wanted, he just ordered what he *thought* I wanted.

He didn't even notice when I pulled my phone out and started texting in the group chat, I have with the girls. I haven't taken my attention off my phone in almost thirty minutes, and he hasn't noticed. I doubt he would even notice if I were to get up and walk out. I'm tempted, oh so tempted.

The truck keys sit on the table in between up, right there. I could easily grab them and wait in the truck. I try to push the thought to the back of my head. My phone dings with more messages from the girls.

> **Sasha: Any change?**
> **Me: Nope**
> **Alyssa: I'm out front**
> **Me: What?**
> **Mona: Alyssa and I are here to pick you up**
> **Natalia: I told them they should**
> **Natalia: If he's not paying you attention**

Natalia: At least let us
Sasha: You said it feels like he wouldn't even notice if you were to leave
Sasha: So leave
Sasha: See if your right
Me: I'm on my way

I glance up at Tanner, hoping he would just look at me, but he doesn't. He's too busy talking to the manager. I mumble something about going to the bathroom, no acknowledgment. I grab my clutch and slip out of the booth.

I glance back at our little corner only to see Tanner is still enraptured by the manager and hasn't even noticed my absence. A pang hits me in my chest. Anger, sadness, loneliness. It was supposed to get better now that his season is over and I'm days away from graduating.

I guess that was wishful thinking.

I climb into Alyssa's small car, and she drives away. The car is silent, my friends waiting for me to say something, but I don't know what to say. Just two hours ago I was the center of my boyfriend's universe. Now I'm not.

I notice Alyssa isn't taking me home, but I don't say anything. We pass by so many buildings and streets I lose track of where we are until they all fade away. Farmland zooms by as we drive down quaint country roads.

Natalia and her mom are waiting outside when we pull into their driveway.

Nate crushes me in a hug the moment I'm out of the backseat. "Are you okay?" I open my mouth just to close it, not really having an answer for that.

"Of course she's not. Do you see her?" Nate's mom pulls me inside and into the kitchen where a cup of hot cocoa waits for me. "Here, have some happiness." I want to smile; I really do but I can't muster up the strength to. She's always called hot chocolate a cup of happiness, I love that she does.

I sip on the warm liquid while my friends scramble around me, talking in hushed voices. Nate's dad, Greg, takes the stool beside me. He doesn't say anything, just offering his comfort.

Someone goes upstairs, the creek of the wood a dead giveaway. A few minutes later, they come back down.

"Here, you can borrow some of my pajamas. There's makeup remover out on the bathroom sink and the spare bedroom is made up in case you want to stay." I look up at Nate and offer her a wobbly smile.

"Thanks."

The front door swings open and Sasha rushes in. She scans the room until her eyes land on me. She's at my side in an instant, her arms creating a barrier around me. "You're going to be okay. I promise. And if you aren't, I'll kick Tanner's ass." She stiffens around me, her head lifting to look at Natalia's parents. "Sorry, forgot you were here."

Gloria, Nate's mom, shrugs her off. "We'll let it slide this time. Just don't make it a habit."

"I won't."

Alyssa rounds the island, joining in on our hug. "Are you feeling any better?"

I want to say yes but I can't, not when that's blaring at me. "It's been an hour."

"It has." She mumbles into my hair.

"And my phone doesn't have a single notification from him."

My fear continues to be fed when another hour passes and still nothing from him.

I've taken over the spare room, Alyssa staying in here with me tonight. Sasha is staying too, though she'll be in Nate's room. Mona fell asleep on the couch half an hour ago so I guess she's staying too.

This is not how I imagined this night going.

I should have acted on the urge to climb into bed and pull him with me. If I had, none of this would have happened.

I shake the thought out of my head. No. This isn't my fault. It's not fully Tanner's either, but it's hard not to feel like it is. Yes, all of those people kept coming over to talk to him. But he could have told them he was on a date. He could have been polite and answered their questions without starting a conversation with every single one of them. He could have paid me even a little bit of attention.

32

Evie

The morning light assaults my eyelids, begging me to open them. My swollen eyes slowly blink open, blinking away the sleepies that have made their home along my water lines.

Alyssa lays in the spot beside me, breathing calm and even. She looks peaceful. For a moment I forget where I am and why I'm here, but the buzzing of my phone is a stark reminder.

I pat around the mattress until I locate the buzzing device and immediately wish I hadn't. Tanner's face takes up my screen with his incoming call. I stare blankly at him until he disappears. Before the screen turns off, I see the flood of messages he left me from last night to this morning.

I don't have the energy to read them yet but I don't want to stay in bed. Gingerly, I slide out from under the warm blankets, careful not to wake Alyssa.

Gloria is in the kitchen when I descend the stairs. Her smile is sweet when she sees me, sliding some bacon across the island while the smell of cooking eggs fills the air.

"Thank you." I can't tell if she didn't hear me, or she chooses not to acknowledge how weak I sound. Either way, I can't bring myself to care.

"Eggs are almost done dearie." She sounds especially chipper this morning, but she's always happy when there's company. It doesn't matter what brought all of us to congregate here last night, she's just happy to have us.

My phone lights up again, another incoming call from Tanner. I hesitate to answer. I know my feelings are valid, but I can't help but wonder if I over reacted.

Yeah, we don't see each other often so our time together is precious, but also, we don't see each other often. He's not used to having to divide his attention. I'm hurt, I shouldn't have to beg for my boyfriend's attention. So, I let the call go to voicemail like all the rest.

"It's alright to feel how you do." I look up at Gloria who's watching me intently. "What he did was not okay, but your relationship straddles a thin line. Yeah, you got together before he became famous, but that's not the case anymore. This situation will come up anytime you leave the house. You have to talk about this and come up with a solution. But it is alright to need some time to wrap your head around what happened."

I return her soft smile, taking a bite of the crispy maple bacon. "Thank you. We usually have really good communication but when I can't get his attention to communicate what I feel, what should I have done? Stayed and hoped he would give me a moment of his time?"

"I don't know dearie. Greg and I have had our fair share of issues, but I never had to fight the public for his attention. I don't think there was a right or wrong thing to do. In the moment, the option you thought was the best was to leave, to get some space between you two. And that's okay. You're thinking more clearly this morning, so I would say you made the right decision." She turns back to the stove to stir the eggs.

Greg ambles in from their shared bedroom down the hall. He once again takes the seat next to me, offering comfort with his presence. He has never been very talkative, more the strong and silent type. But he never really needed words. *The best advice is the one you come up with on your own.* He told me that last year after a headline popped up with an accusation of Tanner cheating. It wasn't true but it hit me hard.

We eat in silence, letting the quiet hum of the morning soothe my racing mind. Tanner has called three more times and on the fourth, Greg grunts and answers. I can vaguely hear Tanner's voice come through the receiver, but I can't make out what he's saying.

"Sorry buddy, this isn't your girl. This is Greg, Natalia's father." Greg's deep timber fills the room earning me a quizzical glance from Gloria. "I'm only going to say this once, you fucked up." Gloria scowls, "sorry honey," she turns, giving her back to her husband. "You hurt our Evie and that's not alright. She needs some time to come to terms with what happened. To come to terms with knowing she fought for your attention and failed. She'll contact you when she's ready." He abruptly hangs up and replaces my phone in the space between us.

"I didn't exactly fight for his attention."

"Did you try to talk to him? Attempt to get his attention on multiple occasions?" Gloria's blue eyes pierce mine.

"Yes?"

"Then you fought for his attention."

A long groan draws my attention to the living room couch where Mona slowly sits up. "What time is it?" Her voice is groggy from sleep. Her ocean eyes are hazy as she looks around, confusion scrunching her pretty face.

"Seven-thirty." Gloria chips cheerily.

Another groan and Mona flops back down onto the couch. "Too early."

"You can go upstairs and cuddle up to Alyssa. She's a bed hog but it's a private room that has blackout curtains and, well, a bed." Without another word, she's up off the couch and is walking up the stairs.

Eggs are placed in front of me and while I eat, I check the messages Tanner sent me.

> **TANNER: Are you ok?**
> **TANNER: You've been in the bathroom awhile**
> **TANNER: Baby?**
> **TANNER: The waitress just said you aren't in the bathroom**
> **TANNER: Where are you?**
> **TANNER: Are you ok?**

TANNER: Baby?
TANNER: Please answer me
TANNER: I'm worried about you
TANNER: Fuck
TANNER: I'm so sorry
TANNER: I just saw the time
TANNER: I didn't mean for this to be how the night went
TANNER: I guess you're asleep
TANNER: I'm sorry
TANNER: Please talk to me
TANNER: Baby?
TANNER: I know you normally get up at this time
TANNER: Are you still asleep?
TANNER: I'm sorry
TANNER: I should have told them I was on a date
TANNER: I should have shooed them away
TANNER: Politely that is
TANNER: If I wasn't kind you would have been upset
TANNER: Please answer my calls
TANNER: I need to hear your voice
TANNER: I'm sorry

The most recent one was sent five minutes ago after Greg hung up on him. I don't doubt he's sorry. I know he is; he always is after we fight. The same as I'm always sorry. There's no doubt in either of our minds whether the other person means what they say, for that, I'm thankful.

A name stares out at me. We haven't talked in a while, but he gives the best advice. Without a thought to what time it is in

Arizona, I call Collins.

"Evie?"

"Hey Collins. Did I wake you?"

"Yeah, it's four am right now."

I cringe. "Sorry, I forgot we're on different times. I can call back later."

"Nah, my alarm goes off in half an hour anyways. What's up?"

I recap everything that's happened in the last twelve hours, letting the words hang between us as he processes the situation.

"Fucking idiot. He told me a few days ago he was worried this might happen. I've seen it firsthand how he struggles to tell people to fuck off. It's a real problem."

"Oh." The words sink in. So, I'm not the only one that experiences this. I can't decide if that makes me feel better or not.

"Are you ok? I can chew him a new one if you want me to." I shake my head, forgetting briefly that he can't see me.

"No, no, don't do that. I know it was a mistake."

"Mistake might not be the word I use but yeah, it was. One he's going to beat himself up over. That man loves you so much it's crazy. Trust me, every time you guys get into a fight our group chat blows up. He freaks out. I've spent more hours than I wish to count telling him you'll forgive him, that it was a stupid argument." I smile despite the conversation. Sean told me the same thing the other day.

"I'm not home so you'll probably hear about this from him later."

Collins chuckles knowingly. "So, I get to lay into him anyways. My favorite hobby these days."

A smile overtakes my face, I can't stop it from spreading.

"We don't fight that often."

"Nah, you guys don't. But that doesn't mean he doesn't talk to me for advice. The sheer number of stupid things that come out of his mouth is shocking. I had to convince him to resign for two more years with Ohio last year. He wanted to resign in West Virginia. It would have paid less, and he wouldn't be any closer."

I didn't realize he wanted to move back here. But Collins is right, there isn't much change in the distance between us.

The conversation shifts and we talk until the girls all wake up and come downstairs. Collins convinces me to go home sometime today and talk this through. I know it needs to be done, I had planned on going home soon, I just didn't know if it would be tonight.

I've gotten a few more texts from Tanner by the time we hang up, all of them along the lines of 'I'm sorry'.

Sasha thinks I should stay a while longer but she's petty.

Hours later, after lunch, I gather my clothes from last night off the bathroom floor where I dropped them in my rush to get the dress off. My clutch sits on the counter next to the makeup remover.

Natalia hangs by the door, just watching. She's offered to have me stay another night, but I turned her down.

Tanner and I need to talk, and I refuse to push it off. We've always tried our best to have a healthy relationship and I'm not about to let miscommunication ruin everything we've worked so hard for.

"I'll wash your clothes and return them later."

"I know you will."

"Thank you for having me."

"Any time. You know that. My parents love you." She

mumbles under her breath about them possibly loving me more than her but we both know that's not the case.

Alyssa waits outside in her car for me. Sasha is already on her way back home. She said she needed to talk to Tanner before I get there, quite frankly, I'm terrified of what I might come home to.

"Ready?" I climb into the passenger seat.

"Yeah."

With one final wave to the Jones's and Mona, we pull out of the driveway and start the longish drive home.

33

Tanner

The front door creaks open, my heart thunders with the thought that Evie came home. Before I can move to go down the stairs, Sasha's voice screams out my name as she comes closer.

Her footsteps thud on the stairs as she climbs them. She enters my room, now Evie's.

"We need to talk." She's seething and I don't blame her. I've already had my ass handed to my, first by Collins, then Sean, then Dillan, and then Oli. I don't talk to the guys very much anymore, living in different states, working different jobs, and all that. But every time I need advice, they're my go to group.

I didn't mean for this to happen.

I had just meant to answer their questions politely and move on with our date. But every time one person left, another took their spot. I heard Evie say she was going to the bathroom but when she didn't come back, I started to worry.

My annoyance spiked when our original waitress came up and I asked her to check on my girlfriend in the bathroom. This woman had the gall to look confused and told me I didn't come in here with someone else. No one I talked to remembered my girlfriend. The girl I love, my forever, walked out on me because of these people. I know I'm partly to blame, not being able to divide my attention. But I had planned to answer their questions and sign autographs. Once I was done, my undivided attention would go to the most beautiful woman in the building.

It took ten minutes and seven photos of Evie later to convince the waitress to check on her in the bathroom. When she returned empty handed, for a brief moment I thought she didn't even check. I sent text after text off to her with no response, that is until I noticed the time. We got here at eight, it was now nearing midnight. I hadn't noticed the restaurant emptying out around me.

A sick feeling has settled in my stomach since then. Evie could have been gone for hours and I didn't know.

I've tried texting and calling to no avail. I was ecstatic when she finally answered, until it wasn't her on the other line. I understand why she wouldn't want to talk to me, why she might need some time. But I hope she doesn't take too much. Selfishly, I want her in my- her- bed tonight. But more so, I need to talk to her, explain what happened.

I tell all of this to Sasha. I watch as her eyes soften with every word that comes out of my mouth.

She rests a hand on my shoulder, squeezing softly. "She's not mad Tanner."

"She's not?" Surprise and hope fill me all the way up.

"No. Is she hurt? Yes. But she's not mad. You're not the only one who talks to Collins ya know" It's moments like this that I'm eternally grateful my friends get along so well with my girlfriend.

Collins had warned me this might happen, and like the idiot I am I didn't listen. I put Evelyn through so much on a daily basis. If I make it in the headlines, she does too. A woman finds her way into my hotel room, I call her first thing, if she doesn't answer I leave a voicemail. So, when she wakes up and inevitably sees the headlines about my potential 'cheating', she knows what really happened.

My head falls between my shoulders, shame eating away at my insides. "I'm an idiot. I was warned about this, ya know? Collins told me to make sure this exact situation didn't happen. And did I listen to him? Of fucking course not! I thought I would be able to handle the situation that was bound to come."

"Tanner?" My eyes slowly lift to meet hers. "Evie doesn't blame you for the actions of others. She understands this wasn't entirely your fault. She knows you didn't want this to happen. Could you have handled it better? Perhaps. She expected something to happen along these lines, she always does. She was just hoping it wouldn't happen the night you got into town."

"I'm one lucky bastard, aren't I?"

"Yes you are Tanner Shaw. You most certainly are." She leaves me alone with my thoughts. I still don't know when Evie is coming home but I know better than to spam call and text her again. Like Greg said, when she's ready to talk, she'll talk. God! I run my hands down my face in frustration, a groan rumbling my chest. I royally fucked up.

I don't know how long I sit there, wallowing in my own self-pity. But when a tender hand lands on my shoulder and the sweet scent of vanilla lavender wafts through the air, I know who's beside me.

My glossy green eyes connect with her warm honey ones, nothing but love shining there. Love I'm not sure I deserve.

"You came home." My voice cracks as a single salty tear slides over my cheek. She wipes the watery droplet away with her thumb, a soft and patient smile on her face.

"Of course, baby. There's nowhere I'd rather be." The floodgates open but I don't bother trying to hide the tears cascading down my face, too fast for my beautiful girlfriend to wipe away. "Don't cry. I'm not going anywhere." She keeps her voice gentle, like she's soothing an injured animal.

I try to speak but a hiccup takes my words from me.

"Shhh, shhh. You don't have to speak, I know. I know, baby." She moves my arms so she can squeeze between them and take a seat on my lap. Her arms come around and wrap my head in them, cradling me as I cry into her.

She continues to soothe me until the tears stop and I can finally speak again. "I'm sorry." It's a quiet whisper but loud in the otherwise silent room.

"I know."

"I thought they would leave at some point, leave us alone. But when you left and I had asked our waitress to check on you, I realized how wrong I was. She tried to tell me I came alone, that there was no one to go check on. None of them remembered seeing you. I was so pissed that it took so long to convince her just to check. They had to go over the cameras before they believed that I came with someone. And when they realized that I did, they didn't apologize or even seem remorseful that they completely overlooked you. I was so mad and scared because you were gone, out of my reach."

"I will never be out of your reach; I was just upset. Last night was supposed to be a romantic dinner and that's not what happened. I know you were trying to be polite but there's a line that needs to be drawn. I will never tell you not to interact with fans, but you can't only talk to them, at least not when I'm there. Hockey is your career, your first love, but I fit into your life as well. Hockey takes most of your time, I would like the remaining." I nod into her neck, my tears dampening her skin.

"I'm so sorry."

"I know you are baby. That's why I'm not mad. I know you didn't do it on purpose. We just have to work to make sure it doesn't happen again." She pulls back to press a kiss to my forehead.

"I love you." She smiles against my hair as my muffled words wash over her, her smile warming me to the bone.

"I love you too." We sat there, cuddled together for a while longer. The front door slamming closed breaks our bubble and we reluctantly untangle from each other. "I'm going to take a bath." I don't move from my spot on the bed as she leaves me to my thoughts.

I hear the bath start and eventually turn off but I still remain rooted to the edge of the bed. She forgave me, yes, but I still feel awful. I took my girlfriend out for a nice dinner to celebrate and ignored her the entire time. On purpose or not, it was a shity thing to do.

I scrub my hand over my face with a defeated groan. I'm an asshole.

A knock on the door brings me out of my self-loathing. On the other side is Mona, I've met her a few times but were not close.

She holds up a brown paper bag with a grease stain on the bottom. "I brought Evie some food, and I guess you as well. Is she here?"

I lean against the doorway, blocking her from entering. "Yeah, she's taking a bath. I can give it to her." I hold out my hand to take the bag, but she hesitates.

"Oh, well, tell her we're going to watch a movie if she wants to join later." She sets the bag in my outstretched hands and disappears down the stairs.

The door closes behind me as I walk into the bathroom where Evie is the definition of relaxed, bubbles up to her throat, hair in a messy bun. She's beautiful.

"Mona brought you food." Her lips quirk up on the sides.

"I know, I heard." I set the food on the counter behind me.

"Are you going to join them for the movie?"

"No, I think we need some time together. I figured we could watch that new show Sean was blowing the group chat up about." Her eyes remain closed, basically speaking to the air.

I hum, that does sound nice. "Just you and me?"

"Just the two of us."

I smile as I push off the counter where I was leaning. "Should I go get it queued up then?" Finally, she turns those brown eyes to me.

"Yeah, you can take the food with you, we'll split it. I'll be out in a minute." I do as she says and by the time I have the show up and ready to watch, the tub is draining, and Evie is approaching the bed in a silk pajama set that should be illegal. "Ready?"

She crawls under the covers and cuddles up next to me. "Yeah." I press play and the opening credits roll.

34

Evie

I'm stressed. I graduate tomorrow and I'm freaking out. Tanner watches from the kitchen island while I pace a hole into the ground. I've been talking myself in and out of a pit for the last hour. I don't know if I'm ready for the next chapter of my life but it's here now and it's not going anywhere.

Next week I move into Tanner's apartment permanently, Mona is moving to Seattle, Natalia is staying here for the summer than she's going to Chicago, Sasha is moving to New York, and Alyssa is moving to Arizona where Oli lives. They've been dating since she said yes to go out with him three years ago.

Everyone is going their separate ways, and it terrifies me. I finally have a chosen family and now we're going to be thousands of miles away from each other.

"We can always fly out to visit them during my off season. Or when I have a game in one of their cities you can fly out and spend the day with them. You can make it work, baby. I mean, Oli, Dillan, Sean, Collins and I are still friends, and we talk pretty regularly." Tanner pipes up from the island with the same advice from ten minutes ago.

"I know but that doesn't make it any less scary." I turn to face him; our eyes lock and my panic subsides slightly. I approach him, stepping between his open legs. "I love you and I'm super excited to see where life takes us but that doesn't change the unknowns."

He tucks a strand of hair behind my ear, a soft kiss touched my temple. "Well, I'll be right here through all of those unknowns. Plus, you still have another week with everyone." I nod. I do, everyone will be together for one more week. "I told you the guys are flying in to attend your graduation, right?"

I jerk back and stare at him with wide eyes. "No! You never mentioned anything about that! They're really coming?"

"Yeah, they land tomorrow morning, a few hours before the ceremony. Unfortunately, you won't be able to see them until after, but they'll be there, right next to me and your mom."

My heart warms at the idea that everyone will be there. I'll be able to see them again. It's been almost two years since we were all in the same place. "You're picking my mom up, right?"

Tanner laughs, we've had this conversation already, but I need another confirmation. "Yes, princess. I'm picking them all up. Now come on," he picks me up like I weigh nothing. "I think you need a nap; you stayed up far too late last night watching tv."

A yawn interrupts my next sentence. I hate when he's right. I'm probably just overthinking everything because my brain is tired. "But the show was so good." Tanner laughs again as he carries me up to the room. "Don't tell Sean I said that it'll give him too big of a head."

"Ok, princess. I won't." He pulls the covers back for me to slide under. I pause when I notice him not following.

"Are you not joining me?"

He shakes his head. "Not this time, I'm going to get started on some dinner." At my questioning look he elaborates. "You mentioned a handful of times last night that your mother's special birthday meal sounded amazing and that you were craving it. I got permission to break tradition because of what tomorrow is, and she sent me the recipe. Though I didn't realize it took almost three hours to make. So, I'm going to get started on it while you take a much-needed nap." He leaves after giving me a kiss.

I watch him until he closes the door. I don't remember asking for that meal. It doesn't have a name since mom never named it, it's her special recipe.

I smile as I snuggle further into the sheets. It's the big things that make you fall in love, it's the little ones that keep you in love.

Tanner

Three hours and one complicated recipe later, Evie's walking down the stairs, stifling a yawn.

"Smells amazing." Her sleepy voice caresses my ear.

"Let's hope is tastes as good as it smells." Her arms wrap around my waste from behind while I stir the pasta for what should be the final time. "Did you sleep well?"

Her head moves up and down on my back as she nods. "Still sleepy though. It would have been even better if you were there for me to cling to like a koala."

My chest vibrates with my laugh. "Good thing, staring next week our sleepovers will be full time."

I feel something push against my arm so I raise it allowing Evie's head to poke through. "You know what's even better?"

I raise my eyebrow in response, waiting for her to fill me in. "You're here to help me pack and do all the heavy lifting." My earlier chuckle grows into a full-blown laugh. Jonny, the new transfer on the team made a similar comment at practice the other day.

I try to school my features, pretending to gasp. I place the hand holding the spoon to my chest, "Is that all I am to you? Some nice looking muscles?" Evie giggles again and I pray that she won't stop. I could listen to her laugh for the rest of my life and never tire of it.

"Of course not," she forces out through her giggles, "you also have an amazing-"

A throat clearing behind us catches our attention. I look over my shoulder to where Sasha stands with a bag so full her work clothes are spilling out. "Voice, right? That's what you were going to say. Right Evie?" The two girls stare at each other for an extended moment.

A mischievous smile breaks free across Evie's face, a small glint in her eyes. "Dick, I was going to say dick."

Sasha lets out a long sigh but doesn't seem even the least bit surprised. "Some days I wish you were still the same girl I met nearly four years ago. That girl would have never uttered that sentence." She turns her attention on me. "I blame you." She points at me the best she can with her full bag in one hand and a dress in the other. "You corrupted her."

I just shrug. "Yeah, it's great, isn't it?" Sasha groans, mummering something about me being the dick Evie seems to think is so amazing and then stomps away.

I look down at the girl who's still stuck to my side, she's already looking at me when our eyes meet. "She may be a little annoyed with my newfound lack of filter."

"She's annoyed by that? Wasn't she the one, during your sophomore year, trying to get you to loosen said filter?" Evie detaches herself from me, using the counter to lean on.

"Yeah. It's not like she hates it, it's more of a playful kind of annoyance." I shake my head, a laugh bubbling in my chest. Women, I will never understand them, but that's part of the fun."

A timer beats on the oven, so I pull out the cookies I tried to bake at the same time. They look sad. There's no way around it, they look really sad.

As they cool, I assemble the rest of the meal and plate it for Evie to try. She takes a tentative bite, chewing slowly. She tries to hide it but a grimace takes over her expression for a split second.

"That bad huh?"

She sets down her fork. "No, it's really good." I sigh as I take her fork and try it for myself. It tastes like somethings rotten and burnt. There's also a tangy taste like sour cream but there's nothing in here that should taste like that. I defiantly messed up somewhere.

Without hesitation, I grab a napkin and spit it out. I applaud Evie for swallowing an entire bite, I just hope it doesn't make her sick. "This is the worst thing I have ever tasted." Tentatively, she nods her agreement.

"I didn't want to hurt your feelings; you spent hours on this." She slowly slides the plate off to the side, almost like she doesn't want to touch it.

"Thank you, Princess, but if you don't like it just tell me. I'm a big boy, I can handle it." Another one of those mischievous smiles graces her face and I know what she's going to say before she says it.

"You are definitely a big boy." She pats my shoulder as she reaches for her phone. "So, what sounds good for dinner?"

35

Evie

The morning went by in a blur of color, makeup, and anxiety. I woke up at three a.m. unable to fall back asleep. I tried taking a bath, didn't help, a hot cup of milk didn't help, reading a book in dim lighting also didn't help.

Tanner was able to sleep until five when my antics woke him up. He offered sex as a way to sleep better, I declined. It was far too early to even think about getting naked with him. Though under different circumstances, I wouldn't have hesitated. I love getting Tanner naked.

Needing something to do to keep my mind occupied, I started packing. I need to get most of it done by Monday so Tanner can take my things with him to his, now our, apartment. The plan was to pack as much as we can and stuff it into his truck, which should be most of my belongings. Whatever doesn't fit would fit into my jeep. All of the big-ticket items like my bed frame and dresser will be donated since I helped him decorate when he moved into this apartment. There isn't much room for extra furniture, so I won't be taking them.

At eight Nate and Mona arrived and the five of us kicked Tanner out of the room so we could get ready. It's a little past noon now, I'm on my fourth cup of coffee and the jitters have set in. Graduation starts at three, we have to be at the venue at two and the planes carrying my friends and family won't land for another hour.

Moms plane lands first at one. Sean and Oli are on the same plane that's supposed to lands at one fifteen. While Dillan and Collins plane is set to land closer to one forty-five. The airport is only twenty minutes from the venue so as long as the planes land around the scheduled time, they should be on time.

There's one hundred and sixty of us graduating today so it should go by relatively quickly. I think they estimated two to three hours.

Mona comes to stand behind me, both of us looking in my mirror. "You okay?" Her hands run my arms where goose bumps have popped up.

My eyes take in my appearance, long perfectly curled hair with a small bun at the crown of my head that took an hour and a half. Peachy eyeshadow with a glittery white on my eyelids that makes my brown eyes pop. Fake eyelashes that Nate helped me put on. A light blush to bring color back into my face. Bright red lipstick that matches the strawberries in my dress. Dimond encrusted gold earrings dangle from my ears, a gift from Tanner for Christmas last year. A matching necklace sits delicately on my pale skin. A pure gold bracelet is on my right wrist, a gift for our one-year anniversary. My shoes sit in front of the mirror, stiletto heels about four inches, black with fake gems that wrap around my legs in thin straps.

I look the part of someone who's ready to take the next step. But I don't feel like it.

"I don't know Mona." I sigh as I fiddle with my bracelet. "These last four year went nothing like how I wanted them to. It's just hard to look back and realize how little control I truly had over different outcomes." I turn my head to face her head on.

"Do you regret how things turned out?"

I shake my head as I look at my friends, new and old. "No, I don't know how I know but I can tell I'm exactly where I'm meant to be. With whom I'm meant to be with. I wouldn't go back and change anything. I think that's the hardest thing to come to terms with. I went into my freshman year swearing off any and all distractions only to come face to face with my biggest one on the first night. I tried to stay away but the longer I tried, the harder it became. Rumors spread about how Tanner no longer went to parties. He stopped being seen hanging out with random girls while they hung all over him. He was heard talking about this girl that he couldn't take his eyes off of. Then there was him. His insistence, never giving up no matter what I said.

"If I told him to go away, he would. But he'd be back a few days later trying again. He changed his whole lifestyle just to guarantee I wouldn't immediately write him off. Anytime I saw a girl hanging off of him he was always trying to get them to leave him alone. From day one he knew what he wanted, and he didn't stop until he had that, had me. I've never been so happy, felt so loved. That man has taken my world and turned it on its head, and I couldn't care less.

"I gave him a chance and within days I forgot that I wanted to keep him at arm's length. I forgot that school was supposed to be the only thing I cared about. I gave myself to him so fast that it gave me whiplash, and yet, I can't bring myself to regret a damn thing. I wouldn't be who I am without him, I wouldn't have the friends I have if he hadn't taught me to trust people. So no, I don't regret anything, I wouldn't go back and change anything, and even though I'm scared of what lies ahead of us, I know I'll be okay as long as he's by my side."

At some point all of my friends had stopped what they were doing and were now watching me, Alyssa was fighting back tears while Sasha had the biggest smile on her face. Natalia eyes had softened and she watching me with love in her eyes. And I returned every look with one of my own.

"I love you guys."

We all awkwardly shuffle together for a group huge. I stand off to the side while they all go back to getting ready. Mona leaves to go put her dress on while Nate applies her mauve lipstick.

It's surreal knowing that in a week none of us will be where we are right now. We'll be scattered across the US.

I've never been very far from Alyssa, where I went, she went and where she went I went. We've been inseparable since we were kids and now, she'll be close to two thousand miles away.

My phone buzzes in my hand, a text from Tanner glowing bright.

> My love: I believe in you
> My love: You deserve everything that's coming to you
> My love: I can't wait to wake up to your beautiful face every morning for the rest of my life
> My love: This is just one more step on the way to forever
> My love: I will always be by your side no matter what
> My love: You're stuck with me now
> My love: No turning back

I smile as the texts flood in. He always seems to know the right thing to say to calm me down.

> Me: I wouldn't even if I could
> Me: There's no one I'd rather be with
> Me: There's no one out there that completes me like you do
> Me: You're my today, tomorrow, and forever
> Me: Though, even if you weren't, I'm sure you'd find a way to become it

The typing bubbles appears and disappears a few time before he finally sends his message.

> My love: Fuck yeah
> My love: I would literally kill any man who tries to take you from me

> **My love: No one else gets to hear your little noises when you get close**
> **My love: No one gets to see you in those special moments reserved for just you and I**
> **Me: Okay my caveman**
> **Me: No one for me but you**
> **My love: No one for me but you**

"Oh, for heaven's sake!" I look up to see Natalia watching me. "You saw him literally forty minutes ago before he left for the airport."

Alyssa laughs from her spot in front of the mirror. "What did you expect. Evie is madly in love with the man."

"Oh, and you're not?" Nate challenges with raised brows.

"I have no idea what you're talking about." Alyssa tries and fails to hide the blush slowly creeping up her face.

"Girl, Evie isn't the only one here with a super-hot, super famous boyfriend. Oli has quite a fan base in Arizona. You're going to have to fight your way through hordes of other girls just to get to him." Natalia crosses her arms over her chest, leaning on the countertop with her hip.

"Oh, I know. But he also knows that that won't happen. If I have to fight for his attention, It's over. I'm not going to battle with other women to get *my* boyfriends attention." Alyssa caps the mascara and sets it in her makeup bag. "What about you?"

"What about me?" Natalia asks.

"What happened to that guy you were talking to? The one in Chicago?"

Sasha comes walking in, completely ignoring the other two in here in favor of me. "Here." She hands me a strawberry gem encrusted clip. "I found this in my hair stuff and wanted you to have it. One it will match your dress, and two I want you to have something of mine, so you know no matter the distance that my separate us, I'll always be with you."

Tears threaten to fall as I take the clip from her hand. "Thank you." My voice is a broken whisper and I stare at the beautiful clip. "Will you help me put it up?"

I turn around and allow Sasha to slip the clip into my small bun. "There, perfect." Her arms wrap around me from behind as she squeezes me. "I know you're scared, but you have no reason to be. No amount of distance could ever keep the five of us apart. If you ever need me, call me and I'll be on the next flight to you."

This time I can't stop the tear that snakes down my face. A knot in my throat stops me from speaking but judging by her expression, I don't need to. She knows just what I want to say.

We stay like that for a few minutes before we all migrate to the kitchen to grab something to eat before we have to leave.

I grab my salad from the fridge and sit down at the dining table that rarely gets used. The others slowly take their seats as we all eat and bullshit.

"Oh, what about the time that Nate wanted to get her belly button pierced."

Nate groans into her hands. "Don't remind me of that day! It was awful."

We all laugh as Mona pipes up. "The lady was about to put the needle through when you practically flew from the seat and ran out of the store." That was the day that I got my first tattoo. A hand drawn heart just behind my left ear. The heart my mom always put on the bottom of every letter she sent me.

"I thought I could get over my fear of needles, but I just

couldn't."

Sasha laughs and Nate pins her with a stare. "What about the time you went on that date with the guy who you *swore* was the 'perfect' man and he turned out to have an obsession with taxidermy."

Sasha shivers, her smile fading. "That was so creepy. When he asked me to go to his place, I thought it was for sex then he opens his door and shows me every animal he's ever taxidermied. Then proceeded to tell me what their names were and their 'back story'. Worst date ever."

She had texted an SOS with her location and Nate went to pick her up. Just listening to the full date story is creepy, I can't imagine actually having to live through it.

"Or that time that a super attractive guy asked Mona out and you froze. It took you so long to answer I thought you weren't going to. Then you pointed to Evie and said she was your girlfriend."

Mona's face pinkened beneath her makeup. "I panicked."

"That guy didn't believe you either. After you left, he looked at Evie and asked if she was Tanner Shaw's girlfriend. Apparently, he's a big fan."

"Oh god, I didn't know that." Mona hides her face in her hands as her shoulders shake with her laughter.

That guy was so confused. I don't blame him, there was a tabloids article about mine and Tanner's relationship a week prior.

"How about when Oli got called up in the draft to play for Texas. Alyssa, you cried for three hours, and no one knew if you were happy, sad, or mad. Oli was terrified."

Alyssa laughs while shaking her head. "It's his fault for

telling me when I was in the middle of my period. Everyone knows I get emotional during that time of the month. He had it coming for him for forgetting to get me the chocolates he promised me earlier that month."

Tanner was panicking right along with Oli. Neither guy could figure out what was going through her mind. It was endearing. Should it have been, probably not. But seeing him so concerned for my friend did something to me.

"Evie's not immune either. I'm still traumatized from the time I saw your collection of BDSM toys."

I give Alyssa a pointed look. "Well, if you hadn't been snooping for your birthday gift you would have never found them. That sounds like a you problem to me." I shrug it off despite how embarrassing the whole interaction had been at the time.

Five timers go off at the same time and the table quiets. One-thirty, time to leave. We clear the table and put our shoes on. Mona and Natalia drove separately, and plan to drive to the venue by themselves as well, that way they can go home right after. Alyssa is driving herself so she and Oli can drive together on the way back. Sasha and I are carpooling so we can split the load into two after the ceremony.

We wait for everyone to leave before we pull out and follow behind.

I look out the window and take a deep breath. In a few hours I'll be a college graduate and despite my nerves, I'm excited.

36

Tanner

The plane Heaven, Evie's mom, was on landed five minutes ago. She should be almost through to baggage claim where I'm waiting. Sean and Oli's plane just landed, five minutes early but they haven't started off-boarding yet. Dillan and Collins's plane shows it's about twenty minutes out which mean that they might land early as well.

If they all land early enough we'd be able to grab something to eat before sitting in a crowded stadium for three or so hours.

I hide away in the corner, doing my best to stay hidden from any prying eyes. I've already been approached twice and I'm trying to keep that to a minimum. Today's not about me, it's about Evie and she deserves to hog all the attention. She's worked so hard for this moment, overcome so many obstacles.

I couldn't be prouder.

Someone catches my attention as they enter the baggage claim area. A shorter, older version of Evie, looking around until she spots me in the corner and laughs.

I almost couldn't believe my eyes when I met Heaven. Five foot two, medium length thick black hair, big brown eyes, pale as the moon. Evie in twenty-five years.

She approaches me at a speed that makes you second guess how tall she really is. I've never known someone short who can keep pace with me easily, then I met Heaven.

"Tanner, darling." She grabs my covered face in her hands, forcing me to bend down and kisses both my cheeks. "It's been far too long. I must thank you for all the help you've been. I hardly leave my house, but I don't feel so lonely when the deliveries show up."

My brows crinkle as I try to understand where this accent came from. "Heaven?"

She hums in response, her hold on my face finally relenting.

"Why are you talking like that?"

"Talking like what, darling?" She peered up at me from under thick lashes, the definition of innocent.

"You gave yourself an accent, like those from high society snobs." Her laugh is low and quiet as her brown eyes soften, finally fully taking me in.

"I've been watching a lot of nineteenth-century adaptations, I guess they're rubbing off on me." Her eyes rack up and down my body, settling on the hickey that's barely visible above the collar of my shirt. "Well, you and my daughter have been busy I see."

I feel the flush crawling up my neck to cover my face. I clear my throat to no avail, a sneaky smile graces Heaven's lips, but she says nothing further on the subject.

"Have the others landed yet?" I blink, trying to go along with the subject change instead of fantasizing about her daughter tying me down, or me tying her down, both some great right now.

"Sean and Oli should be coming this way soon; their plane landed not long after yours. Collins and Dillan's plane keeps updating." I look over her shoulder to where the screen reads their flight is now expected five minutes sooner than last time. "When I got here it said it might be late due to the weather but now it's saying it will be twenty-five minutes early, so we'll see I guess."

"I wasn't aware of any weather conditions. Is it supposed to rain?" I shake my head, returning my attention to her. She's a lot like Evie in more ways than her looks. When in a group setting, she prefers to blend in, but when alone with someone, she better be your main focus. Quiet but somehow also loud when need be. Sweet and kind, but fierce and loyal. How Evie's fucked up father landed Heaven is mind-boggling to me.

I met Heaven during his trial. I watched the whole thing live from the audience, the entire time wanting to strangle him and watch the life seep from his useless body. The world doesn't need him anyway, no one would miss him. The only reason I didn't was because Evelyn said he wasn't worth my breath, which is true, he isn't. He got the longest sentence of everyone involved since he was a grown man raping a fourteen-year-old while the others were all under eighteen. Last I heard he wasn't the most popular guy in the prison.

"Not here, there's a storm going through Kentucky that the airline was worried about, but we must have missed it. The path didn't change so maybe there was a lull in the storm or something." I shrug nonchalantly, keeping an eye out for two guys dressed 'discretely' like me. A few flights just landed so a hoard of people just started through the door to the baggage claim and I'm hoping they're in the crowd. Heaven has turned her back to me and stared scanning the crowd for the guys as well.

I hesitate to ask but I want her permission before I go through with my plans for tonight. I know Heaven is really important to Evie as her mother and protector and I also know this is typically asked to the father but fuck that, I hope he dies in prison.

"Heaven?"

She turns around to look at me. "Yes, darling?"

"I was hoping to get your blessing." Before I even finished my sentence her arms are encasing my neck and squeezing me so tight it's hard to breathe. She squeals, drawing a few looks from other people passing by.

"I thought you would never ask." She leans back just enough to look me in the eyes. "The day Evie met you was the luckiest day of her life. And those aren't my words, she tells me almost every day. I would be honored to be your mother-in-law. I see the way you look at my daughter. I never doubted you were the one for her after I learned about you. The way my daughter always talked about you made me know. A mother's intuition and all of that."

My smile stretches across my face so tight it almost hurts. "Thanks, Heaven."

"Now where's the ring, I want to see it." I chuckle as I fish it out of my pants pocket and open the box for her to see. "Oh, it's beautiful." It is, I saw it two months ago and knew it was perfect. A diamond in the shape of a snowflake is surrounded by smaller diamonds that rest on a rose gold band.

"I asked Alyssa and Sasha to bring up the idea of looking at rings and Evie apparently gravitated to this style so when I saw this in the store, I knew it was perfect." Heaven sighs dreamily as she stares at the ring in my palm.

"Damn dude, that looks great. She's gonna love it." My eyes fly up to meet Sean's gaze. Oli stands a foot or so behind him, also looking at the ring.

"Thanks, man." I snap the lid closed and tuck it back into the safety of my pocket. I grasp his hand and pull him into a hug, doing the same to Oli when we pull apart.

"When are you proposing?" Oli pipes in.

"Tonight, Jensen should be arriving at the house any minute to get the backyard set up."

"Oh," Heaven mumbles, "he's not coming to the ceremony?"

"He's watching the live feed instead. He was going to come but when I expressed my worry about how I would set up without Evie finding out, he offered to do it for me."

We fall into easy chatter while waiting for the rest of the group to arrive. Heaven met the guy's last year when we flew her to Ohio for the summer. Announcements sound over the intercom saying which flights have landed at this small West Virginia airport. Eventually, Collins joins us, and Dillan a few minutes later. No one checked any bags since none of them can stay very long so as soon as everyone is here, we head out to where my truck is waiting. It's a tight fit, Heaven in the middle of the front seat squished between Sean and me. While the other three get to cram themselves into the back.

"Anyone hungry?" A chorus of yeses fills the car, so I queue up the nearest fast-food chain into my GPS and start that way. We have just over an hour before the ceremony starts so we have some time. However, my nerves for tonight don't seem to care that it's still hours away.

37

Tanner

Breathtaking.
That's what she is as she walks across the stage. Her long black hair is styled to perfection in beautiful waves that cascade down her back, the small bun I know is there almost indistinguishable.

The sadness I felt when we lost so close to the Stanly Cup finals dissipates as I watch the love of my life accept her diploma, now allowing her to permanently move in with me.

She can't see me where I'm hidden. Todays about her, not

me. It was bad enough when I graduated, and I stole the thunder of so many of my classmates. I know a lot of them didn't care, but I did. They worked just as hard as I did but I got far more recognition than I deserved. Evie always said I was being too harsh on myself and maybe I am, but that doesn't ease the guilt I felt when the paparazzi showed up and ruined the ceremony for so many people.

That's why I'm sitting in the far corner surrounded by all of her friends and family. We're hidden away so there is no way for us to steal the show.

Evie steps down from the podium, head on a swivel. I'm sure she's looking for us but she won't be able to see us, we're too far away. I can't see her facial expression but I'm sure she's disappointed when she doesn't spot us on the way back to her seat.

I pull out my phone and zoom in, snapping a photo when she glances over the crowd in our direction.

More names are called but my eyes stay glued to her as she stands and claps for her friends.

A few hours later we're making our way down the stairs searching for them in the mass crowd in the middle of the building. Kids scream and run between guests mulling about, causing a ruckus.

I've always wanted kids but now as I see them and imagine them as mine and Evie's, I know that want has turned into a need, as long as Evie will have them. We've had the discussion a few times, but it was never serious, now it will be.

Oli stops in front of me causing me to run into his back. "Why'd you stop?" I glance over his shoulder to where he's looking. Sasha stands with her back to us talking to her parents.

Next to her is Evie and Alyssa.

As if sensing our eyes on them, the three girls turn to look over their shoulders at the same time. A smile blossoming on all of their faces. Sasha shoves them both lightly in our direction, following behind them when they finally move.

"Alyssa." Oli's voice is choked as he fails to catch his breath. I had a feeling when Oli met Alyssa that he had a small crush on her but I never anticipated for them to be a couple, let alone one that's as strong as Evie and I. "You look like an angel." Said woman blushes as she pulls him down for a kiss.

A throat clears next to me bringing my attention to the most beautiful woman in the world. "Hello, princess."

"Hi, are you done watching our friends make out?" She crosses her arms with her eyebrows raised. "I'm waiting for my kiss and I'm starting to get impatient." My smile grows impossibly bigger as I pull her into me and let her kiss the smile off my face.

"Better." I rasp against her lips.

"Not yet." She pulls my mouth back to hers. Loud groans arise around us from our single friends while Heaven squeals again. She loves PDA even when it includes her daughter.

As I pull away, I peer down at her, "God, I love how short you are." She scoffs, turning her back slightly to me.

"I'm not short." Evie protests to the sound of the guy's laughter. "I'm average." She looks too damn cute with her arms crossed ever her chest as she pouts. I pull her into me by her waist as I nuzzle into her neck.

"Princess, there's nothing about you that's average." That earns me another kiss as she giggles against my lips.

She pulls back to look at me sympathetically and pats my

chest. "Too bad you're the very definition." I scoff at her but let the comment fly this time, she'll make up for it tonight and she knows it.

"Evelyn! Oh my, you look like a princess. My baby girl is all grown up now." Heaven's words blur together as she pulls Evie from my embrace into hers. She cries into her daughter's shoulder as they rock together on the concrete.

"Thank you, mom. I missed you." They continue to have a hushed conversation while Natalia and Mona approach the group with their families.

Over the next hour we talk and congratulate other graduates as we slowly, and I mean very *slowly*, make our way out to the cars.

Evie climbs into the passenger seat while Dillan and Heaven take the back seat. Collins and Sean are riding with Sasha; Oli and Alyssa said they'll be late getting to the house. I wonder why.

The car ride is filled with Evie and Dillan catching up, they have never been super close but are still fairly good friends. Evie tells him about the job she currently has and how she is not a big fan of her boss. My jaw clenches as she continues to describe the creep.

I've never personally met him and hope I never do. He takes every opportunity to flirt with Evie knowing damn well I'm her boyfriend. I remember her telling me he didn't believe her at first and it took photos from a gossip magazine to convince him.

When Evie told me about that incident, I almost flew from California back here to meet him in person and introduce myself, so he knew she was taken. Unfortunately, I wouldn't have made it back in time for my game, so I had to make do with knowing she was able to 'convince' him she had a boyfriend.

I hate men like that. The ones who think every girl who says they have a boyfriend is lying. Like seriously, if they're lying it's for a reason, take the fucking hint and leave them alone.

"Have you looked into other employers?"

Evie turns around to face him as best she can. "I'm in contact with this author who is new to the publishing world and is looking to make a team. She has three books out right now which sounds impressive, which it is, but she has had them written for like four years and just now got the confidence to publish. One blew up so she decided to continue writing. She offered me a job and I'm really considering taking it. I loved working for that first author for the summer, I think I'll benefit from a small intimate team instead of a chain publisher."

"Yeah, I remember how happy you were when you first started with her. Why'd you stop anyways?"

"Oh," Evie quiets. "Uh, I took over for her pregnant editor who didn't know if she wanted to come back or be a stay-at-home mom. She chose to come back."

I pull into the driveway as the garage slowly opens revealing Jensen's van. Evie is still looking at Dillan, her attention fully on him so she doesn't notice until I'm helping her out of the truck.

"Jensen's here?" When I nod and move to the door, she follows behind wearily. "Why wasn't he at my graduation?"

I stay silent as I pull her into the dark house.

"Tanner? What's going on?" I lead her up the stairs, leaving Dillan and Heaven in the kitchen.

"Nothing, princess. He just texted and said he wouldn't make it on time. An accident on the freeway, I think. So, he came here instead." She digs her feet into the ground outside the bedroom door, forcing me to stop.

"So why are we up here instead of saying hi?" I sigh as my hands travel to her waist and pull her flush to me.

"Because I'm going to have to share you for the rest of the night. I was hoping to get a few minutes alone before everyone else got here." Good, keep stalling. I just have to keep her up here until Alyssa and Oli get here. I don't want to do this without them. Hopefully, Oli doesn't get carried away and remembers the plan for tonight.

"But I want to say hi to Jensen." Evie pouts but doesn't resist as I steer her into the room.

"I know." I kiss her neck as I push her against the door. "You can in a moment, but I've needed to properly kiss you for hours. Forgive me if I can't wait any longer." She giggles as my lips ghost over her neck and down her collarbone. The front door opens downstairs as voices float in. "Ten minutes, then we can go mingle. Deal?"

She sighs into my hair. "Deal."

38

Evie

I don't believe him. Tanner's hiding something but I'll let it slide for the moment.

We've been up here far longer than ten minutes and he won't let me go back downstairs. I figured something was up when I didn't see Jensen at the graduation, but his car was here.

The noise downstairs has grown exponentially louder which would be the perfect cover if we wanted some sexy time, but that's not what's happening. Tanner is checking his phone every couple of seconds while I sit on the bed watching him.

"Tanner, baby." He looks up at me. "Let's go downstairs and mingle. I'm part of the reason they're here, it's rude for us to hide away and not even do anything."

"But," I cut him off with the raise of my hand.

"You can stay up here, doing whatever it is you're doing, but I'm going downstairs." He looks like he wants to say something more but doesn't so I take the opportunity and open the door.

"Alyssa, you guys are finally here. What took you so long?" Sean's voice carries up the stairs.

"Oh, shut up Sean." Oli's voice, almost as loud, comes next.

Like a switch was flipped, Tanner joins me as I descend toward the party.

"Changed your mind already?" I eye him wearily.

"Yup." Nothing more is said as we join everyone in the kitchen.

I search the group for Jensen but notice pretty quickly he's nowhere to be seen. I tap Dillan on the shoulder to gain his attention. "Where's Jensen? I was hoping to say hi." Dillan looks over my shoulder to where I thought Tanner was still, but when I look, he's gone.

"Uh, I think I saw him outside, come on, I'll come say hi with you." Dillan speaks obnoxiously loudly, earning the attention of everyone in the room.

My brows furrow further as I follow him toward the backyard while everyone files behind me. A nervous energy leaks from my friends and my worry heightens.

Before I can ask what's going on, I see the yard. Balloons line a white carpet with red rose petals. Everyone around me pulls out confetti canons and Dillan steps aside to reveal Tanner standing at the end of the carpet.

As if he materialized, Jensen takes my hand and guides me to the opposite end of the carpet as Tanner and leans down to whisper in my ear.

"You look beautiful today. Congratulations on your diploma. I'm so proud of you. "The simple words undo me as tears stream down my face.

It's obvious what's going on. It looks like a makeshift wedding. I'm too dazed to move so Jensen takes ahold of my hand once more and leads me to where Tanner waits, his nerves painted on his handsome face. Like a father hands off his daughter at a wedding, Jensen gives my limp hand to Tanner, who takes it gratefully.

"Evelyn."

"Tanner."

He smiles, big and bright, making my heart melt. Then he gets down on one knee. I shouldn't be surprised, I knew from the moment I walked out here what was happening, but I still gasped, covering my mouth as tears stream down my cheeks.

Tanner keeps my left hand in his as he stares up at me. "Evelyn Campbell, you are the most wonderful person I have ever met. I knew you were special from the first day I met you. In that diner, I met the love of my life at nearly eleven at night. I could have never imagined that you would be there when me and my idiot friends were sat behind you. I remember having this feeling that I needed to turn around and there you were, typing away on your laptop. I had only briefly glanced at what you were writing when you noticed me creeping and shut it off only to slap me moments later when I foolishly tried to reopen it.

"It was at that moment that I decided I wanted you. I know it took half a year and a lot of pestering but look at us now. I got you, and I will never let you go. You are my light in the darkness, the sun to my moon, and my one and only. I'm hoping to make it official by making you my wife. So, what do you say? Evelyn, will you marry me?"

My nod is slow but very much prominent. "Yes." The ring slid onto my hand while I'm still dazed. Before I know it, Tanner's on his feet spinning me in the air and yelling at the top of his lungs.

"She said yes!"

Cheers erupt around us as my lips crash on his.

"Is this why Jensen wasn't at my graduation?" Tanner at least looks sheepish.

"He may have heard me say I didn't know how I was going to get everything set up without you seeing, and he may have offered to do it after you left." I sigh as I rest my forehead against his.

"You're insufferable sometimes, you know that?"

"Yeah."

"Do you also know I would have been happy with none of this? You didn't have to plan anything. All I need is you, obviously bonus points for everyone being here."

"Obviously." I stare into his sage eyes once more before kissing him with all the love I have. He knew I would want everyone here even if I never said it aloud so he planned it when everyone could be here.

With each passing day, I fall deeper and deeper in love with him and I hope to never find my way out.

Epolog

EVIE

Two Years Later

The shrill cry of Analise cuts through the otherwise silent house. I reach over to shake Tanner awake to go check on her since I'm still bedridden from the emergency C-section one week ago that brought our beautiful daughter into the world.

My hand lands on the empty mattress and my eyes crack open to make sure I didn't just miss him. Nope, he's not here. I groan as I slowly sit up, all while my baby girl wails her lungs out in the corner.

"What are you doing?" I look up to see the outline of my husband now holding our infant, and the sight warms my belly, and a little lower.

"Sitting up, what does it look like?" At my voice, Analise quiets down, her chubby hands reaching out into the darkness toward me. "Now be a good obedient husband and bring my daughter to me."

He chuckles as he walks over to where I've rested myself against the headboard. I hold my arms waiting for our little bundle of joy to be placed there.

"Here's your mommy." Tanner's voice drifts over me, almost putting me back to sleep.

These last few weeks have been tough. I was thirty-six weeks pregnant when the pain started. Tanner was at an away game, and I was home alone. Near midnight I couldn't take the pain anymore and called an ambulance.

I called Tanner on my way to the hospital, and he was on the next flight home.

We moved to Seattle a few months ago when Tanner was transferred mid-season to the team here. We didn't complain because it meant being closer to my mom who took the opportunity and sold the house to the first bidder.

She was my second call and was halfway to the hospital by the time I arrived.

Hours and multiple tests later, no one knew what was wrong. I wasn't having contractions, and nothing was wrong with Analise, but the pain wasn't coming from nowhere.

By the time Tanner arrived the pain was unbearable. He

tried to calm me down with whispers in my ear as he argued with the doctors. Finally, my delivery nurse came in and noticed blood between my legs.

I was rushed into an emergency C-section right as my contractions started. Three hours later Analise came into the world and her daddy was the first person to hold her.

After much discussion, it was decided I wouldn't be breastfeeding, worried my body wouldn't be able to handle it, so after Tanner set her in my arms, he went to get a nurse to get her milk.

"Shhh, pretty baby, mommies got you." I rock her in my arms singing softly to her to calm her cries. The bed dips next to me as Tanner crawls into his spot and hands me her bottle.

We only have one more week before he has to go back to work and my mom will stay with me full time. The season is in full swing, and the team needs him.

While I want him to stay, I want him to win this year just as much. The finals are weeks away and his team is on the way to being the winners of the Stanly Cup.

"Do you want me to feed her?" I pass her off so I can gingerly climb out of bed to use the bathroom. Ten minutes later I can't get up. As if guessing I need help, Tanner materializes and helps me off the toilet and back to bed. "Get some sleep. I've got the baby."

Tanner

I'm in awe of my wife.

A month after giving birth she's wobbling on the edge of the ice as my team passes around the Cup we just won. Heaven stands beside her with my wonderful baby girl in her arms.

I look to my new teammates, thankful to find everyone already looking at me. The captain skated over and placed his gloved hand on my shoulder. "Go get your damn baby so we can put her in the cup."

I skate over to my family so fast that it surprises Evie.

I help her on the ice and take Analise from Heaven. "Go, I don't want to get on the ice." I nod and slowly move back over to my team with my wife and baby.

The guys crowd around us, Ooing and Awing at my baby as I place her in the Stanly cup and raise them both over my head. Cameras flash off in the distance, catching the moment and cementing it in history.

With Evie's blessing, Analise is passed around in the cup, getting photos with all of the guys.

"Congratulations." I smile down at my wife and my heart swells.

We found out we were pregnant two weeks before our wedding ten months ago. It was the best day of my life. That is until she was born, and I saw her perfect chubby face.

She's a daddy's girl, no matter what her mother says.

"Thanks." I lean down to give her a sweet kiss that she turns into a steamy one. "Careful, princess. Keep it up and I'll have to put another baby in you."

Evie swats playfully at me. "Don't even think about it Buster. You're stuck with your hand for another two months." I groan into her hair. It's been torture to see her naked and not be able to touch her, but I'll do whatever needs to be done so she can heal properly. But if she thinks I'm kidding, she's sorely mistaken.

I want my own hockey team.

"We can try again in a year." Hope blossoms in my chest.

"Really?"

"Yeah, that way they have a year in between them and my body won't be put through the wringer. But dammit if I don't already want another one." She smiles longingly as the assistant captain takes Analise out of the cup and snuggles her against his cheek.

"The team loves her." Evie nods into my side.

"At least I know she'll be safe from some random boy breaking her heart. No one wants to go up against this group." I laugh as I kiss her hair.

"Yeah, she'll be safe. But that's because she's never going to be allowed to date." Evie scoffs but doesn't respond, instead reaching out to take Analise back into her arms and pepper her with kisses.

"Good luck, baby girl. You're going to need all you can get with this man for your father."

The team chuckles behind me but nobody challenges her, whether it's because they agree with her or because they don't want to argue with a new mom, I'm not sure. All I know is she's right and I'm one lucky bastard.

Acknowledgements

When I started writing this book, I didn't know if I would ever finish. This wasn't the first book I started writing but it is the first I finished and for that, it will always hold a special place in my heart.

I'm thankful to all my friends and family who believed in me even when I didn't. Without all the love and support from everyone I don't know if I would have ever been able to do it.

A special thank you to my friend Patti who, from the moment I mentioned writing a book, believes that I will make a name for myself.

To my friends Halie, Megan, and Bridget; thank you for sitting through my numerous rants about this book without getting annoyed.

Finally, thank you to my Mother, Father, and two brothers. Thank you to my mom who has been in my corner from day one, believing in me every step of the way. Thank you to my brothers who had to listen to me talk about books my entire life and will now have to listen to me talk about publishing one myself. Thank you to my dad who told me to let him know when my book becomes a movie so he can watch it instead of reading it; and for wondering why books need covers.

I'm eternally grateful to have everyone by my side, supporting me through my journey to becoming a published author, to fulfilling my dreams. Whether your support was through comedic questions or words of affirmation, thank you.